SADDLE TRAMPS

By

CAROLE T. BEERS

W & B Publishers
USA

W & B Publishers

For information:
W & B Publishers
9001 Ridge Hill Street
Kernersville, NC 27284

www.a-argusbooks.com

ISBN: 9781942981756

Book Cover designed by Dubya

Printed in the United States of America

ACKNOWLEDGEMENTS

To write and publish a book takes not only a village, but a whole country -- to tweak a phrase of my favorite photographer, Jenny J Jaks Grimm. But not to worry. Here I will thank only God -- my personal leader -- plus a few helpful citizens.

My late parents, Vern and Neva Thompson, along with other dear relatives, encouraged me to write early and often. My husband, Richard Peterson, not only cheers me on, but also tolerates my travails, travels and time-taking fits of creativity. My Jones and Thompson family members offer steadfast support. My friend Marjorie Lewis spurs me on.

Without the support and encouragement of my writing group, Monday Mayhem, I might not have made it this far in my writing. Meeting bi-weekly for nine years, they offer praise, tips and well-considered criticism exactly where due. Tim Wohlforth, whose dark-edged books and stories are a beacon of smart writing, tenders dead-on directives about voice, tone, detail and action. Actor-writer Clive Rosengren gives incisive notes about drama, continuity and -- commas! International thriller writer Michael Niemann has fresh insights on story arc and plot points. Literary former-professor Sharon L. Dean provides advice on how to make stories stronger, more compelling, while Jenn Ashton targets grammar, syntax and viewpoint issues.

Others without whose help and support this book would not have come together, include: William Connor of A-Argus Books, who saw the value in my work and brought it to the world audience; Melinda Bargreen, fellow arts critic/writer and bosom buddy since our Seattle Times days; and a village of fabulous other friends and role models who offered quips, quirks and fictional characters for the book. So, thank you, Jeanne Wolfe, Ann Shriver, Sandy Thorne, Candy Morasch, Tamara Chastain, Patty Ann, Nancy Hanson Panner, Larry Chastain, Mike Edwards, Judith Hovlund and the Cedar Tree Stables Family, plus the late wit and arts critic, John Voorhees.

The big black-and-white stallion stopped chewing alfalfa from the stall's corner manger. He raised his head and flicked his ears forward. Aside from the usual stable sounds of horses munching, blowing, or drinking from automatic waterers, he heard sounds he didn't recognize.

He sniffed the air. His nostrils flared, intensifying the barn smells. His eyes grew wider, scanning the stall and aisle in the dim light of overhead bulbs. He stepped up to peer through the bars but drew back with a snort when his nose touched cold steel.

The stallion knew all was not right. He was unsure how to react.

A few other horses in their twelve-by-twelve stalls whinnied nervous greetings toward a new creature or human in their midst. They, too, seemed unsure.

Out in the covered arena, which the stallion's stall-row backed against, he heard cantering hoof beats. Someone—probably that skinny bald man he liked—was out there riding after everyone else including the chatty women had left. Riding the brown-and-white mare the man recently had taken as his own.

The stallion was not concerned by whoever was out there, though he swept back one ear to catch arena sounds that might be of interest. Later that man might come and offer the stallion an oat-molasses treat.

There it was again. That sound. Someone walking. It was not a walking sound the black-and-white knew. Nor a smell he recognized. Not right.

Still he wasn't really afraid. He had never been afraid of humans, as the horse had been handled by humans all his life. Yes, he'd been hit with spur or crop. Or felt a chain tighten across his nose or chin, when he needed correcting, or when the human reckoned he needed correcting. But it was rare, if he kept trotting or galloping in round circles or straight lines at cadenced gaits with graceful body carriage, sometimes over low jumps. Such corrections, when he'd let his attention slip, were always fair.

The strange sound and smell stopped outside his stall door. The stallion arched his neck and tucked his chin toward his chest. He blew softly, and stared. His skin rippled in anxiety.

A human hand in a black glove slid back the iron bolt, then slowly slid open the door. The other gloved hand held something tubular and white. The human wore dark, rustling clothes and a black head cover with eyeholes. Close up, the person emitted a familiar smell mingled with a medicine scent from the tubular object.

The stallion wrinkled his nostrils. He snorted again and stepped back, making hoof dents in the piled-up pine shavings that served as his bedding.

He still was unsure. Was this someone he knew, or should know?

A hand lay on his shoulder to steady him. The hand stroked his coat. A rope tightened around his neck. That meant stand. The horse waited.

"OK, boy. It'll be OK. Take it easy now." A monotone voice. Somehow familiar, yet not. Pinched, and higher.

Another hand rose. It held something with a silver point that glinted in the light.

The stallion's head jerked as the hand on his shoulder clutched at his throat. Strong fingers slid down. They groped the pulsing vein, and pulled it out a little.

In the silence the horse felt a quick, sharp prick. He winced, and jerked his head again, bumping the human back a step. But the horse kept his hooves still. He had been trained well. This procedure was nothing new for a champion show horse. Often these injections relaxed him, eased another pain or sent him into a pleasant dream state.

Sometimes shots left a sore spot. But they were just part of his life. He accepted them, as he'd had to accept many different things over the years.

The present dull pain lasted a few seconds as the fluid pushed into his vein. Then the stallion watched the human slowly pull the rope off his neck, leave the stall and shut the door. The footfalls receded. As the sounds died away, the horse's ears relaxed.

Within minutes his head swam. His eyes closed. He felt sleepy. Slobber ringed his lips. He tried to take a step but his knees buckled. He slowly sank into the shavings.

That was the last thing he knew.

1

Lost in the bouncy strains of "All My Exes Live in Texas," I began to spin under the arm of my partner, a middle-aged Tony Curtis lookalike. Halfway through I flashed on how much fun my gal pals and I had at country dance lessons, and how fit we'd become. Nonstop high stepping for a few hours made you sweat like a horse.

As I finished the spin, a red-hot pain stabbed my shoulder.

"Ooo-ow!" I jerked away and clutched the hot spot as other couples blew by in a lively Western Two Step.

My partner froze. His relaxed-fit jeans stayed relaxed. But worry skittered over his face, flattening one black eyebrow under his fringe of silver hair.

"Sorry, Pepper," he said.

"Me, too," I muttered. "My shoulder hasn't been the same since I fell off Bob."

Tony's eyes widened. His head tilted, making him resemble a curious cat. He took a slow step back.

***

"I fell off Bob" seemed a perfectly reasonable explanation. It was the truth. But I saw wheels turning behind Tony's curly-lashed eyes and detected a stiffness in his spine. He must have wondered what-in-heck kind of woman he'd hooked up with.

"Oh," I said. "Bob's my horse. He bucked me off a few months ago."

Tony's face softened. He nodded, but didn't use that as an entrée for further chat.

"You all right to go on?"

"Oh, yeah." I rolled my shoulder. It felt better. "I rode him through five bucks. Landed hard, cracked some ribs. But almost made the horn."

Tony gave me that curious cat look again. Not the brightest bulb in the box. Definitely not life-partner material. He didn't get my jokes. Also the dude had not recognized me from dancing with him the previous Thursday. Capital crime.

"They sound a horn in rodeo when you ride a bronc for eight seconds."

"Oh." He held out his arms to resume the Two-Step.

Mercifully, the music ended just then.

"I need a drink of water," I said, not really fibbing but mainly to escape Tony. I did feel dehydrated. My back ran with sweat. My joints creaked as if needing a shot of WD-40. Not only had I spent the afternoon practicing horse-show patterns on my cute Paint horse, Chocolate Waterfall. but also had danced for the past two hours.

In the hall near the restroom I bumped into Tulip.

"Watch where you're goin', Tule," I grinned.

* * *

Tulip Clemmons, whom I've known since childhood, is my buddy at Dutch and Donna Grandeen's Brassbottom Barn. It's where a dozen gals and one or two guys keep horses in training for show events such as trail, western pleasure and horsemanship.

She turned her baby blues on me and looked down, her face haloed in frothy red-blond curls. I'm five-four, a diminutive Reba MacIntyre lookalike, but Tule stands five-ten, and there's not an ounce of fat on her. In her white dance boots she tops out at an even six feet. A blond and footloose Susan Sarandon.

Naturally I hate the witch. Who wouldn't? But Tulip Clemmons is my best friend. She helped me raise a couple kids and lose a couple husbands, so I must make the effort. Besides, she helps at—and buys tack and clothes from—The Best Little Horsehouse in Oregon, my tack-and clothing store a few miles from home outside the town of Gold Hill, and also from a trailer I haul with my red, dual-rear-tires pick-up to horse shows.

"Why, I declay-ere. Miss Pepper Kane. What all happened there with R2D2?"

"You mean Tony Curtis from Madame Tussaud's?"

I filled her in, eliciting her famous mule-bray laughter. Tulip's store-bought boobs in her low-cut red top threatened wardrobe malfunction with every shake.

"Pep, y'all are too funny! Why'd we ever think to find boy toys here? We never shoulda quit playing senior co-ed softball."

She was right. I adored softball, never mind that I could barely run, throw or hit. We'd played ball last spring, but quit when it ran afoul of our horse show schedule. We still held tickets, though, to Medford Rogues Wood-Bat Collegiate Team home games.

"Tony didn't recall dancing with me last week," I said, "Thought I was a new girl."

As Tulip brayed once more, I bent down and pressed the water fountain button. A wet plume blasted my forehead. I adjusted the stream and drank. Then I went into the restroom, used the toilet and repaired minor damage to my hair and makeup.

Leaning into the mirror I combed over my blonde-streaked red hair. New smears of peach gloss across my mouth minimized lines and enlarged my thin lips. Pink dabs on my freckled cheeks made me look passably healthy, which cleaning stalls and riding horses did to some extent, but whose effects tended to fade come evening.

I turned sideways to stand on the tiptoes of my pink and brown cowgirl boots, the better to assess my muffin top. I sucked it in. That nearly made it disappear under my swingy brown tee and low rider jeans.

Not bad for fifty-something, I mused.

The door burst open, nearly smacking me. The va-va-voluptuous Victoria Smith, another barn buddy, popped into view. Vic didn't give a rip about muffin tops. The more lady layers, the merrier, was her motto. No wonder this chiquita had a waiting list of Lotharios despite her reportedly happy marriage.

Victoria was ever on the quest, as were many of us, for a perfect mate and perfect horse, neither of which probably could be found. Until they materialized, Vic bought a new horse every year, and amused herself with flirtations, mostly semi-harmless. According to her.

"Come on in, Vic. I'm about done. Can do only so much with a hysterical relic."

"You mean historical."

She grinned and pursed her Botox-enriched lips.

"I'm desperate, Pep. Bladder control not what it used to be."

She hustled her full, lace-trimmed figure toward the toilet stall. Long black hair caught up top with a feather contraption billowed around her shoulders. A whiff of Oriental perfume hung behind her.

"Any luck with the boys tonight?" she said, closing the toilet stall door.

"Negatory."

The toilet flushed rapidly three times. I paused mid-exit from the restroom, ready to apologize in case I'd left a rude memento in the bowl.

"Shoot!" Victoria whined. "Dang toilet has a flush attack before I even settle down to business. Don't you hate when machines are smarter than you?"

"Gettin' used to it, Vic. Ain't aging great?" I gave my 'do a final lick.

"By the way," she said, "how are your parents doing?"

"Still stubborn, and not in the best health. But they refuse to go into a retirement home and let Tulip and I turn their farm into a guest ranch. Between them, my grown kids' troubles and my hump-busting work at the store, it's a full plate."

"Hmmm. Yet you still find time to ride and even dance. Superchick."

"Gotta have that 'me' time," I said. "Without it I'd go flatline."

In the hall I met another Brassbottom buddy, the svelte, mustached and purposely bald Freddie Uffenpinscher. Yes, like the dog breed, but whose last name starts with a "U" instead of "A." And whose tight, flat ears bore multiple earrings.

***

I was shocked. He'd often threatened to come dancing with us, but not made good on it until now. There were no men for him to dance with in the couples part. But I often argued some gals didn't mind playing the male. Another story entirely.

"Pepper! Oh, thank God!" said Freddie, his eyes flashing.

He pressed a hand to his chest in its tight black tee. His close-set dark eyes bored into mine. Grabbing my hand, he pulled me down the hall to a lounge room replete with recycled fridge, spavined sofa and mug-filled sink.

"What's up, F U?" I said. "You look like you've seen a corpse."

His shiny head snapped back, animating the half-dozen gold hoops and diamond-stud earrings in his earlobes.

"Practically," he said with dramatic emphasis. He once had starred as the guileless nephew, Patrick Dennis, in an off Broadway production of "Auntie Mame," so he knew his drama. Freddie rode hunter-type horses, tall greyhoundish affairs fitted with flat English saddles. He rode them very well, too. And he looked way sleeker in tight breeches than some of us gals.

"What do you mean?" I pressed.

"Oh my God. You've got to help, Pepper. You were a reporter."

"What is it, Freddie? What happened? Can you slow down?"

"OK." He took a deep breath and ran his fingers over his head. "Dutch and Donna don't want us to get upset. And the law is all over it. But I wanted you to know since you were such a fan. And I had to tell you in person, not by phone or text. Let's go in here."

He pulled me into the lounge and locked the door behind us.

"So what's got you aflame, Freddie? More than usual, I mean."

Freddie collapsed into me. I put my arms around him. He began to sob. I loosened him after a few seconds. I heard faint dance music start in the ballroom down the hall.

Freddie looked up, briefly touching his thumbs to the inner edge of his eyes.

"OK, brace yourself. It's Vader. He's ... DEAD! Collapsed in his stall."

"No!" I said. "Not Vader!" I felt a thud in the pit of my stomach. I covered my mouth with my hands, as if I had delivered the news. The gorgeous black-and-white stallion could not be gone. There had to be some mistake.

"For real." Freddie sniffed. I pulled paper towels from above the sink and handed them to him. He dabbed his eyes and blew his nose.

There was a knock. We looked at the door it as if we could see through it.

An older alto female voice spoke. It sounded like our dance instructor.

"Everything OK in there? Need any help?"

"No, we're fine," I lied. "Just be a minute."

I waited until I thought she'd left. I turned back to Freddie. He stood straighter but his cheeks were flushed and his eyes were huge. His mustache quivered.

"I was at the barn late. You know I ride after evening appointments at the salon. I was doing stall checks like always when I'm the last one there. Vader was lying flat on his side. Usually he's at the door begging for treats. When I called he didn't look up."

"Did you go in? You sure he was dead? How did Dutch and Donna react?"

"I touched him. He was stiff and cool. Dr. Givens came right away but Vader was gone. The Grandeens were devastated. I am beyond devastated. That stallion of theirs took me to the top of the nation in my amateur group. This was our year to win the world championship. I so wish I could've found a way to keep leasing him."

"I know, Freddie." I patted his shoulder, trying to keep back my own tears, but with little success. "This is unbelievable. No horse can replace Vader."

"And the worst part, Pep? I saw blood running down his neck from the jugular area. I touched my hand to it, tasted it." He lowered his voice. "I think he was killed."

My skin went clammy as I let that sink in.

"You're saying it was deliberate? Vader didn't die of natural causes?"

"That's what I'm saying. What the vet and Grandeens are saying, too."

My pulse pounded in my temples. I searched Freddie's eyes. They never blinked, showing helpless shock and fear.

"The horse had not been ill," he said. "The Grandeens knew nothing about any injection for maintenance reasons. You know, to keep him sound."

"I see." But I didn't see, really. This was a huge loss. The Grandeens, in fact their whole stable and clients, would be crushed. Who would do such a horrific thing to that wonderful horse? Who would do it to such a decent couple, who ran the operation on a shoestring, but often beat the biggies at their own game?

"That's mainly why I came," Freddie was saying. "I knew you were here tonight, and would want to know right away. You've got to help clear our names. And superfast not only because of the big California show next week, but also because all of us are persons of interest. Sheriff took names and will interview everyone tomorrow."

I gave Freddie a blank look.

"Surely they don't think it was one of us?" Prickles of fear skittered on my forearms. "We were all here, dancing. Except you and the Grandeens, of course."

"And Jody and Carlos."

"The stall cleaners?"

"Can you believe it, Pep? Sheriff even took the names of farriers, and the hay and shavings suppliers."

"Part of being thorough, Freddie. Gotta check everyone no matter how unlikely they seem. Killer could have acted for somebody else. Or have a grudge."

"The worst part is," he said, "the sheriff and the Grandeens must wonder about me as I've been pretty pissed since that 'reech beech' Marietta Von Sustern bought the horse out from under me before my lease was up."

"I hate to say it," I said, "but that's routine, too, to look at the person who found the body. Don't worry. Everyone knows you loved Vader and would never hurt him."

"God. I hope you're right." Freddie examined his bitten-down fingernails.

"The Grandeens might be hurting financially and emotionally," I said. "But they're good, decent people. They can't really suspect you."

"Especially since Marietta and I were good right after the sale. Remember, she had me style her hair the very next day."

"And gave you a hundred-dollar tip."

"Supposedly to ease my pain. The sheriff sure asked me a lot of questions. The same ones different ways. I'm freaked."

"I see that." I stroked his arm and looked into his dilated pupils.

"We are all people of interest, if not suspects," he said. "Even you, Pep."

"No doubt. They might think I had time to kill Vader on my way here, or to slip away for a half hour."

"And not be missed," he said. "Just playing devil's advocate here."

"Thanks for the compliment," I said, pinching his arm. "That I'd not be missed."

"You investigated a suspicious show-horse death in Seattle before you retired from the newspaper," he said. "Olympic Games hunter-jumper sliced up in his stall?"

I shuddered, reliving the revulsion I felt working that story. The owners and every competitor were suspects. The insurance company was all over it. But due to a fortuitous hunch I had, a dinner-party invite I'd wangled at the owners' home, and my acquaintance with the party caterer, I'd uncovered the killer. Won a reporting prize, too.

"Not sure I can repeat that success," I said. "My skills are rusty after five years in retirement. But I'm still a pretty good gossip-girl, and way-too-curious a cat for my own good. Already used up some of my nine lives being so nosy."

"And you're super competitive," he said. "You will solve this, Pep."

"True. I will surely try. But just one more thing."

"And that is?" He cocked his head and narrowed his eyes.

"Just what you said, Fred. I'm a person of interest, myself."

2

Warmed by an early sun over the hills, I paused at the double doors at the front of Brassbottom Barn. I scanned the parking lot, shuttered house and outdoor arena. Except for the sad call of mourning doves, nothing.

Why was my favorite horse haunt so quiet? It wasn't that early, being a little after seven. A valuable show horse had been killed. It had doubtless been a late night for all. But I'd thought the sheriff, insurance folk and the Grandeens would be up and at it.

I tapped my French-manicured nails on the door handle. Gracie, a rescued Rottweiler, rubbed against my jeans. I stroked her head.

The dog whined. Horses neighed. A rooster crowed somewhere out in the valley. At least it sounded normal, almost like at my own home, a modest acreage with a small barn and Western-themed doublewide ten miles down the pike.

I pulled open one door, walked in and inhaled the earthy, horsey odors that one former boyfriend called "Pepper's Chanel No. 5."

The whinnies increased. Horses know any human can bring breakfast, which in this case was six-inch-thick, twenty-by-twenty alfalfa "flakes," or hay bale sections.

"Hi, kids," I called down the alley bordered by stalls on each side. "Mom's here," I said to Chocolate Waterfall, my brown and white Paint stalled halfway down. His neigh rose above the rest. He often neighed at the sound of my truck pulling into the lot.

On the left I saw a yellow "Do Not Cross" crime tape stretched over the door and front wall. Feeling a chill, not knowing what I might find, I walked closer. A brass plate read, "Dark Vader, APHA Champion." The tape suggested more investigating was in order, doubtless in today's daylight.

I peered between the bars. My heart jumped when I saw a blue tarpaulin covering a large oblong lump that could only be Dark Vader. Four black hooves poked out from under the tarp, facing toward me.

He hadn't been removed, then.

It got very quiet in the barn. Even the horses stopped their neighing, as if they knew the seriousness of what I was seeing and processing. This doubtless was what Freddie, the Grandeens, Dr. Givens and the sheriff had seen last night.

My forearms prickled with fear. Again, despite the warm morning, I felt cold. It wasn't the revulsion. I had been around dead horses before. But none like this.

I shouldn't go in. It was wrong to go in. It was illegal to go in. But I had to go in.

I'd be careful. Touch nothing. Disturb nothing. They'd never know I was there.

But I'd better be quick. People would be coming to the barn soon, maybe in minutes, to feed, clean and investigate further.

Making sure there was no human activity outside or inside the barn, I softly but swiftly picked open the yellow tape knot at one end of the stall bars. I draped the tape's end through the door handle. Carefully, trying not to make noise, I slid the bolt and opened the door. The low grind of metal-door cap in rusty iron runner unsettled me. Horses began to whinny again.

I had no time to waste. I left the door open and took two steps into the shavings, setting my feet into places already dented by hoofprints. I quickly knelt near Vader's head and neck, and folded back the tarp.

There was the tiny needle hole, the black hair around it stiff from dried blood. A dried brown trickle ran from the wound over a patch of white hair, as if the blood had partly coagulated when Vader was still upright, then finished thickening when he fell.

It also looked as if someone had disturbed the flow. Was that a bloody partial fingerprint? Probably a gloveprint, if it had been the killer's hand. It looked as if it had already been dusted in an attempt to lift a print, though it couldn't have been real clear because of the hair.

But, I thought, this also could have been Freddie's print, when he touched the fluid. He had told me he'd done so to try to learn what it was.

Freddie, Freddie, Freddie. Why did you do that? You must have known that would give them more reason to suspect you.

Well, I reasoned, we all do weird things, unreasonable things, when emotion takes over. Just like me, right now, in this stall where I was very much not supposed to be.

Wait. Were those footsteps on the gravel out front of the barn? Better get going.

As I lay the tarp back over the beautiful, black-and white head and neck, I stared for one sad moment at those glazed brown eyes with half-closed lids. Then I quickly turned and started out of the stall. When I reached for the yellow tape to re-secure the scene, my gaze dropped to Vader's hooves, frozen as if in mid-gallop. They lay sideways, the hoofs walls shiny and shod, the soles gray and partly packed with dirt, shavings, and – what was that?

A thin shiny object, so tiny it might have been missed by investigators, glinted like a pinhead amidst shavings inside the left front hoof.

I knelt again. With trembling hands I picked out the shavings clump with its shiny flake, pocketed the object, jumped out of the stall to re-secure the door and yellow tape. All the horses were in full hungry-neigh mode now, so the grinding of the door might not be heard by anyone near the barn.

My heart beat hard. My cheeks burned. But I was home free. I would examine the flake after I went to work at my store, The Best Little Horsehouse, set to open at 10.

I took a deep breath and resumed walking in as easy a manner as possible toward my own horse's stall.

I jumped at hearing a familiar male voice behind me.

"You're here a little early."

I looked over my shoulder although I knew darned well who'd stepped up to give me some grief.

Dutch Grandeen, all lanky six-feet of him in a white tee and slim denims, a straw hat on his head, loomed dark against the light at the barn entrance. He strode forward to stand about ten feet from me, just past Vader's stall.

His blue-grey eyes twinkled. His lips parted in a grin that revealed uneven teeth and animated his weathered face. No wonder most of the dozen ladies in the barn, and at least one male, had a crush on Dutch. Those darned horse trainers. Even the plainest and pudgiest among them had a special way, a charisma that made them almost irresistible to anything with a pulse. In most cases they were "taken," as in married or in an equivalent relationship. But some trainers didn't let that stand in their way if they wanted a romp.

"Yeah," I answered. "Early bird gets the worm." As soon as the phrase left my lips I regretted my word choice. Was I too casual? Had he seen me leaving the stall? I doubted it, but couldn't be sure.

"Don't be frisky, now," Dutch said with a wink. The next second he'd moved down the aisle to attend to chores. Soon he'd be followed by Donna, his shapely blond wife of thirty years, who helped the workers clean stalls while Dutch fed and turned horses out in the pens.

I scolded myself. I'd been so surprised to see him, and yes, guilty, that I'd forgotten to ask a few questions about Vader's death, before the day got busy.

Putting together a quick list of things I wanted to know, I jogged down the aisle after Dutch.

"Wait," I said as I drew up behind him.

He turned to face me. His eyes narrowed, as in a protective response. Just as quickly they softened. Deep bags sagged beneath them.

"Terrible about Vader, isn't it?" he said, slouching. He knew exactly what I was thinking. Reading minds is another implement in a horse trainer's toolbox.

"Unbelievable," I said.

I was a little surprised at how normal Dutch seemed, under the circumstances. I'd expected more emotion. Then again, he was a pro. He'd lost dozens of horses over thirty years in the business. Probably he'd already accepted last night's tragedy and now was focused on next week's big show.

"Quite a shock," he said, blinking a few times, almost like he was trying to blink back tears. "But the sheriff took a look last night, and Dr. Givens is on it. Samples are being overnighted to the Oregon State University lab. And the insurance people are sending someone. They'll figure it out."

The Grandeens weren't the biggest trainers on the block. They didn't travel to all the shows as did better-heeled trainers. Partly it was because of the cost of diesel and the Grandeens' being far from the middle and southern United States. But major California wins would give them and their clients a needed leg up in the national standings. A badly needed leg up, as the show year so far had disappointed some Grandeen clients. There'd been whispers that the couple might be losing its touch.

"Well, my condolences on your loss," I said. "How's Donna taking it?"

"We're fine, thank you." Dutch seemed about to say something else, but didn't. Instead he gazed through the barn's open back doorway toward the pastures and pens making up the fifty-acre Grandeen ranch. Horses dotted the pens that spilled down toward treed slopes, distant low hills and a pale blue June sky. Already the warmth promised a day in the mid-eighties, typical for the month in southern Oregon.

"So the sheriff plans to talk to each of us?" I ventured.

Dutch seemed almost relieved by that question.

"Think so. He'll be here soon to wrap up. Not sure he'll spend a whole lotta time on a dead horse, though. That's for the vet and insurance people to check out. But stick around if you can. That would help us tremendously."

Dutch sniffed. He ground his teeth. His left cheek twitched. Sure signs of distress. Usually the trainer was loose, easygoing, calm as cold butter. But worry brought out a cornucopia of twitches, tics and spasms.

"I'll stay as long as I can, Dutch. Anything to help."

I felt like twitching myself. There was no escaping this tragedy. Vader's death weighed on us all, could seriously affect our performance next week and tarnish the Brassbottom Barn reputation. Maybe forever.

We couldn't let that happen. I couldn't let that happen. I had to get to the bottom of this, and fast. Freddie, and the other barn buddies I'd called last night, had sworn to keep their eyes and ears open. But they looked to me to solve the mystery before we headed off to sunny Cal. We didn't want this to drain energy or blur our show focus. Huge wins would give us prestige and position us for even more impressive wins at the fall's World Open Western Show in Fort Worth, Texas. WOWS, for short.

My plan was to ID Vader's killer here. Talk to the vet and other locals, and try to pry something out of the insurance investigator, whoever that turned out to be. If I didn't get it done before Cal, I'd be forced to continue to sleuth there, as all of us and our main competitors in riding and training would be there. As if I didn't have enough to do making sure my aging parents would be okay having my adult son, Serrano, watch them while housesitting for me. Never mind showing my horse and running my business, another worry. I wasn't even sure I could make this month's rent.

I folded my arms and looked into Dutch's bottomless eyes.

"Any idea who was involved last night?"

Dutch sighed. "Could be anybody. Any reason. Could even have been one of our own, though I sure as hell hope not." He glanced around. No one else was here yet. Most riders came midday, if they didn't have jobs, or after work, if they did. Yet soon enough the place would be abuzz with the Grandeen morning routine as well as a crime investigation.

"Ditto that. I hope it wasn't anyone we know. And that the insurance was paid up. Maria's deal on Vader was finalized, right?" I attempted a grin that I didn't feel. Still it was important to keep up a positive attitude. Fake it until you make it, kind of deal.

"Assume so. There were some details to work out. Well, back to work. Or the worm's gonna get the bird." He winked, turned and strode outside.

Lost in thought, I moseyed back toward my horse's stall.

My conversation with Dutch left me still needing an answer as to the timing and details of Vader's change of ownership. I also needed to know details of how Vader's lease was worded and how it ended. The fine print.

I'd ask Freddie that afternoon, when he cut and colored my hair. I also planned to talk to Donna, get her take on things. Dutch's wife might be more forthcoming than her husband. She and I were a little closer. She was a good customer of The Best Little Horsehouse. Also, like me, she was the mother of adult children who sometimes gave her fits, whether getting fired, job hunting in a tough economy, or breaking up with partners of whom we'd grown fond.

I didn't have to wait long.

"Well, Pepper, my favorite Spice Girl!" Donna Grandeen's lilting, upbeat voice trilled down the aisle. I turned to see her statuesque form and fluffy blond hair outlined in the light from the barn's open front doors.

3

"Hey, Donna." I said, sliding open the door to my horse's stall. I looked up the aisle as she strode forward, her assistant stall cleaners a few steps behind. "Terrible about Vader. How you doing?"

"Don't ask," she said, pausing to stand up a pitchfork that had fallen over a blue muck tub. Her helpers, Jody and Carlos—she round and blond, he squat and dark—moved past me. Their eyes met mine but quickly looked away. Residents of the brown and tan trailer behind the barns, they weren't the talkative kind. But they surely felt unnerved by Vader's death last night. Crime interviews, not to say death, did that to people.

Donna checked the whiteboard up front to see what riding lessons she was giving today, and to whom. Then she came toward me.

"Just so sad," I said when she stood beside me. "Who'd do such an evil thing?"

"No idea," she said with an exasperated-looking smile. "None. Nada. Real kick to the gut, for sure. Damn nice horse. Great sire, too. One in a million."

I waited for more, but none was forthcoming. I tried another tack.

"He was special, Donna. We'll all miss him. Freddie is beside himself. Because of Vader's death, but also because he's now a suspect. He was so angry at Vader's being sold before the biggest shows of the year. He hoped to earn big bucks from wins so he could finally buy out the salon and score world trophies to bling it out with."

"Yeah, I know," said Donna. "And this was supposed to be his last best chance."

"Right," I said. "It was coming down to the horse or the salon. Hard to support a horse habit costing nearly two grand a month when you only make three or four grand."

"It was unfortunate timing," said Donna. "But he knew the horse could be sold if someone offered our asking price. Marietta was that person. That's the horse business. It's a damn tough one. We have bills to pay, too. Remember we have added pressure since Mad Mattie sicced the State Labor Department on us."

"Oh, that's right."

I nodded, indeed recalling "Mad" Mattie Henderson. That tiny, tough little Valley newbie with a mouth like a stevedore had worked for the Grandeens cleaning, exercising and prepping horses for seven months part time with no contract, as did many helpers. Yet when she was let go last spring after handling horses recklessly and working for Grandeen's clients on the side, she filed for unemployment benefits.

The Grandeens subsequently had to lawyer up and produce financial records dating back years.

"Hmmm," I said. "Mattie had a definite axe to grind. Is there a chance she might be behind Vader's death?"

"I doubt it," said Donna. "She's getting her unemployment benefits. Besides, she wouldn't know how to do what was done to Vader. That took somebody experienced with horses. Mattie barely knew the end that eats from the end that poops. She never could tell the two bay Paints apart. And, Jello is a mare, Domino a gelding!"

Donna's eyes sparkled at that. Then they darkened again. I couldn't be sure what she was thinking or feeling. Another horse-trainer trick that kept clients guessing.

"But the sheriff will talk to Mattie?" I said.

"I imagine so," she said, swatting at a fly.

"Well, I believe I might talk with her, too."

Donna lifted her eyebrows. She shot me a curious look.

"Why would you talk to her, Pep? Assuming you can even find her?"

"People in the barn want me to look into Vader's death. Mainly Freddie wants me to. He knows I was a reporter. So-o-o, if you don't mind, I'll just nose around a little."

Donna stiffened, and then sighed.

"I guess it won't hurt, Pepper. If you have time with your business, showing and all. And if you come up with anything, I'd appreciate if you'd let me or Dutch know. Before the sheriff. Bounce if off us first so we know what's up."

"Sure. And, oh yeah. What do you mean, 'if I can find her'? Meaning Mattie."

"Nobody's seen her since she filed. You know she's a real rolling stone. Lived all over the world. Might have moved back to California to help her aging parents."

"Do you know where in California?"

"Somewhere like Stockton. Sacramento. Started with an 'S'."

"O.K.' I said. "I also need contact info on Marietta Von Sustern. I only saw her from a distance, never talked to her, when she came up to try out Vader."

"You got it," Donna said. "Hey, thanks for any help you can give, Pep. This might be the final straw, the horse business and clients being as flighty as they are. You never really know who your friends are in this racket."

"No kidding," I said.

Competition for world titles and the money and future business that came with it, turned friends into enemies and enemies into so-called friends. But even with Donna's talk about vulnerability, I wondered if I was hearing the whole story. It almost seemed she was protesting too much, as they say.

Something just kept wiggling around the edges of my consciousness. As with Dutch, I was struck by how normal Donna seemed. She said the expected things, yet didn't appear to deeply feel Vader's loss. I thought I'd see a little more stress, emotion, anything.

Then, I reasoned, giving my longtime friends the benefit of the doubt, maybe they were still in shock, holding pain without feeling it completely. It had been quite a night. Besides. Donna was one tough cowgirl, a true professional like her spouse. They stood united in many things but notably that. Their motto was, "Don't show your fear, and don't let 'em see you sweat." That applied to people as well as to horses.

"Well, off to work," Donna shrugged, her eyes and voice brightening. "Those stalls don't clean themselves." She walked down toward an outside stall where the wheelbarrows and pitchforks were kept.

Like I said, one tough cowgirl.

***

As I stood in the open stall door, Choc nuzzled my arm and sniffed my breath. He was assessing my health, my mood and my most recent meal. It was an equine greeting I happen to love. I stroked his neck and bent to unfasten the belly and leg straps on his blue and white stable blanket.

"Hey, Handsome," I said, leading him to the grooming area. I gave him a quick brush. Then I tacked up with my Western saddle and bridle and led him through the passage to the covered arena where we rode night or day, rain or shine.

I lifted a long whip and a twenty-foot cotton rope from a hook. I snapped one rope end to Choc's noseband, raised the whip, and paid out rope, called a "longe line," as the horse drifted away. When I clucked, Choc trotted in a large circle around me.

This "longeing" lets horses warm up and play safely before a ride. As my gelding moved into a lope, or slow, western-style canter, I thought of how pretty he looked. I also thought of Vader. My horse, in fact few horses anywhere, could ever hold a candle to that leggy black and white. Vader had been the ultimate show horse, in almost any English or Western class. A sure bet to have beat them all, even the top horses from leading Southwest trainers, at next week's Western Horse Nationals at Rancho del Cielo Equestrian Center south of Sacramento

His death couldn't have been more timely, from a major competitor's viewpoint. Somebody needed Vader seriously disabled, even dead. That way the horse would never make the record books as the World Champion, and sire of World Champions, he was meant to be. He'd also be stopped from winning much of the million-dollar prize money offered by the new and powerful World Western Horse Association. This was a consortium of uber-rich and influential owners and breeders of Quarter Horses, Paints, Pintos, Appaloosas, Buckskins, Palominos and other stock-type breeds.

"Ow!" I said, feeling a powerful yank from the longe line. I tightened my grip, braced my feet and bent the rope across one hip to block Choc's leaping and bucking.

That same instant a quick movement in the passageway caught my eye. Someone in a white T shirt ducked around the corner before I could focus on who it was. It didn't look like Dutch or Donna. Maybe Jody or Carlos, the barn cleaners. Had they been spying on me? If so, why? Whatever, it unnerved me. It took a minute to settle my nerves.

Bringing Choc back under control and reversing his direction, I eased him into a gentlemanly lope. But he still looked sideways and launched into another few bucks.

"No!" I shouted. "You have twenty-three hours a day to do as you like. I wish I had your job, working one hour a day, five days a week, my every need met."

Choc tossed his head, but loped his circles without further ado.

It was approaching eight o'clock. I needed to have my own daily ride for mental and physical fitness, though Dutch later would school Choc and check for errors. I also had to rocket myself to Gold Hill to open my tack and clothing shop.

Most days, I arrived at The Best Little Horsehouse by nine-thirty. I liked to clean and organize stock, put out new items, and go over the previous day's receipts, if any, before customers started dropping by. Truth to tell, business had been slow, and the landlord recently upped the rent on my small building. I feared I'd soon have to work solely from the long, live-aboard trailer I set up at horse shows.

I returned the whip and longe line to the wall by the gate, and mounted my horse. Gathering the reins in one hand, I clucked, and brushed Choc with my calves. He aligned his body between my legs.

He was a good boy. Knew his job well. He should, after four years of training and showing at about a thousand dollars a month. Which didn't include shoeing, vet work and extras like tack or my show clothes.

Having a show horse was not for the faint of heart or light of wallet. Not remotely doable on a shoestring, like dancing or softball. That's why I still worked, trying to run a business during my so-called retirement. It also explained why I, like many other single horse owners, was constantly on the lookout for a Sugar Daddy or Mommy.

I rode Choc at a jog, sitting lightly as I worked my hands and legs, driving him in circles and diagonals. I made each part of his body move away from pressure of my legs.

As I rode I flashed on another aspect of Vader's death. The horse had been priced at fifty or sixty thousand dollars, according to Freddie. Had the Grandeens in fact been paying on an insurance policy in that amount for him that covered theft, mortality, colic, and loss-of-use? Donna Grandeen once mentioned to me that she and Dutch never carried horse insurance. From the thousands they saved by not paying premiums, she said they could afford surgery or the loss of a horse. But a horse like Vader? Doubtful. No one could afford to lose a horse like that without insurance. They had to have had some on him. Then, if the sale were finalized as Dutch implied, Marietta would now have her policy in place, meaning she alone stood to collect.

I'd ask the Grandeens again, but at a less stressful time. I could ask the vet, too, though she probably would not feel comfortable answering me. But in an investigation you had to ask many questions of everyone even remotely connected. Also ask these questions many times, many ways, until something gave. Which it usually did.

Today from work, I'd try to take a stab at scoping out Vader's insurance status. The answers might not be forthcoming They would tax all my investigative powers, demand all my bulldog pushiness. But I'd find a way.

Now I put such speculation aside and turned my attention to riding Choc. His body rose and fell under me, responsive to every cue. The saddle squeaked agreeably. Earth and barn smells mingled pleasantly. This was the Heaven part of my day. It would prepare me for anything the Underworld could later pitch my way.

Little did I know the Devil was about to throw me a slider from Hell.

4

Dolly Parton belted out "Here You Come Again" from the phone on the truck's middle seat. I glanced down as I drove the gray ribbon of I-5 that snaked through the Southern Oregon hills from Brassbottom Barn to The Best Little Horsehouse.

The phone screen lit up with a photo of Choc and me enjoying a blue sky day much like this. A carefree day from another year, long before last night's tragedy at Brassbottom Barn. The killing of Dark Vader would represent, I was sure, a turning point for us horse people, when our innocent pursuit of equestrian dreams turned to paranoia and a sobering awareness of evil. Did we really know each other or our friendly competitors in other barns? Whom could we trust? Should we trust at all?

On the third line of Dolly's song I picked up the phone. Keeping an eye on the road, I slid the arrow to answer the call. But before bringing the phone to my mouth, I glanced around to check for yellow license-plates indicating "Smokies." Good. Only a few civilian cars and one semi truck.

"Hello?" I said, holding the phone tight to my cheek.

"Pepper! Where are you?" It was Dutch Grandeen.

"Halfway to work. Why?"

"Sheriff Jack Henning's here. You were supposed to wait to talk to him."

"Oh crap. I was in such a hurry to go to work. My mind's preoccupied."

"No kidding. Well, circle back. He doesn't have much time. Has another case. Says it's more important than a dead horse. His words. Oh, wait a minute."

"Okay. But hurry. I'm driving." I heard muffled voices over the phone. I frowned and looked around. The coast was still clear but I couldn't count on that for long, this being mid-morning on a work day.

"Jack says he'll catch you at your store. He's headed that way for the other case."

"Cool. I'm almost there. Don't need to backtrack twenty miles."

I pulled up to the cement building I rented for The Best Little Horsehouse. It sat off the main drag of Gold Hill, an itty-bitty city founded in the 1850s at one northerly bend of the Rogue River near Table Rock mesas. Two prospectors found a giant gold nugget there after the 1849 California strike, making Gold Hill an important name in Rogue Valley history. Recently it fell into hard times. No police department and very little revenue. But it was a great business location, halfway between Grants Pass and Medford, and Seattle and San Francisco. It drew customers from a wide area.

I parked my dually in the shade of a horse-chestnut tree beside the building, fished keys from my purse and opened the door, turning the "Closed" sign to "Open." I stooped to pick up a flyer slipped through the mail slot. Just an ad for the local pizza place. Once inside I flipped on the lights and disabled the alarm.

The air in the twenty-by-forty building felt fresh and cool. It smelled of good leather and new clothes. Racks, shelves and stand-alone kiosks overflowed with hats, boots, saddles, bridles and grooming gear.

Cheered, I walked over to activate the cash register and credit-card machine. Reaching over the tall captain's chair behind the counter, I turned on the radio.

Soon a rockin' country tune played over speakers in the four ceiling corners. They were the brainstorm of Sonny Chief, my former part-time boyfriend and full-time tribal policeman on South Dakota's Standing Rock Reservation. I wondered what Sonny was up to. Probably hitting on a new winyan, or "woman." Or being hit on himself. As I stood behind the counter, nostalgia swept me. I looked back at our five-by-seven photo with the beaded frame. It stood among others, including ones of my adult son, Serrano, and daughter, Chili, on a scarred tan bookcase. It showed Sonny and me holding the reins of horses we'd ridden on his Rez.

I still marveled at how much he towered over me. Six-foot-six, he'd once lifted a freezer as if it were a hatrack and carried it across a room when I needed it moved. His smile could light up an arena.

Dolly burst into song again, spoiling my reverie just as it was getting juicy.

"Hello?" I said into the phone.

"Hell-o," drawled a deep male voice, emphasis on the double-bass "o," which made my toes curl and my neck tingle.

Sonny!

My heart did a flip. I was happy, sad and mad at the same time. I tried to stay calm, however. Tried to sound cool and collected, though he'd see through it.

"Wow. I don't believe it's you. Sonny?"

"What they call me. How you doing?"

My heart beat even faster. He always made my heart beat fast. Sometimes from passion or anticipated passion. Other times from anger. "Well, I'm fine," I said. "Kinda. There's been stuff happening. I was just thinking of you out of the blue. Then you call."

"Not surprised. How they work."

"You mean the Spirits."

"Ho."

A few seconds passed. I heard Sonny breathing softly on the other end of the line.

"Been years, Sonny. Heard you got married, and went on the pow-wow circuit with your kids. How are your wife and kids? How, no, where, are you? What's up?"

"Kids are fine. Pook and I are no longer together. Don't want to talk about it. I have been told you are in trouble. Care to share?"

"The spirits again, I suppose. Well, I am not in trouble. Yet. But friends of mine are, so I'm investigating. A valuable horse was killed here last night. Sheriff is on it, but I'm digging on my own. Better not turn out to be my own grave."

Again, soft breathing on the other end.

"Uh-huh. That's Pepper. Curious cat."

"You didn't answer my question, Sonny. Where are you?"

"Not far. Thought I'd come to see you. Maybe I can help."

"Well, I don't know." Trying to sort through the jumble of emotions the sound of his voice produced, I rolled my upper lip under my front teeth, and played with a topless red pen. After a few rolls it flipped, leaving a bloodlike ink blot on my hand.

Very funny, spirits. But you do have my attention.

Because I undoubtedly would encounter trouble and probable harm in undertaking this investigation and in reupping my friendship with a man I considered the love of my life, as dangerous and unpredictable as I knew him to be.

Still, Sonny might be able to help. Pull strings with law enforcement and other entities touched by the case. But I had to keep control, and convince Sonny to proceed with utmost care. The relationship between mainstream cops and tribal police was historically tainted and tricky.

"Sounds like a strong maybe, for me to come" he finally said. "Take it as a yes."

"As if anything would stop the famous, much-feared Sonny Chief. Hey. Sonny?"

The line was silent. The red light indicating an active call turned gray. I didn't know if the call was dropped, or Sonny had cut it off. What was up? Was he coming? Then, when? You didn't know with Sonny. Our relationship was never what many considered traditional, with exclusivity, etcetera. But still, it was a relationship.

Not knowing what else to do what with too many questions bouncing in my brain, I went to the restroom, grabbed Mr. Coffee and set him percolating. Sounds of simmering water and dripping brew soothed my brain.

As I awaited the French roast, I climbed into my captain's chair to call Donna regarding Vader's insurance. I had to get back on task, no matter what was up with Sonny. I might see him, I might not. But I wasn't going to let it distract me.

I punched in Donna's cell number. She would be easier to chat with than Dutch. Sometimes he could be intimidating. You never knew for sure what thoughts passed behind those beguiling blue-grey eyes of his.

My call to Donna went to voicemail. I left a message asking if Vader'd been insured, and if so, with whom, by whom. That was a reasonable question.

Then I pulled my old laptop from its tooled leather case, and powered up.

Damn! Only twenty minutes tops, left on the battery. I'd been meaning to replace that sick puppy, as it no longer held a charge very long. But I couldn't ever scare up any spare change for a new battery. Usually I just left its cables plugged into the charger.

I typed hurriedly, entering "horse insurance agent" in the search pane. While I awaited results, I thought about Sonny again. Not exactly the distraction I needed at a moment like this. Crime investigation going on, super big horse show coming up.

Jees, Sonny, your timing is so weird. You are so weird.

Yet somewhere deep inside I believed there was a purpose to his call and possible visit. A purpose beyond venal cravings, although that would be enough for Sonny, who had a girl in every port, as it were. No, he was sent by powers I didn't quite understand yet had seen results from often enough, in the fifteen years I'd known him.

A list of horse insurance groups came up. I scrolled through them, and began writing the names and numbers of the top picks, names I recognized from ads in the influential horse magazines.

Dolly sang out. I grabbed the phone. It was Donna. "Hey, Donna."

"Hey. Not sure, but I thought Marietta said that Vader was insured, or going to be, when we signed over his registration papers. Maybe Sterling Mutual. Or Stanton Group. Always get the two mixed up. Both start with an 'S.' Used to be one company."

I had to laugh. Donna never could remember details when names started with an 'S.' Like where that former barn helper's folks lived, somewhere east of San Francisco.

"Then I assume you haven't heard from an insurance investigator yet."

"You assume right. Maybe later today. Possibly tomorrow."

"Also assume you've talked to Marietta. How'd she react?"

"We talked briefly last night. She was hysterical."

"I can imagine. I would be, too. She in town?"

"No. Traveling in Nevada and California. She'll be at the show, though. To look at another horse to buy"

"Really."

Boy, I thought, that woman doesn't let any grass grow under her feet. So much for mourning time.

"I think she had her eye on this other horse for awhile. A different type than Vader. Different events."

"Well, she is the ultimate showgirl," I said. "Win at any cost. Literally. Do you have her number, Donna?"

"I'm still down at the barn. But I can look it up when I go to the house for lunch, if there's enough time. Pretty crazy here. Sheriff talk to you?"

"Not yet, Donna. Did he say when he was coming over here?"

"No. Just that he'd drop by on his way north."

"Almost forgot. Did the vet verify what was in the syringe that killed Vader?"

"Not yet. Likely one of the heavy tranquilizers. Dr. Givens said the lab will pin it down in a few days. Probably by the end of the week."

"Sure hope so. And that this was an isolated case. Anything else, Donna?"

"Nada. Sorry. Gotta go."

"Okay. Thanks."

I could just imagine the scene at the stables. Clients would be whispering, the sheriff or a detective might still be working, and Dutch probably would be tractoring Vader's body out to bury in the back pasture. Glad I wasn't at Brassbottom.

But Tulip was meeting me for lunch after she rode her horse in late morning. I'd hear the latest from her, and we could hash out a battle plan then. We'd teamed up more than once when trouble bubbled. She often had insights from out of left field. Where, by the way, was where she'd played in our short-lived senior softball career.

Rich coffee smells filled the store. I got up, filled my hotel brownware mug, and wrapped my chilled hands around it for comfort. I stood a moment, staring into space. Then I took a few deep swallows of the hot dark coffee.

I found the numbers of the horse-insurance companies Donna had mentioned on the list I'd scribbled earlier. I called Sterling Mutual first. I was pretty sure neither they nor Stanton would give out information, but it was worth a try.

Years ago, for the paper, I'd been making random calls to insurance companies and then gotten lucky when a harried executive assistant accidentally said the first syllable of a name that turned out to be pivotal in the case.

My call to Sterling, however, brought the expected predictable result.

"That is privileged information," said an officious sounding woman after I'd introduced myself and asked my questions as professionally as I could.

"Marietta said her policy on Darth Vader was with you," I pressed, expanding only a smidge on what Donna had told me.

"Still, this would be private between us and any client. I'm sure you understand."

I said I did. Then I hung up. I called Stanton. Same results. I looked down the list of horse agencies I'd made earlier. No more beginning with 'S.' But there was a West Best, with several 'S's in it. Oh well. No matter. I'd wait. Their investigator certainly should show soon, what with a probable six-figure payout pending.

My watch read ten-thirty. It felt like I'd been at the Horsehouse for hours, not minutes. No customers yet. But it was still early.

What I needed was physical work, to give my busybody brain a break. Picking up the broom, dustpan and industrial mop from a closet by the restroom, I set to work cleaning the speckled linoleum floor.

***

Jason Aldean's rockin', stompin' "The Only Way I Know" played over Sonny's speakers. "Don't back up, don't back down, full throttle, wide open." That'd be me, on the case, from now on. It was the only way I knew.

Pushing and pulling the mop in swirls and circles, I did a hip-hop line dance while making piles of lint and the odd stall shaving that had dropped off someone's jeans cuff.

Halfway through, I stopped. I leaned the mop against a shelf of designer jeans.

Jeans. Shavings. I'd been so busy with phone calls and brain work that I'd forgotten about the shiny something I'd found that morning in poor Vader's hoof.

I'd been moving around a lot since then. Grooming and riding Choc. Driving to Gold Hill. Visiting the restroom. Cleaning The Best Little Horsehouse.

Hopefully that shiny something was still in my jeans pocket.

5

I propped my mop against the jeans rack and moved behind the counter. I didn't want the shiny speck I'd taken from Vader's hoof to accidently drop out of my jeans onto the lint on the floor.

Just when my fingertips felt the metallic speck tangled with a thread inside the pocket, a shadow fell on the windowed top of the Horsehouse front door. Next thing I knew, the door opened.

A brown-uniformed man resembling an overfed grizzly, complete with hairy, humped neck and beady eyes, loomed in the doorway. Daylight haloed around his "Smoky Bear" hat and glinted off his stars and badges.

I'd never met Sheriff Jack. But I figured this was one and the same, a local hero known for conclusion jumping and criminal thumping. He'd often had his hand slapped for "unnecessary roughness" in arrests or incarcerations. Or been rumored to have had a slight gambling problem. But it never seemed to get in his way. And for decades voters let it be known they didn't give a rip about his issues or policing style, as long as he brought home the bad guys.

"Pepper Kane?" he said, his close-set eyes drawing even closer together over a long upturned snout.

"Um, yes," I said, standing straighter behind the counter. "Sheriff Henning, I presume? I've only seen you on TV. Nice to meet you in person."

"The media sucks," he said. "Anyway, I need to ask a few questions regarding the horse killed out where you board your horse, Brassbottom Barn in Sam's Valley."

"Yes, I was expecting you. Dutch said you were dropping by on your way to another crime scene down the freeway. Didn't know you guys would be so involved in a horse death, beyond a first response."

"It may be a Class C felony, animal abuse, for starters. Serious matter."

For starters. That sounded interesting. I moved out from behind the counter and stood a few feet away from the sheriff as he took out a pad and pencil.

"Animal abuse," I said. "For starters. What's that mean? That other crimes are possibly involved."

"Can't say. Too early. If we learn more we'll release a statement. But animal abuse is serious enough to get us involved."

Now I had something else to look into, and to ask the Grandeens and others about. Animal abuse was a medium priority crime for law enforcement. They'd go with it for a time, work the usual angles, then let the case languish as other cases took priority. Let it languish, that is, unless another angle turned up in their animal abuse investigation. Say, drugs, trafficking, or money laundering.

"Sounds fair," I said. "Please have a seat. Want some coffee? Just made." As I pointed at an overstuffed leather loveseat and chair by a coffee table stacked with glossy horse magazines, I thought of also offering him a stale cinnamon doughnut-hole from a bag in the mini-fridge. Then I felt ashamed of thinking that. Not all cops subsisted on java and pastry. But he definitely looked like one who could.

"No, thanks," he said. "And I'll stand."

He asked for and I gave him my address and phone numbers, details about my business, what work I did before, and how long I'd known the Grandeens.

"Had a horse with them coming on five years," I said. "Known of them, as trainers, maybe twenty."

"Consider them friends?"

"Absolutely."

"Know about any legal trouble or serious disagreements they've had in the past? Clients, horseshoers, suppliers, contractors, other trainers?"

"Any business has disputes with customers, suppliers and competitors," I said. "They have been in business forty years."

"Of course. Just narrow it down to the past year."

So I told the sheriff about "Mad" Mattie Henderson, the Grandeens' former helper who had been fired for insubordination, among other things.

The sheriff stood up straighter, and brightened considerably. I gave him what I knew of Mattie and the situation as he eagerly jotted notes.

"Anyone else? What about Freddie Uffenpinscher. Understand he was upset over the horse that was killed, being sold out from under his lease."

"Yes, I'd say he was very much disappointed. Understandably so. But he knew it was a possibility in a horse lease."

"He wasn't just disappointed, Miss Kane. He broke into sobs during our interview. Screamed. Went way over the top."

I slowly smiled as a thought came to me.

"Freddie always has been a drama queen," I said. "Pun partly intended."

The sheriff's already hard face turned to stone.

"Are you taking this lightly?" he said, tapping his pencil against the notepad.

"Oh, no, sir," I said, chastened.

"He said he drove the fifteen miles to the dance hall to tell you the night the horse was killed," said the sheriff. "Why single you out? And why make a twenty-minute drive so late, when he'd already been through a lot, and he simply could have called?"

"Freddie and I are friends. He trusts me. Needed face-to-face support."

I'd felt pretty relaxed when the sheriff started the interview. Most questions had been routine, like those I'd asked people thousands of times as a newspaper reporter.

But now, as the interview doubled down, the questions became increasingly and annoyingly more personal, almost accusatory.

My body tensed and my palms began to sweat.

"So you were at the dance hall when?" said the sheriff.

"Left home at six-thirty, got there at seven, stayed until ten; then drove home and texted or called our barn buddies about Vader."

"Any of them react unusually?" he said.

"Not that I recall," I said.

"Do you regularly go to the dance hall on Thursdays?" he said.

"Yes," I said.

"Why not tell your friends about the horse when they were at the hall?"

"They were busy dancing."

"Did you take any breaks at the hall last night? Step out for air? Use the john?"

I answered as briefly as possible, not elaborating. Longer answers could cast a shadow of collusion or guilt on the person giving them. Newspapering had taught me that. So had aware living.

The sheriff stopped writing and fixed me with a sharp stare.

"So," he said. "You took a break of maybe fifteen minutes, you say, from dancing last night. We can check that. And after we interviewed Freddie at the barn last night, he drove over to tell you about Vader."

"Yes, to both questions."

I dropped my gaze to the floor in front of me, a panorama that took in the badly scuffed toes of Sheriff Jack's size-twelve boots. I amused myself by thinking, "So he's not obsessive-compulsive, not a polisher, probably not a former Marine."

It was not totally clear if that held meaning. But it was possible that either through laziness or minus points in the IQ department, infinitesimal details got past him. He'd no doubt caught crap for that. Hence the gruff exterior and extra pro-active demeanor.

"I think we're done, for now," he said. "Thank you for your time. Nice little place you got here. Like the name. How long you been here?"

I was caught off guard by his change of subject and demeanor. He seemed almost cordial. For a griz. "Oh. Uh, almost three years."

"Ever had any problems?"

I wondered if he meant paying rent, handling unruly clients, or something else.

"Not really," I said. "What kind of problems?"

"As you must know, Gold Hill break-ins are not uncommon. No police force, so near the freeway, drug culture and all. Have a good alarm system?"

"I do." I thought but did not add, *Thanks again to multi-talented Sonny Chief.*

Sheriff Jack nodded. He slipped his notepad into a pocket, touched the brim of his hat, and left the store.

I stood there a moment, a little dazed, chastened and distracted. I wondered why he'd dwelled on my store and its security. *Was he being thorough? Was he saying I should be more watchful, since I might know something I wasn't saying, about the horse's death? Or was I just being paranoid?*

Probably the latter. I'd bet my mini-farm that everyone else even lightly involved with the Grandeens, as well as other local horse owners and trainers, felt paranoid about now. Everyone would feel vulnerable at this point in the investigation. Another barn, another horse, might be "hit," if the killer were just some whacko seeking attention.

I'd sure be locking my stable at night.

***

Sheriff Jack also had intimated that Freddie and I might be suspects, or at least that we might know more than we were saying, since we'd behaved in ways that he considered unusual in the aftermath of Vader's death.

Was he warning or threatening us in some way? Trying to bluff us into confessing guilt, collusion, or knowledge of a cover-up?

Well. Sheriff, roger that. Warning taken.

But not necessarily obeyed. I'd simply have to use a higher brain octane as I went about this sleuthing business. Definitely more stealth.

***

Dolly Parton broke into my thoughts again. What now? Today the phone seemed bent on bringing up an increasing number of questions and emotions.

"Pepper?" My mother's creaky voice came on the line.

"Mom! Sorry I didn't call to check you two this morning. How are you and Dad?"

"Same ole. Caught him smokin' again on the back porch."

I had to laugh. Mom always said smoking would stunt his growth or drive him to an early grave. But retired CPA Vincent J. Kane was eighty-five, and that didn't classify as "early" in my book.

"Nicotine patch didn't work, I take it."

"Pulled it off after the first day. Mean as a cut snake, since. Say, Pep, could you bring us some milk and bread today? And pick up our prescriptions at the Wal-Mart? We're out of everything."

Oh, boy. Just what I needed. More errands and worries, with the day already filled to the flood level. I still had people to talk to, places to go, and was paddling as hard as I could just to stay afloat.

My left temple began to pound.

"Can it wait until tonight, Mom, or tomorrow? I'm up to my armpits in alligators, stuck at the store until lunch, which I'm having with Tulip. I also have important calls to make, and a hair appointment at three with Freddie."

"Oh, he's such a nice boy. So knowledgeable about music and the theater. Could you schedule me in with him next week?"

"I'll try. Remember, I'll be off all week at the horse show in California?"

"I guess Serrano, or Dad, can drive me. I really need a color."

My son, Serrano, was coming down from Seattle to house-sit my place but also spend days with my parents. I finally agreed to Mom's requests, signed off, and jumped down off my chair.

Resuming my normal store routine, I swept the lint into the dustpan, nuked the French roast and returned to my chair behind the counter. My stomach rumbled, so I grabbed a doughnut hole from the mini-fridge. Brittle, but edible.

I wiped my mouth and settled back in the chair. Time to examine that little thing in my pocket. I groped in my jeans pocket again, then pulled at the tangled thread. The shiny flake or whatever seemed to be coming loose, and had more substantial hardness than I'd thought. Like a grain of sand. Maybe that's all it was, a shiny bit of local quartz with glints of real or fool's gold embedded in it.

As I finally dug the bit out of my pocket and held it up to the light, the front door opened again.

I looked over, still holding the speck between thumb and forefinger, to see two familiar-looking women surveying the place. A willowy young blonde, and a nipped, tucked and streaky-haired replica of herself, doubtless her mother.

At last. Customers.

I smiled, stood up, and stuffed the shiny speck back in my jeans pocket. It would have to wait. Again. Business always came first.

6

"Hi, Ladies," I said. "Welcome to The Best Little Horsehouse. May I help you?"

The younger woman ignored me. She fondled a show bridle with chunky silver straps and Texas-cross conchos where the straps supported twin ear loops. The bridle hung on a peeled-pine rack beside the loveseat, in front of a row of silver bedecked Western show saddles.

The older woman, wearing tight, low-cut jeans and a bright slink top like her daughter's, stepped forward, smiling. Her extended hand clanked with a queen's ransom of turquoise bracelets. They matched her thickly mascara'd eyes. A pale turquoise pendant the size of a credit card nestled at the top of her cleavage.

"Ha-eye. You all must be Peppah Kane, the owner? I'm Patsy Ann Carpenter. My daughter, Honey, and I are up from Texas for a family reunion. Saw your ad in the Journal, and decided we just had to check out your store."

"Well, great," I said. "Nice to meet you." I recognized their faces and augmented figures from costly full page ads in the Western Horse Journal. They were among the top show riders in the nation. Tulip once told me they had more money than God. Daddy Carpenter owned the majority share in a generic-drug company.

"So nice to meet you, too," said Patsy Ann. "You show Paints, don't you? You're with the Grandeens. The horse show world is a small world."

"Way less than six degrees of separation," I said with a smile.

"I beg your pardon?" said Patsy Ann, raising her lightly brushed eyebrows.

"We know everyone at least by name and reputation," I said, keeping it simple.

"Oh, so true," she said. "We don't travel to the Coast much, mainly follow the Midwest and Southwest circuits. But we'll be hitting the Rancho del Cielo show next week, as I expect you are. That show just gets bigger and bigger."

"Oh, yeah," I said. "We're pretty excited about it."

"Honey," said Patsy Ann, turning to her daughter. "Say hello to Miss Kane."

The young woman turned, holding the bridle in her hand. She had turquoise eyes, too. But her taste in jewelry ran to silver with pink and orange coral stones.

"Nice to meet you. I like this headstall. No price tag, though."

"Sorry. It and the saddle behind it came in on consignment as I was rushing out the door yesterday. I got sidetracked this morning before I could tag them."

"Saddle has Texas crosses, too," said Honey. "Did you see it, Mommy?"

"My, my, now that's what I call pretty!" said Patsy Ann, turning back to me. "Who consigned it?"

"Jane Pardee," I said. "Quarter Horse gal. Used to train with Mark Gordon."

"Oh yes," said Patsy Ann. "We heard she had a bad fall, and may never be able to ride again. So sad."

"Yes," I said. "Jane has amazing medical expenses, and is getting out of the horse business for now. Her show clothes are on the other side of the loveseat. Near the jewelry case. Why don't you ladies have a look while I check my book about prices on the bridle and saddle?"

Patsy Ann and Honey glided to the clothing racks. I was struck by their erect yet relaxed posture and balletic stride, even in high-heeled crocodile cowgirl boots. No wonder they beat almost all challengers in their Hunt Seat Equitation and Western Horsemanship events.

Which horses do they own? Oh, right. Honey has Royal Flush, and ... oh, dear! I remembered with a pang that Patsy Ann owned the black gelding, Dark Victory, who'd won a reserve Western Horse world championship last year. Victory was related quite closely to Dark Vader. Half brother, something like that. I wondered if Patsy Ann had heard about Vader's death.

"Oooh, I like this red jacket," cooed Honey, absorbed in the clothing display.

"Real pretty, Honey," said her mother.

I pulled a three-ring binder from behind the counter, and thumbed through the names, arranged alphabetically by consignee or vendor and cross indexed by date the item came into the store. I had been meaning to put all my business records on the computer, but hadn't gotten around to it. There was always so much happening.

"I like your sound system," said Patsy Ann, nodding her head in time to a Carrie Underwood tune while doing a little jewelry looking. "That speaker system makes it sound like there's a live concert going on down the block."

"Thanks," I said. "A friend set it up."

Patsy Ann held a few earrings to her ears, already decked out with turquoise-ringed diamond studs as big as peas. I had displayed no pieces near as spendy as hers. Mine ran to fabulous fakes. Some were new, others were consigned.

I put my finger on Jane Pardee's binder page that listed chaps, hats, show tops and pants, as well as the bridle and saddle. I hadn't called Jane yet about her minimum prices. One of those things I'd been meaning to do, probably today, before I got sidetracked.

Patsy Ann held out a pair of giant hoop earrings, whose gold and silver wires were twisted to resemble mating snakes complete with fierce heads. She carried them to the counter. "These are adorable. I'll take them while my daughter decides."

"Great," I said. "They are pretty cute."

"The snake is my spirit animal," she said. "A native American medicine man I know told me that."

"Really." I said. You never knew what customers would tell you. It was the old comfort-in-confessing-to-captive strangers routine, I guessed.

"You all have them priced at $60," she said. "Would you take $50? Cash?"

I tucked my lip under and tried not to grin. Richer than God, but still trying to save ten bucks, with no concern for the little guy. Or gal just barely squeaking by. "Sold," I said, hoping to create a loyal customer for the long run.

Patsy Ann fished in her handbag and pulled out a hundred-dollar bill. I put it in the register, made change and wrote a receipt.

"Thank y'all," she said.

"You're welcome. And regarding the bridle, I believe it will be in the two-thousand dollar range, but I need to call Jane to verify that. She paid a lot more, I think. It's custom. I'll call her now."

I touched Jane's numbers on my phone, and waited through a half-dozen rings.

"By the way," I said to Patsy Ann, "what's the name of the family having the reunion, and when is it?"

"The DeYoung Family, they have a vineyard near Roseburg? DeYoung Cellars?"

"Oh, yes," I said. "They have a wonderful Zinfandel."

"And a mad Merlot," said Patsy Ann. "The reunion was last weekend. We've just been taking in the area's other attractions We hardly ever get up this way. Finally made it to Crater Lake. What a wonder. So blue."

There was no answer on my call to Jane Pardee. I left a voicemail, hung up and asked Patsy Ann how her horses were.

"They're doin' just fine," she said, "thank you."

"Well, one of ours isn't. You know Dark Vader. Related to your Dark Victory?"

Patsy Ann's eyelids flickered once, then resumed their normal neutral position.

"Oh yes, such a lovely horse," she said.

"He died last night," I said.

I figured a direct question might shake loose a reaction or information I could use. That is, if Patsy Ann were privy to any information. Being a bigwig in the horse show game, owning a Vader relative, and all.

Patsy Ann's jaw dropped open. Her artfully made-up face took on a look of shock, then dismay. She put one hand to her chest.

"What? Vader died? Oh. My. God. That's just … so sad. Honey, did you hear what Pepper said? That Dark Vader died?"

The younger woman's head popped up, and she looked blankly at us.

"Really? So sad."

Patsy Ann turned back to me.

"How did he die? Oh, that's just terrible. And right before the California show."

Patsy Ann began rolling her bracelets around on her arms. She fluttered her thick black eyelashes again.

I thought it an overly dramatized reaction. But, then, Patsy Ann was all about drama. It might mean nothing more than genuine concern.

"The cause is being checked out," I said. "They don't know anything at this point. Just died in his stall. Found last night."

Patsy Ann tapped her bright fingernails on the counter. The shadow of a wrinkle passed across her surgically tight forehead.

"Is there a chance it was colic, or a heart attack from too many supplements?" she said. "That's how a lot of them drop dead. Oops. Poor choice of words."

"Yes. About the words, I mean. Probably not colic or a heart attack." I hesitated to say more. Patsy Ann still was a stranger, and her reaction to the news of Vader's death seemed off, a bit overdone. Was she really here for a family reunion? For all I knew she might already have known about Vader, what with her horse's ties to him. She could even have some connection to the crime. You never knew.

"Well," she said, settling. "Who all found him, then? And what time was it?"

Those questions, too, seemed odd. Not things a normal person just hearing the news would ask.

"Freddie Uffenpinscher," I said. "The man who leased him before Marietta Von Sustern bought him a week ago."

"Oh, yes," she said. "Isn't he the hairdresser who rides hunters?"

"That's the one." I didn't want to tip my hand any more to this relative stranger. A stranger and a competitor who, with her daughter, had a lot to gain with Vader dead.

Then I brushed off that thought. Man, I was jumping to conclusions. No reason at all to suspect Patsy Ann. Yet you had to examine everyone, no matter what, no matter who. When it came to crime and its investigation, there were very few coincidences. I had learned that through thirty years of newspapering. And if there were coincidences, they'd reveal themselves as such fairly early.

Or not.

Patsy Ann leaned her elbows on the counter. Bracelets banged and rang against the glass. She lowered her voice to a whisper.

"Do they suspect foul play?"

I wondered why that question had popped up. That wouldn't be the first thing I thought of if I'd heard a horse had died.

"His blood and urine are being checked out at the state lab," I said. "Could take a few days, even a week."

"Well, that is just terrible news. I should call Marietta. Offer our condolences."

Now this was something. These two women knew each other well enough to have exchanged telephone numbers. They were among the Top 10 western riders in the world. Patsy Ann and Honey were with the famous Royce Ball and Rogers Valentine of the Diamond Double R in Texas. Marietta was with the rival Pinnacle Performance Horses in Oklahoma. Both women competed in the same events, so of course they knew each other.

"You have Marietta's number?" I said. "If no, I can get it from the Grandeens."

"Well, I think I have it," said Patsy Ann. "Let me look." Patsy Ann pulled out her phone and checked it. "Yes, there it is." She made the call.

Honey carried the show bridle over to the counter.

"I just have to have this, Mommy," she said. "The saddle, too. How much is the saddle, Pepper?"

"I haven't been able to reach the seller yet, but I left a voicemail," I said, at the same time marveling at the narcissistic rudeness of the daughter. "Probably twelve or thirteen thousand."

"Sorry to hear about Dark Vader," Honey said, as if reading my thoughts. "He was a nice horse. We tried to buy him a long time ago, but they wouldn't sell."

That was news to me. And even more food for thought.

***

"Marietta!" Patsy Ann's voice trilled loudly through the store as she spoke into her phone. "Yes. We're at The Best Little Horsehouse. In Oregon. Wonderful place."

For thirty seconds it was quiet, except for the music playing over the speakers. I turned them down a hair.

Patsy Ann spoke into the phone again.

"We just heard about Dark Vader, Marietta. So sad. Our condolences. Yes, we're coming down to Rancho. Royce and Rogers are bringing our horses out from Texas even as we speak."

I gestured to Patsy Ann as she listened to her phone.

She put her hand over it and looked at me.

"When you're done," I said, "I need to ask Marietta a question about Vader."

"Pepper Kane, she owns The Horsehouse and has a horse at Grandeens', wants a word," said Patsy Ann. She handed her phone to me.

"Marietta?" I said. "Sorry to break in, and I am super sorry about Vader. I hope you're doing okay?"

"Thank you, so nice of you," she said. "And I hope dear Freddie is okay."

"He's working through it," I said.

"Do tell him hello," she said.

"Will do," I said.

"So," she said, "do they know anything more?" Her voice was gracious and low, as I remembered from hearing it a short distance when she came to ride Vader. I tried to recall what she looked like. I'd only seen her from afar. Short, squat, long and graceful neck, dark hair with silver streaks. Plus, expensive jewelry up the yin-yang. Very expensive, some of it in the shape of hearts, spades and diamonds.

"Nothing yet, Marietta. But the sheriff is on it. Treating it as a Class C Felony."

"Yes," she said. "He and I talked on the phone last night."

"Marietta, I have a question. Had the transfer of ownership and insurance on Vader been finalized, I mean before his death?"

"Well, I, assume so." There was a pause. "My husband, Richard, was handling the transaction. He handles all our business affairs."

I thought that odd. Most riders I knew handled all their own equine affairs. Some excessively so. They liked to be deeply involved in every aspect of their beloved horses, from health and riding to training and showing. In fact most horse people obsessed with winning were micromanagers, often to the chagrin of their trainers. I would have placed Marietta and her friend, Patsy Ann, in that group.

Now I wondered if Marietta was the horsewoman I'd supposed her to be.

"Do you at least know what agency held the policy on Vader?"

Silence on the other end. Followed by a long, phlegmy cough. A smoker's cough.

"I'm sorry, but I barely know you, Pepper. Why do you want to know?"

A pinched, suspicious sounding tone. Dang. I'd pushed too far. Yet, I reasoned, and often said aloud, if you don't go too far, how do you know how far you can go?

I had to take my approach down a notch, make it casual, no biggie.

"Sorry, Marietta," I said, switching to full improvisational mode. "We're all just so worried about you, is all. Somebody, I forget who, asked if I knew."

"I am under a lot of stress right now," she said. "And such matters really are no one else's business. I'm sure you can relate."

I guessed it was possible that Richard Von Sustern, Marietta's influential spouse, had handled Vader's transfer without her and even taken out the policy on the horse. I had heard that Maria was almost as rich as God, but had neither the mind nor time for business. In fact I'd heard she'd run her husband's prior venture, delivering luxury vehicles to discriminating customers, into the ground.

"You're right, it's none of my business," I said, now in full placation mode.

"If anyone official must know, they'll have to ask my husband. He'll be at the show next week. Right now he's in Europe on business, fairly hard to reach."

It was as I'd figured, but had been worth a try.

"Well, thank you, Marietta. We'll see you at the show. I understand you might be looking at another horse there."

"There is one that came up," she said. "Of course none could replace Vader."

"Of course," I said. "Take care."

I handed the phone back to Patsy Ann. She completed her condolence call with a few moments of casual chatter.

"Okay, Marietta," she said. "Again, so sad about your loss. We'll see you soon."

When Patsy Ann hung up, I told her I'd hold the bridle and saddle for twenty-four hours, if she was sure she wanted it, and would leave a deposit of two hundred dollars.

"How long will you be in the area?" I said. "I should have an answer by tonight or tomorrow morning. Jane is that rare bird who listens to voicemail and returns calls."

"We're on our way to California," said Patsy Ann. "Have to make Sacramento by dinnertime. Can you believe? We're dining at the Governor's mansion with the Governor and First Lady herself."

I could believe it. Patsy Ann made no attempt to hide her wealth or connections. Simply not her style. I also was not surprised she was on calling terms with Marietta. They ran in the same orbit, socially and financially.

"Lucky you," I said. "So I'll call when I hear the tack's price, you can charge by phone or do a wire transfer. I'll bring it down to the show with me, in my tack trailer. Here's some paper. Write down your contact info."

She did so, and handed me two crackling new hundred-dollar bills to hold the precious tack.

"Thank you," I said. "I'll guard it with my life."

"Hopefully that won't be necessary," Patsy Ann twinkled, signaling her daughter it was time to go. The two headed out the door to their sleek black Lexus bearing dealer plates and a temporary license sticker.

Must be nice, I thought, looking over at my red dually pickup, which should have a wash before my trip. I had pretty fair makings for bug soup baked on the windshield.

"Drive safely," I called.

As I stood looking after them, letting the hot air blow into the store, I felt relief. It was wonderful to actually meet these semi-celebrities, at least in horse show circles, and probably be doing big business with them. The sale of Jane's saddle and bridle should bring me several grand. Enough to keep the store's power on and the landlord from changing the locks a few months.

But their visit also had raised some questions. How close was their relationship with Marietta? Was it in any way a business connection? And did they, or Marietta, know more than they were saying?

Their reactions to Vader's death, their questions, the connection with him, their showing up the day after, and knowing Marietta well enough to call, all seemed significant. I just didn't yet know in what way.

Back in the Horsehouse, I rinsed my mug, flipped my store sign to "Closed," and checked the mail before walking to Katie's Kitchen, "Home of Sky-High Pie," for Tulip's and my regular Friday lunch. I needed me some "Sky-High Pie." As well as Katie's fabled "Cowgirl-Up Burger." Made with hot melty pepper-jack, of course.

Dang. That yellow envelope was a second reminder from our landlord Vern Brachmeier to pay the Horsehouse rent. Both last month's and this month's, totaling two grand. This envelope had bright gold paper showing in the address pane. Every month, as I was later and later to pay, the address colors got hotter and brighter. Every month it was harder to make rent.

Hopefully, the tack sale to Patsy Ann would go through, and I could finally give Mr. Brachmeier his due. But I wondered how much longer I could hang on.

At the café, I slid into my favorite red leatherette booth by the window. Roly poly Katie, herself, set a frosted glass of raspberry iced tea in front of me.

"How you doin', Pepper?" she smiled, setting her giant rhinestone-hoop earrings in motion and showing the gap in her front teeth. "Meeting Tulip? Having your usual Friday Special?"

"Yes, and I'm fine, thanks. Probably have my usual. But I'm also gonna check what's fresh today. Might shake things up, try something different."

Katie jumped back in mock shock. The floor quivered under our feet.

"Whoa! What's up?" she said.

"Little trouble over at Brassbottom Barn. Horse died last night."

"No! Oh, that's just awful, Honey. Not yours I hope."

"No, thank the Lord. We're just shaken up, is all."

I shrugged as if this kind of thing happened sometimes with animals, and that was that. This wasn't the time or place for a tell-all. Besides, Katie and I weren't that close. She'd find out, anyway, using her own sources, by day's end.

Katie frowned, and patted my hand.

"See why you're down. Let me know when you're ready to order."

I nodded as she left to tend to other customers. I took a few swallows of tea, and savored the sweet-sour taste as I rolled ice shavings around in my mouth.

Glancing around before checking the menu board on the wall, I saw Jesse Banks dip his straw cowboy hat at me. That ten-years-younger, tan and hard-bodied fireplug often fixed things at my farm down the road. We always greeted with steamy kisses there, but that's as far as it went. He was tangled in a long, messy divorce.

Looking back through the front window, I saw Tulip's pink '56 short-bed Chevy pickup drive past, probably trolling for a shaded parking spot. She was fashionably late, as usual. But not too late.

What I saw next shocked me. Sheriff Jack Henning in his green-and-white SUV crept into view, then did a U-turn and pulled into an open spot in front of the café. He unloaded his bulk from the SUV, crossed the sidewalk in one step and shoved open the café door.

What the heck? Was this my favorite smoky's favorite lunchspot, as it was Tulip's and mine? Wonder what his favorite dish was on the menu?

But I could tell from his jowly frown and on-a-mission stride that lunch was the farthest thing from his mind. I also knew it could be me on the menu.

7

My blood iced up as I watched Sheriff Jack Henning chug toward my booth at Katie's Kitchen. The chill came more from my fear of his hurrying, plus my guilty feelings, than from Katie's cranked-up air conditioning.

How had he known where I was? More important, why was he rushing to see me again mere hours after our interview at my store?

In seconds his sweaty face and brawny chest filled my vision at the table's end.

"We meet again," I said as neutrally as possible. I sipped my iced tea and fiddled with the salt shaker.

"Miss Kane, you're in big trouble," he rasped, glancing around as the waitress and a dozen or so café patrons stared. "I'll ask you to come outside. We need to talk."

I shifted nervously. My jeans-clad bottom and thighs sweated against the vinyl.

"Okay. But would you please tell me what this is about?"

"In the unit," he said, motioning for me to rise.

I did so slowly, as my friend Tulip pushed through the door. Her eyes grew wide seeing the sheriff take me by the elbow and guide me past her.

"What's going on?" she said, worry lines dividing her eyebrows.

"Nada," I said. "Hold that booth, Tule. I'll be back in a second."

She half-smiled, making her way to the booth where I'd been sitting.

The hot noon air hit me like a blast furnace. Sheriff Jack opened the passenger door of the SUV for me, then got in the driver's side while I tried to settle myself.

"Are you detaining me?" I said. "Because you do need a reason to do so."

He turned toward me, spittle lining his lips. A flush rose to his cheeks.

"I will do the talking, Miss Kane. I have reason to believe you trespassed on a crime scene. Possibly compromised the investigation of a horse's wrongful death. A felony, I must remind you. You lied earlier, and undoubtedly obstructed justice."

Shards of fear pricked my body. What did Sheriff Jack know or not know? Had someone actually seen me enter or leave Vader's stall that morning? Dutch, Donna, or even the stall cleaners? Could someone have seen me put the shiny speck in my jeans?

No. They couldn't have. I had been too quick and careful. Checked and double checked. I was sure no one had seen anything.

Yet here was Sheriff Jack, showing up unexpectedly, putting me in his vehicle as if I were already under arrest, and delivering statements in a done-deal, accusatory way.

Well, two could play Blind Man's Bluff.

"Sheriff, I don't know what you are talking about," I said, looking over at him.

Sunglasses masked his tiny eyes. But his left hand resting atop the steering wheel jerked every few seconds.

"You know damn well," he said. "Just heard you were at the barn before anyone else this morning. Why there so early? May as well confess here and now. Help get this case solved. Save a helluva lot of trouble down the pike."

So, I thought. He sure sounds like he is either fishing or bluffing As he was doing earlier. Maybe both. Guy has nothing on me, or at least nothing convincing. Otherwise at this point he might have added a tidbit to support his so-called information. Surely he was just putting the old cop squeeze on me, intimating he knew more than he did so I'd say more than I should.

"I always ride early," I said. "So you'd better have a darn good reason for hauling me into your SUV. If not, I'm outta here."

I put my right hand on the door handle and gave it a pull.

Of course it was locked.

He merely smiled.

"What if I said someone saw you in the stall this morning?" he said.

"Okay. Name a name. Then I'll play your game."

"Watch the mouth, Miss Kane. Coulda been a Grandeen, or an employee."

"You say, 'What if?' and 'Coulda'. Sheriff, you got nothing, or you would have taken me downtown or arrested me already. Unlock this door, now, or I will bring charges against you and your department for harassment and unlawful detention."

"This is a routine interview," he said coolly. "Nothing to put your britches in a twist. Answer my question and you're free to go. Were you in that stall this morning?"

I paused before answering. I was sure no one had seen me. Yet here was Sheriff Jack, acting like a griz discovering a honeybee hive. Well, I wasn't giving up easily. I'd have to do some stinging myself to buy me more time.

"If someone said that, Sheriff, they lie," I said, emboldened. "And if you want me to go further with this, I respectfully request to have an attorney present."

He sighed and dropped his hand off the steering wheel.

"Your call," he said. "But gonna go hard on you, you obstruct justice in any way."

When the door lock popped, I was out of that SUV like a scalded cat. As I went straight into Katie's Kitchen I heard the SUV start and motor away.

The café was quiet as I entered. I gave a perplexed grin, glancing at the tower of pies on my right, as if nothing had just happened. I lingered there, studying a lemon meringue slice that stood in excess of six inches at its swirly peak. Then I sauntered across the cafe and plopped down opposite Tulip in our booth.

The staring heads returned to their lunches and conversations.

"What you done now, Miss Peppah?" said Tulip. "To get the law down on you?"

"Sheriff Jack's a piece of work," I said, shaking my head. "Tried to bluff me into believing someone saw me at the barn before anyone else got there. Tried to get me to say I'd snuck into Vader's stall and poked around."

Tulip sat back and frowned.

"Not good, Honey. Well, did you?"

"Did I what? Cave and confess?"

"No. Sneak into Vader's stall and poke around?"

"Sheriff has no proof. No one saw. Crime tape just as I found it."

"Uh-huh." It was the unconvincing, I-know-better "uh-huh" some wise grandmas make when they know you're putting them on.

"All I'm saying, Tule. All I'm saying."

"Well, you know I won't rat you out. What did you find, Miss Marple?"

"Not sure." I straightened my body up and dug into my jeans pocket. Then I gently tugged out the tangled threads containing the shiny speck. I held it between thumb and forefinger and picked it free of its nest. As I held it out a little, I bent over to study it.

Tulip leaned forward.

"You did find something."

"Not saying where I got it," I said.

"No," Tulip said. "And if you told me, that would be hearsay, not usable in a court of law, as you reporters say."

"True." I turned the speck around in my fingers. Then I pulled my white paper napkin out from under the silverware at my setting, and carefully set the speck on it.

"Well, it's gold," Tulip said.

"Might be a flake off a gold-toned lead-rope chain," I said.

"Or off a button from a jacket," she said.

"Or else ..." I said.

Tulip looked at me. She raised her eyebrows.

"Or else what?" she said.

"Off a piece of jewelry," I said.

"Uh-huh." This time her utterance sounded more like "Ah-hah."

We both sat back and stared at the napkin and the shiny speck. The more I looked at it, the more I became convinced it was part of a piece of jewelry. It could be a broken part of a hinge mechanism from an earring.

"But everyone wears jewelry," Tulip finally said, more to herself than to me.

"Some more than others," I said. "Victoria, Donna, Jody, even Carlos."

"Know what I think?" Tulip said.

"I'm breathless to know."

"Gotta be Freddie's."

I took a quick breath. Of course.

"It could be," I said. "I forgot about Freddie. He does love the gold hoops. Has a boatload in each ear. And he did go in the stall last night to see why Vader was so still."

"Exactly," Tulip said. Then she sighed. "On the other hand it could have been in the stall awhile."

"Yes," I said, "maybe sitting along the wall, then remixed when fresh shavings were put in to top off the old ones."

Both our shoulders sagged simultaneously. All we were doing was opening up new possibilities of where the speck came from and how long it had been there.

"Where exactly was it sitting?" Tulip said finally.

"Inside Vader's hoof," I said. "He was lying stretched out."

"Really," Tulip said.

Part of me wished I hadn't said quite so much, even to my best and most trusted buddy. However, what I said was still hearsay, if anyone asked her anything. We had collaborated in the past. I also knew naughty tidbits about her, should it come to that. Besides. Tulip sometimes had flashes of insight I could only dream of.

"Yes, inside the hoof. But at the outside of the packing. So it had to have been picked up by him recently. Before other dirt and shavings pushed in over it."

"I think you're right," Tulip said, leaning in on her elbows. "It probably got in there before the horse went down. Maybe Vader struggled to stay standing and milled around before he died."

A chill rolled through me. Picturing that vital, shining show horse struggling to live, brought tears to my eyes. I hoped he hadn't suffered. But he'd felt something.

"You and I make a good team, Tulip," I said. "Thanks, buddy. But you know nothing, heard nothing, saw nothing. Right?"

She flopped back in the booth.

"Are y'all kidding me?" she said.

We high-fived. I wrapped the gold speck tightly in the napkin and slipped it back into my jeans pocket.

Katie showed up with her pencil and pad. Our conversation would continue later.

"What'd the sheriff want?" Katie said, her eyebrows rising.

"Just something about that horse that died," I said.

"Does he think you had anything to do with it?" Katie said, leaning in.

"Just routine," I lied. "Questioning everyone."

Katie looked disappointed. But my answer satisfied her for the moment. For sure she would shake down other customers who knew the Grandeens, or Tulip and me. She also would have more questions for us another day. Katie, bless her heart, was a Gold Hill equivalent of jungle drums. Faster than Twitter or Instagram. Or whatever light-speed communication was hot now. The way tech-speak was headed, people would know your thoughts and actions before you did.

Tulip and I both ordered a Cowgirl Up Burger and agreed to split that towering slice of lemon-meringue pie.

A bit later, up to our elbows in melting pepper-jack, lettuce, onions, meat and mayo, I brought Tulip up to speed on my visit from Patsy Ann and Honey. Told her they'd had me hold Jane Pardee's saddle and bridle.

"Huh," said Tulip between bites. "Hopefully we'll have a sale. Sure could use it. And very interesting that they all own a horse related to and competitive with Vader."

"What I thought," I said. "Think I'll just ring the DeYoungs in Roseburg to check Pasty Ann's story." I wiped my hands, and did a quick white pages search on my phone.

"Say you're trying to reach her and heard she was in Roseburg," said Tulip.

I gave her a thumb up.

"DeYoung Cellars?" said a male voice on the other end of the line.

"Hello, I said, "this is Pepper Kane, owner of a little horse tack store in Gold Hill? Am I speaking to a DeYoung?"

"This is the owner, Mason DeYoung, How can I help you?"

"Patsy Ann Carpenter stopped by today and had me hold a saddle and bridle. She said she was up your way for a DeYoung family reunion?"

"Yes, she and Honey were here."

"Just last weekend, right?" I kept my tone breezy.

There was a momentary silence.

"That is correct. But why do you ask?" The voice now had a suspicious tone.

"Oh. Sorry. I misplaced her number and wondered if you would give it to me?"

"I could have her call you."

"I'd appreciate that."

I gave De Young my number, and hung up.

"Guess Patsy Ann had a legit reason for being here," I said, returning to my lunch.

"Whether or not she had mayhem in mind," Tulip said.

I considered this while finishing my lemonade.

Tulip and I mapped out the rest of the investigation. I'd take the lead, logging whom we'd each talked to and what they said. The smallest detail or some offhand comment could open a path for further sleuthing.

I'd tackle Freddie as he did my hair today at the salon in Grants Pass, and also call Victoria, Lana and Barbara. Might even run back to the Grandeens' to take on the barn cleaners, Jody and Carlos. I burned to know if they or either Grandeen had seen me in Vader's stall that morning

Tulip agreed to reach our other barn buddies.

"Oh," I said, "and I'll call Stewie." He was Brassbottom's sole entry in Walk-Trot events for kids eight and under. I had my eye on that little freckle-face to lease my Bob, the bay Paint who threw me and hurt my shoulder. Bob was temporarily retired at home while he "grew up" mentally.

When our lunch plates at Katie's Kitchen were picked clean, Tulip and I tucked into our lemon pie. A puffy crust cradled yellow-and-white gooeyness gone wild.

"I'd want lemon-meringue pie as my last meal," said Tulip.

"Me, too," said I. "Eight hundred calories don't matter if you're about to die."

That was an interesting choice of words. Hopefully, Tulip and I weren't about to die. Although with a horse murderer around, and the two of us cowgirls looking for the killer and already taking flak, you never knew.

8

Full and happy, I paid my lunch tab with my nearly maxed out card and reminded Tulip she'd promised to staff The Horsehouse while I kept my hair date with Freddie.

I broke into a sweat when I stepped into the searing sunlight. My hunky red truck now stood only partly in the shade of an oak in front of a faded Victorian. Typical of houses in Gold Hill, "Pop. 1220," according to a sign on Old Highway 99, now an I-5 frontage road that bisected the town.

A jay flew screeching off my hood as I climbed into the dually, started the engine and turned the AC to "flash freeze." I punched my tasks and notes into my Smartphone. At home in the evening, I'd make more calls and transfer everything to my laptop. Keeping track, keeping focused, just like in my reporting days.

That was the boring part of investigations. The "paperwork." But keeping it up was essential. One forgotten fact, one omitted time of an event or meeting, could set a curious cat back for days, even blow the whole case.

A glance at my dashboard showed the time as one o'clock, the outside temperature at ninety-five. Would hit a hundred or better by five. It would be nice to be inside the salon then. But first I had to get home to let out my dogs and make sure Bob and Lucy, the brown

Quarter Horse mare I boarded for a friend, had plenty of water.

Over the river and past the woods, a nine-hole golf course, and hay fields dotted with cows, I drove up the narrow road to my ranch-style doublewide. I opened the galvanized gates manually, and parked under my own oak near the garage. Home. How welcome it felt after a so-far stressful day, and it not even half over.

The horses neighed and hung their heads over the gates of adjoining pastures that stretched from a two stall barn backing up to the garage, out over four acres. It was the perfect setup for a girl who hadn't outgrown her horse-crazy youth.

Finding the water troughs clear and nearly full, I climbed the steps to the deck and opened the French door, letting out a tumble of black and white Boston terriers. Charlie and Shayna were only two dogs. But in bright-eyed motion they seemed like seven.

Another sound bored through all the commotion. The land line. Ringing off the hook. I dashed into the cool bright kitchen, and picked up.

"Hello?" I said, answering just in time.

The Caller ID flashed with a number I did not recognize. A robotic female voice said, "Call from … Von … Sus …tern … Ent."

Von Sustern. Ent. Maybe an abbreviation for "Enterprises."

My heart did a somersault. Maybe Maria had information to share about Vader.

"Hello?" I said.

"Richard Von Sustern here. Am I speaking to Pepper Kane?"

A man's voice. Not what I expected. Cultured, slightly nasal. But it apparently was indeed from a Von Sustern, likely from Marietta's husband, Richard.

"Yes, this is Pepper."

"Oh good. I believe you know my wife, Marietta."

"I know of her though we've not actually met. Lovely lady, beautiful rider."

Curious and still breathless, I sat down on a padded kitchen chair at the counter. The dogs brought toys, which I tossed absentmindedly to keep them busy.

Why was Marietta's husband calling? Was he going to give me Vader's transfer of ownership and insurance details, which Marietta claimed to know nothing about. But that seemed unlikely. After all, what was I, what was this whole affair, to him?

"I understand you talked with my wife this morning," he said.

"I expressed my condolences about Vader," I said.

"Very kind of you," he said. "We appreciate it."

"Wish I could do more," I said.

I had never met Richard Von Sustern, so I couldn't picture him as we talked. But I imagined him to be tall, pinstriped and distinguishedly gray at the temples as were some upper class men I'd known. In short, a proper gentleman, with old school manners and a decent golf handicap.

"That is why I am calling, Pepper. So let me get to the point. You asked some odd questions, about ownership, and insurance."

"Your wife wasn't clear on those details, Mr. Von Sustern. She said you handled her business affairs. So can you tell me if the horse was transferred and insured?"

There was a pause.

"We understand your concern, Pepper," he said. "You sound like a nice person. But, since you are neither a friend nor a business associate, we wonder why you'd ask such things. Everything regarding the horse is our concern, and under control. I am asking you not to call again. Let's just leave it at that, shall we?"

Whoa, Daddy. Richard Von Sustern had just told me to back off, in the most polite yet certain terms. Further, his cultured, carefully spoken words had taken on a steely edge. He'd issued me a clear warning, even a threat. I had no doubt he'd take stronger action if he learned I was not only investigating each detail of the case, but paying particular attention to the Von Sustern angle.

The question for me loomed large and bright. Why threaten me, unless he or Maria were hiding things they didn't want me to know?

I took a deep breath and gathered my thoughts. I used my most businesslike voice.

"Just one more question, Mr. Von Sustern."

"And what would that be?"

"What makes you think I'd call again?" A little angling couldn't hurt. It might even attract a nibble.

The line went silent. I heard a rustle of paper in the background, and a squeak from what might be someone shifting his weight in a cherrywood executive chair.

"Look," he said. "No need to waste both our time. I am a busy man. You are busy, too, from what I hear, running a store, showing horses. Simply put, Pepper, you are for some odd reason poking your nose into our affairs. Things beyond condolences, that don't concern you. No need to continue this conversation. Goodbye."

The dial tone buzzed on.

I sat there stunned. Richard Von Sustern. Not one to mess with. I seemed to be making a lot of people mad, and the investigation of Vader's death had barely begun.

My dog Charlie, the smaller of the two Bostons, jumped up and snapped at a fly beating against the glass door. He finally caught the offending insect, and devoured it with much licking and satisfied chomping.

"Good boy," I said, giving him a pat. Well, I planned to be like Charlie. Let the guilty beat themselves against an unmovable barrier, and watch until they weakened. Then go in for the kill. I just had to figure out how to do that. And more important, to whom.

***

After watering hanging baskets on my porch and fastening mesh fly masks over the horses' faces, I changed into shorts, slathered on sunscreen and donned my Medford Rogues baseball cap. Their pirate logo suited my crusading, sword-swinging mood.

It took twenty minutes to drive I-5 north to Grants Pass, where my parents lived and Freddie had his salon. I had just enough time to pick up my folks' milk, bread, and the prescriptions they'd phoned in. Luckily my son, Serrano, was free to housesit for me and look after the folks when I was in California. Not lucky that he was free, as in unemployed, but lucky for me and my parents.

Oh, Serrano, my dear, redheaded, 35-year-old dreamer. When will you decide on a career that pays actual money, on a regular basis, and not keep creating paintings that might or might not sell? Occasional landscape design or building the odd bookcase for friends doesn't pay the bills, let alone build a future. No wonder Wendy left you after eleven years of marriage.

Chili, my thirty-two-year-old daughter, was just the opposite of Serrano. She was into it all – marketing, real-estate and wholesaling tons of high-end jewelry.

Everything that girl touched turned to gold, except her relationships, of course. The longest had lasted a year.

But I loved them both with a purple passion. Never mind that I rarely heard from them unless they needed something.

We all got our first names, by the way, courtesy of Dad. He grew the hottest and greatest variety of peppers this side of New Mexico. He used to sell them at a Weekend Market. Now that he didn't drive, he had an Internet site that pulled in customers from around the world. Even so, my parents barely made ends meet. Their place had been deteriorating for years.

Before I knew it, I'd wound through oak-and-madrone clad hills and dropped off the freeway into Grants Pass, the Josephine County seat. Leafy, laid back and hot as the blazes in summer, the 37,000-person town billed itself as "The Gateway to the Oregon Caves National Monument."

It also is known as "River City," as the Rogue River bisects its southern part where I once nearly bought property. That cluster of faded riverfront cabins I coveted, similar to one in which Zane Grey wrote adventuresome Westerns downriver, reportedly once served as a hideaway and an outdoor adventure mecca for early Hollywood stars such as Wallace Beery, Clark Gable and Carole Lombard.

I pulled into the Wal-Mart parking lot. Campers, compacts and pickups with pit bulls in back stood in rows or played chicken for desirable parking spots. The store's cool interior presented a noisy, colorful and weird but wonderful slice of America, if not the world. Many voices, ages and figures, plus the ever-present baby screams, formed a crazy quilt of sights, smells, sounds and motions. How could those workers endure the rude customer day in day out for low pay?

Hey, it was a job.

I gave the pharmacy clerk my information and was told the prescriptions would take "about twenty minutes." It was Friday so I thought she sounded a bit optimistic.

Meanwhile I commandeered a cart with a clanking, spinning front wheel, and made for the grocery department. I turned at the coffee aisle when I smelled U-grind designer coffee in bins and bags. I needed French roast. Didn't I always?

A firm but curvy female crashed into my cart as a heavy floral perfume mingled with that of rich coffee.

"Sorry. Oh. Pepper! What are you doing here?" Victoria shook back her heavy hair, and smiled.

"Slumming in Grants Pass," I said with a nod to my Brassbottom Barn buddy

"A Gold Hill-ite sure isn't one to call Grants Pass a slum," she said with a grin.

"Whatever," I said. "Picking up stuff for my parents. Remember, I'm a Grants Pass High grad, too. Class of Tickety Boo. Go Cavemen!"

"Yay." Her hoot and laugh turned heads and animated her gold pendant earrings.

Earrings, again. Dang. Well, it figured. Since I found that shiny speck in Vader's stall I'd started to obsess about earrings, and other things made of yellow metal.

"So," I said. "Did the sheriff talk to you yet about all things Vader?"

"Oh my yes," she said, lowering her voice and glancing around. "I got the third degree, as we all did. 'Where were you when, how well do you know the Grandeens, what was Freddie's reaction,' all that stuff."

"Same here," I said. "Sheriff has zeroed in on Freddie as a person of interest. But he also seems awfully interested in me, for some reason. He seems to think I saw, did or heard something I'm not confessing."

"Why would he think that?" she said

"Not a clue." I said. "Have you heard anything?"

"Nada. We all wonder how Vader died and who is responsible. Some of the other girls figure one of Marietta's competitors had something to do with it."

So Victoria, honest as she was except regarding her love affairs, wasn't aware of anyone seeing or hearing anything about me that would explain the sheriff's bluff that I entered Vader's stall this morning. Also she, like Tulip and I, gravitated toward the jealous-competitor theory. The image of Patsy Ann Carpenter popped into my mind.

"That's a relief," I said. "That you've heard nothing concrete about any of us."

"But I, and probably you, too, am feeling paranoid since we go to the barn so much and also are competitors. We could still be persons of interest."

"True," I said. "Well, Vic, nice to see you, have a great day."

"Ditto, Girlfriend," she said.

I picked up my grocery items, doubled back to the pharmacy for the prescriptions, and climbed into my hot truck for the five-mile drive southwest on old Highway 99, also called the Redwood Highway. In fifteen minutes I reached my parents' forty-acre farm in an area known as Jerome Prairie.

The oaks along the gravel drive shaded my truck as I approached the century-old yellow farmhouse with its sheltering willow and numerous outbuildings.

Mom stood on the porch. Her white hair rippled in the rising wind, which had set the wind chimes ringing. Her high-cheeked face shone with sweat, and her jeans and pearl-snap blouse bore white globs.

I learned why the globs when I hugged her and took my shopping bags inside the house. Peach pie. She'd been baking even on this hot afternoon. As she said, when her baking gene kicked in, there was no stopping her. Although the house drapes were drawn to keep out the outdoor heat, the oven was still full on. Amazing.

"Smells good," I said, setting the bags in the kitchen next to two cooling pies. I turned off the oven. Mom might remember eventually. I saved her the trouble.

"Can you stay for a slice, Honey?"

"Not so much, Mom. Hair appointment in Old Town. With Freddie, remember? Plus I just had a huge slice of lemon meringue at Katie's in Gold Hill."

"Well, take a pie home, then. What you don't eat you can freeze."

"I will. Where's Dad?" I looked around the yellow and white kitchen, my eyes lingering on the black and white barrel racing photos around my grandmother's china hutch. Mom was quite the "can-chaser" back in the 1950s, earning nickel spurs and batwing chaps riding a red horse named Cootie. He did look like a bug, with those bulging eyes, lanky legs and knobby knees. Cootie was the first horse I ever rode.

"Dad's tinkering in the barn," Mom said. "Lawn mower on the fritz again. We oughtta scrap it, but can't afford a new one."

"I know," I said. "Wish we could remedy that. Well, tell him 'I love you'."

"Will do." She peered at me closely. "You look tired, Honey. What's going on?"

"Oh, some bad stuff at Brassbottom Barn. A prize horse died under mysterious circumstances last night. I'm looking into it for my buddies and the Grandeens."

Her face tightened with concern.

"Not again, Pepper. You always get yourself tangled up in these things better left to others, to professionals. Your health suffers, your looks suffer."

I had to smile a little. I loved her concern about both my health and looks, as she always held out hope I'd hook another husband. But just as often it drove me crazy. "I'll take care, I promise," I said, hugging her frail shoulders. "I love you. Mom."

"Love you, tell Freddie the same and that there's a couple pies in it if he'll squeeze me in next week," she said.

"Will do. Your hair still looks nice though."

"Nah. Dark roots poking through. Gotta keep the platinum Harlow look for Dad."

I laughed, put the pie in a bag and made my getaway.

"Serrano still coming Monday?" she called as I stepped up into my truck.

"Last I heard," I said. "But I'm sure he'd still love a call from you."

"Well, stay safe and good luck at the show," she said, waving me away.

"Thanks," I called back over the wind. "I'll need it." I'd indeed need both, the staying safe and the good luck. Not only for the show, but for dealing with pushy sheriffs and the even pushier husband of a fellow competitor.

Meanwhile, I had to get my hair color on and my rear in gear. I was late for my appointment with a leading suspect in the mystery of the murdered horse.

9

Freddie was sweeping up his station when Mom's pie and I reached the Manes 'n Tales salon. I pushed through the glass door. It was painted with a scene of horses with polished hooves and curled manes chatting under hair dryers.

I'd always loved the name and concept. Freddie's idea, of course. But the salon owner liked it too, as her family owned trail riding horses. My son, Serrano, painted it one summer when he'd come down for a long family visit. His signature graced the picture's bottom, the "o" painted to resemble a hot pepper.

I grimaced at the salon's ammonia and hair spray odors. But I grinned at Freddie waiting with open arms at the end of the row of busy hairdressing stations.

"How you doing, Pep?" Freddie sat me down in his swivel chair and wrapped my torso in a silky black cape with the "Manes 'n Tales" logo.

"Good," I said. "But this sack of Mom's pie needs to go in your fridge."

"I'll take it back when I go mix colors," he said. "But you gotta give me a slice."

"You got it. So, how are you doing?" I said, temporarily nesting the pie in my lap.

"Okay, I guess," Freddie said. His eyes looked puffy as he peeked over my shoulder at my face in the mirror. "Not the best day of my life. Any news?"

"Too early. But there have been interesting developments." I filled him in on most of the day's events before he went to the backroom to mix my hair-streak colors, ash blonde and dark brown.

Freddie listened eagerly as he ran his fingers through my hair.

I stared at his reflected face, and counted earrings. "Freddie?"

"Yeah?"

"Do you normally wear six earrings?" I said. "Gold, silver, studs and hoops?"

His fingers tightened on the nape of my neck. They felt strong, probably the result of riding and hairdressing. He rolled his eyes.

"Honey, ain't nothin' normal about me. Don't know how many. Whatever I feel like on a given day."

I thought about that. I hadn't been aware he changed earrings or didn't know how many he usually wore. Was Freddie really unaware, or was he evading the question? If he were evading, why? Surely he could not have killed Vader.

But a shiver tickled my vertebrae. It was a remote possibility. I didn't want to think it. But what if Freddie wanted to prevent another from having "his" horse? I peered harder at his reflection, concentrating on his earlobes. There was an empty hole on the left lobe, above a diamond stud and a silver hoop.

"So you purposely left that one ear hole empty? Or did you lose an earring?"

"Why?" His close-set eyes narrowed. "What's the big deal about earrings?" He raised his hand to the empty hole in the ear. Then he shrugged.

"Just curious," I said.

"Must have forgot when I dressed today," he said. "Been a tad distracted."

That answer would have to suffice.

"I can imagine," I said. "We all are distracted. Sheriff's been pretty intense with the interviews."

"Oh yeah. Hold that thought, Pep. Gotta get the pie in the fridge and mix colors. Want the same, a little blonde, little brown, to brighten your own slightly faded red?"

"Sounds good, Freddie. And you don't have to be diplomatic with me. It's very faded. Sun's bright, and I don't always wear a protective hat."

While he was gone, I analyzed his reactions to my questions. I decided he was acting normal. Except for that missing earring. I wasn't completely satisfied with his answer. But then I was annoyed with myself for thinking bad thoughts about Freddie, possibly one of the nicest men I knew. He'd do anything for a friend, was honest to a fault and rarely reined in his emotions or gossip. In fact, he sometimes joked that "gossip" was his middle name.

In fact he might already have heard about Pasty Ann's visit to the Horsehouse that morning. Wildfires weren't the only thing that spread fast in the valley.

Freddie returned with aluminum hair-wrapping papers, color bowls and a brush for applying the hair colors. He gave me the small square papers to hand to him individually to wrap around each flat, narrow hank of hair.

"You'll never guess who stopped by the Horsehouse today," I said.

"Try me."

So he hadn't heard. Goodie. I would be the first to share news he could use. "Patsy Ann Carpenter and her daughter, Honey. From Texas. They own a Vader relative. They were up for a family reunion in Roseburg."

Freddie's jaw dropped.

"Oh, really. Now that's interesting." He chewed his lower lip. "Another jealous competitor. The plot thickens."

"I know, right? Turns out she and Marietta Von Sustern are buddies. Patsy Ann called her from my store to offer condolences on Vader."

"Oh, so they're pretty tight," he said. "Besties, even. Co-conspirators, perhaps?"

"Perhaps," I said. "You can bet I'm checking out that possibility."

"Wow," he said. " Okay. So … what if Patsy Ann killed Vader, as he and Marietta would have been her closest rivals for the world championships?"

"I know," I said. "Sounds plausible, right? But very petty and dang stupid."

"For sure," he said.

I also told Freddie about Richard Von Sustern's call to me, warning me away from bothering him or his wife with questions about Vader. Freddie reacted with a derisive snort.

"Really?" he said. "So Big Daddy's now involved. Maybe I don't have to worry so much about my being a suspect. There are plenty to go around."

"So it seems," I said, handing him another wrapping paper.

Freddie was silent a moment. Background chatter from other customers, as well as syrupy love songs piped over the salon speakers, filled the void. Finally he leaned down to whisper over my shoulder, "This investigation has become quite the tangled web, a regular Gordon's knot."

I stared at his reflection in the mirror. I couldn't tell if he was joking.

"You mean Gordian? For that ancient puzzling tangle that no warrior except Alexander the Great could break apart?"

Freddie smirked, and play-slapped my shoulder with his paintbrush. "No, silly. Gordon. For Mark Gordon. That ancient puzzling bisexual trainer in

Seattle, whose love affairs are so twisted that no one who enters one with him survives. Remember the snake-hipped bull rider he dumped? Who one night climbed in a pen at the Ellensburg Rodeo to commit suicide by Brahma?" Freddie shuddered.

I gave a shoulder shake myself. I'd had a hand in solving that case, having flown up to stay at my Aunt Connie's guest ranch during Rodeo Week. My Aunt had some serious mysteries of her own, but that was a whole 'nother story.

"Purely awful," I said. "That bull rider case was a tough one to solve. We had to determine whether it really was suicide, or a cleverly staged murder."

"Right," Freddie said. "Result was the same. Vader's killing also was likely a jealousy thing. Or possibly a payback for a perceived wrong committed by Dutch, Donna, even me. Although I can't think of anyone I've offended that much."

For some reason a recent headline about a teenager shooting a barking dog in the back of a pickup at a farm store came to mind. Any animal abuse raised my hackles. The teen later confessed to stabbing his father-in-law. I had read about murderers starting out torturing or killing small creatures before they started carving up or shooting people.

"Or," I said, "consider this, Freddie. What if it was some animal-hating whacko going in for a thrill kill?"

"Now that's a possibility," he said. "Wasn't there one kid in the Valley shooting dogs last fall? Who later killed his father-in-law in cold blood?"

"In his confession he mentioned he had started out hurting animals," I said.

In the mirror, Freddie's reflection lifted its eyebrows. He rested his wrists on my black-caped shoulder.

"So," Freddie said, "you're saying that maybe this horse killer was putting in a little practice, revving up his courage before working his way up to us humans."

"That's a very real possibility."

10

Cold beer in hand, I slouched in a chair on the deck overlooking pastures sloping down to the southeastern hills. I felt like I'd been running a three-minute mile all day. Now I didn't want to move.

One dog lay in the low sun rays near the grapevine woven railing. The other dog nosed around a blue bumpy ball, trying to stop it from thumping down the steps.

Wild turkey gobbles sounded from the oaks and pines dotting the back neighbor's property. I looked across. Hens, roosters and half grown chicks pecked and strutted through the dry grass under oak and pine.

A volley of shrieks scattered them and rattled me. I looked harder, but couldn't see the cause. Surely it was a coyote. Cougars didn't come out this early. Although I'd once spotted fresh tracks while riding Bob one day on Starvation Heights. I'd turned around to head for home, when I saw the cougar tracks had followed mine all along.

Now I always pack a gun when out riding trails. You never can be sure someone or something isn't watching or stalking you.

That line of thought made me flash on Richard Von Sustern's warning call before I'd driven to Grants Pass to get prescriptions and have my hair done. Marietta's husband had sounded angry in a calculated way, sure of getting his point across, certain of getting his way. Which was for me to butt out of the matter of the murdered horse.

Maybe I would, maybe wouldn't. I hoped I wouldn't need to. But I definitely would bother others about him and his wife. Who, a mystery herself, seemed to be making it a point to stay outside the case.

However if it were me, if my horse had been killed, I'd be all over it. I'd be at the location and in the faces of people recently close to or involved in its care and training.

My chunky little bay, Bob, walked up to my barn a hundred feet away. He looked up at me on the deck. His blue eye flashed in the low sun. He neighed.

"Where's my feed?" he seemed to say. "There's a starving horse here, a starving barefoot orphan horse in the snow."

"Bob, you lie," I said. "You've been eating all day in a pasture of grass, and it's a hundred-degrees, so you're not that hungry."

"But I need my treat and supplements," said his next whinny.

"Okay, coming," I said, in plain English. "Don't be a nag. Horse joke. Get it?"

Grinning, I finished my allotted half beer, I was allergic to more than that, capped it and stashed it in the fridge beside Mom's pie, missing a slice for Freddie.

The barn, with stock mesh along the top half of the stall walls, smelled good inside. Alfalfa hay, wood-pellet bedding and a well-groomed horse made it so. I mucked Bob's stall each morning. I dumped soiled bedding a hundred feet the other side of the barn. That kept down the flies. It also guaranteed a healthy atmosphere.

After tossing Bob an alfalfa flake, a three-inch thick section of bale, and giving him powdered supplement in a feed tub, I topped off his and Lucy's water buckets.

Next I sat down on a hay bale and pulled out my cell phone. I dialed Jane Pardee, who'd consigned the saddle and bridle that Patsy Ann Carpenter and her daughter had on hold at my store.

Jane answered on the third ring. She sounded bright.

"Hi, Jane," I said. "How are you doing? Did you listen to my voicemail?"

"I did," she said. "And I'm doing pretty well, Pepper, thanks. I was just about to call you."

"Well, let's get this deal done, then."

"Fifteen grand for both the saddle and bridle," she said. "They cost eighteen new, you know."

Whoa! I stood to make three grand.

"Right. Sounds good. Soon as I get Patsy Ann's charge approved, I'll take my twenty percent, send you a check and ship her the saddle."

"Good deal. Sure can use the money."

"You're not the only one."

I told her the short version of my cash-flow troubles. Jane responded with a short version of her health issues post buck-off. I said I was glad I hadn't suffered such severe injuries in my own buck-off.

***

Back in my house, where I could better take notes, I sat at my hundred-year-old oak dining table, which I noticed needed dusting. I tapped in Patsy Ann's number. I half expected to leave a voice mail. It was after seven o'clock. She likely was knee-deep in veal Parmesan or whatever with the governor.

But she answered on the first ring.

"Patsy Ann, here," she said in a breathy Southern Belle voice.

"Pepper here," I said. "Hope I'm not interrupting your state dinner."

"We're not having steak," she said, mishearing me or not getting the reference. "We're having veal Parmesan and it's terrific."

I heard a buzz of conversation and a clink of cutlery on china in the background. I remembered I hadn't eaten since the lemon pie around noon. My stomach rumbled.

"Glad to hear it," I said, not wanting to correct her on the state-steak mishearing. Patsy Ann didn't strike me as the snappiest whip in the stable.

"Got my charge card all ready," said Patsy Ann. "What's the asking price of the saddle and bridle?"

"Fifteen thousand for both."

"I'll pay thirteen."

I sighed.

"Jane is firm," I said. "She paid nearly twenty."

Why did they always have to haggle? They who could afford the moon.

"The price is fifteen, Patsy Ann. It's more than fair."

"Fourteen, then."

I knew Jane would probably take it. Bird in the hand. Costly tack didn't always move quickly. Jane needed the money. Besides it also was a bird in the hand for me.

Patsy Ann and her ilk didn't become rich paying full price. I'd take the hit off my commission rather than bother Jane again. But it galled me.

Patsy Ann gave me her card numbers. I jotted them down and also entered them onto my phone, as backup.

"So where are you staying during the show?" I said.

"My husband is driving our motor home over to the area," she said.

"Lucky you," I said. "That's so convenient." I imagined one of those custom-built forty-footers with quadruple slideouts and popups, real wood or marble finishes, and flat screen televisions in every room. The going price for those could top a million dollars.

While I had Patsy Ann on the line I saw a chance to glean more information.

"By the way, I misplaced your number, so I called Mason DeYoung for it."

"You called Mason?"

"Since you'd been at their family reunion? How are you related, again?"

There was enough of a pause to make me wonder. Were they related?

"Well, it's a long story," said Patsy Ann, with a small sigh. "The mother of my first husband, Charles Belmont, Lord rest his soul, was a DeYoung."

"Oh." It seemed strange that Patsy Ann would travel all the way to Oregon for the reunion of her ex-mother-in-law's family.

She must have picked up on my skepticism.

"Mama Belmont and I stayed close even after I remarried," Patsy Ann said. "Like mother and daughter. She had four sons but never a daughter, so we bonded right away."

"Oh," I said. "I wasn't so lucky with my former husband's family."

"How sad."

"Yes," I said. "So. We're all set with the saddle and bridle, then. When will you be arriving at the show?"

"Our trainers will have our horses there tonight," she said. "Give them three days to settle in at a strange stable and acclimate to the area. So different from Texas."

"Right about that," I said. "So are you heading there tomorrow?"

"No, Sunday," she said. "We all are meeting Marietta and Richard in Reno to see shows and hit the tables over the weekend, then shooting over to Rancho on Monday. My husband, Carson, is in Reno to open a townhome and casino project, and Marietta was celebrating her birthday at Tahoe, so we decided to meet up in Reno for fun and games before heading to the show."

"You're meeting the Von Susterns?" I said. So Patsy Ann was even closer to Marietta than I'd thought. "Marietta told me Richard was in Europe."

"Oh, no," said Patsy Ann. "He flew back when he heard of Vader's death. Plus for her birthday."

"Sure," I said, still processing. "Well, Patsy Ann, don't lose all your money."

"Those casinos better watch out they don't lose all their money," she said.

I shook my head after we hung up. I not only was annoyed at the haggling, but also at hearing how casual Patsy Ann was about the upcoming do or die horse show. The weekend before a big out-of-town show, I'd be running in circles preparing my gear and assembling papers before leaving Sunday night or Monday morning. The show started Tuesday and ran through the following weekend.

Of course, Patsy Ann had people for that. She apparently also loved to gamble. Further, the Von Susterns liked to gamble. Oh well, what did they have to lose? They were rich beyond imagining. They could afford to spend their money as they chose, whether on trips, cars or horses.

But I could not shake the feeling that all this activity, all these questions, all these people were somehow connected to the death of Dark Vader.

***

I was sorry I hadn't had time or energy to swing by Brassbottom Barn that day to interview Jody and Carlos, the barn cleaners. They'd been at Brassbottom, early as the Grandeens, maybe earlier. I didn't have their phone number.

What were their observations on the night Vader died? Had they seen or heard me enter or leave Vader's stall this morning after, as the sheriff had implied? If so, had they told him? Or was he merely fishing, as I suspect.

I entered the day's notes in my computer, then called Barbara and Lana, my other barn buddies and line-dance cohorts. I asked each what they had overheard or seen regarding Vader, and if the sheriff asked them any unusual questions.

Barb and Lana were best buds though different in lifestyle. Barb, a stocky older woman with myriad health issues, was married to a heavy equipment dealer. Lana, a scarecrow-thin and buzz-cut loner drawn to her own gender, worked as an assistant in a hospital emergency room.

Each woman expressed paranoia about the Vader case and whether they might be persons of interest. They also had concerns similar to mine.

"I hope other horses in our barn won't be hit," said Barbara, ever the worrier.

"This affair put Dutch and Donna on high alert," I said, "so that won't happen."

Lana, who on the phone sounded as if she'd been nipping the honey Seagram's again to ease stress from her job, offered a new twist. Seagram's can do that to you.

"Off the subject," Lana said, "but want to know a little secret?"

"Always," I said. "What's up, Lan?"

"One of the Saddle Tramps has broken up with her boy toy."

I laughed at Lana's quirky name, Saddle Tramps, for us at Brassbottom Barn, for ladies and gents who laid all on the line not only for horses, but also for sons and lovers.

"So," I said, "is this somebody a male or a female?"

"Female. And married. Little Miss Vixen, of course."

So Victoria, whom Lana called "Vixen" for short and for fun, had been having a fling. Maybe with Dutch. Many of us had suspected as much. Vic would never tell.

"First off," I said, "how'd you find out?"

"Pepper, just my powers of observation."

"But I saw her at Grants Pass Wal-Mart today," I said. "She seemed normal. Just sad about Vader."

"Sad about her and Dutch," said Lana. "They had a knock down drag out today. I heard her threaten to take her horses out of Brassbottom after the show. Might send them to Royce and Rogers in Texas. They are the tops. Then, like Marietta, go head to head in shows against Patsy Ann."

"Ouch," I said. "That's two horses. The Grandeens can't afford to lose them, especially after losing Vader. What else, Lana? What was the fight about?"

"You mean, 'who.' That part's unclear. I think she yelled something about two-timing. Maybe she was more than a client to Dutch. You know how we all thought he spent too much time on her and her horses since she was a big-money client? Maybe those two had a little fling. Been known to happen."

"Sad but true," I said. "So who would he have his eye on besides Victoria, if he had it on Victoria?"

"If it is one of us, I can't imagine who," she said. "Most of the Tramps look for a hookup with a future, for a more stable relationship. Ha ha, pun intended."

"Very good, Lana. An oldie, but goodie."

"But if you're gonna hook up," Lana continued, "you gotta stay cool, don't act special, keep the feelings buried. Our Miss Vixen forgot the Saddle Tramps creed."

"Right," I said. "I guess. Huh. I'll take all this under advisement."

"And with a grain of salt," Lana said. "Or a jigger of scotch. See ya."

I chuckled and hung up.

As it was after nine o'clock. I pulled my found gold fragment, still wrapped in the napkin, out of my pocket and set it on the table. I looked at it but drew a blank.

Then I texted little Stewie, our youth rider. It probably was past his bedtime.

I finished the evening with warmed-over TV news, a cool shower and a hot steak. My body seemed to crave red meat. I pulled on my cotton sleep tee, figuring I was about done for the day when my phone sounded the incoming-text alert.

The message pane showed only a local phone number. But I felt surprise reading the square text bubble, "I saw something. Stewie."

So it wasn't past his bedtime. I texted him back immediately. My thoughts ran like a snake stampede, wiggling every which way at once.

"What did you see?" I texted.

In a moment the text alert sounded again.

"Barn, afternoon, strange ladies, black car. Saw Vader before Dutch buried him."

My heart skipped a beat. Could it have been Patsy Ann and Honey? If so, why?

"What time? Get their names?" I tapped out.

There was a pause as Stewie typed his answer.

"After one. School out early. No names."

It could only have been Patsy Ann. She and Honey must have taken time to swing over to Brassbottom Barn after they left The Best Little Horsehouse. While I lunched with Tulip and was re-grilled by the sheriff.

This seemed strange. Why would they go to Brassbottom? What was their stake in this case, that horse? Other than Patsy Ann owning a close, competitive relative to him?

Further, did Stewie mean that he had seen Vader before burial, or that the ladies in the black car had seen the horse?

"You, or they, saw Vader?" I texted.

"Both," Stewie texted. "Dutch hauling him to field. Ladies walked to see. Talked to Dutch."

I pressed my lips together and shook my head. Curiouser and curiouser. What in flaming heck was happening?

Stewie's texts raised another question. Did the Carpenters actually drive down to California? Have dinner with the governor? I supposed they could have made the five-hour drive, even with stopping by Brassbottom. But maybe they had been dining out somewhere else when I called about the tack. That would explain the clinking and clanking dinner sounds.

Or was the governor thing a complete fabrication? Maybe Patsy Ann and Honey were still in this area nosing around for whatever reason. You never knew where people were, when it came to cell phone calls.

"Any more info?" I texted Stewie.

"No, just rode my horse."

"K," I texted, adding "TTYL", text slang for "Talk To You Later."

We disconnected. I sat there for a minute. It was too late to call Dutch and Donna. No doubt they were exhausted after the previous twenty-four hours. I would swing by Brassbottom in the morning. It probably was also too late to call Victoria, nudge her into talking about her rumored affair with Dutch. Maybe I'd see her at the barn.

I was as tired as my Boston terriers, who lay snoring away on afghans in my two leather recliners. But my mind was awake. Crazy awake. So I poured a fresh glass of iced tea and sat down at my desk, fired up the PC and began to search for everything out there about Patsy Ann, Marietta and Richard Von Sustern

I just knew Patsy Ann was up to no good. Why would she go to over to the barn, poke around Vader, scope things out? To report to her friend Marietta about how the investigation was going? Who the main suspects were? That Vader was really dead?

11

The ice-tea glass stood empty, the light burned late and my dogs now snored in a doggie bed under my desk where I sat hunched over the keyboard. My butt checked out early on, numb as a brick. The rest of my body would have to wait.

Reference after reference had come up on my screen about Richard Von Sustern and his international business ventures. Mainly commercial construction, road building and luxury vehicles. He held oil and natural gas company board positions, and was a successful defendant in lawsuits alleging he'd pulled political strings to obtain once-vacated oil and natural gas leases in the Southwest.

He also was touted as a possible Republican candidate in his district. He would naturally be wary of possible bad publicity.

What you'd expect of someone rich although not necessarily famous. None of the legal actions had succeeded, of course. Marietta's husband was one wiley wabbit, as Elmer Fudd says of his nemesis Bugs Bunny.

As an afterthought, I emailed my daughter, Chili, in Seattle, about Von Sustern. It was a stab in the dark. But you never knew what course that high-level business news or gossip might take, and Chili in her dealings might have heard some about him. She also was a computer whiz.

The information on Marietta included her heading up a Las Vegas Night charity ball in Phoenix, a gambling extravaganza that netted some $100,000 for Parkinson's Disease. But most mentions involved her horse show honors, both in the Paint Horse breed and in the World Western Horse Association, to which she and her distinguished husband were major donors. I mean in the over-$100,000 range.

What else was new, when it came to eye-popping donations to nonprofit groups, especially gifts that could benefit you or your interests? It was fairly well known that top owners, breeders and trainers regularly greased the palms of those who controlled the purse, prize and potential horse-sale income strings.

My findings were about what I expected. But they brought me no closer to the question of whether the Von Susterns were connected to the death of their own horse.

My search on Patsy Ann Carpenter mainly involved her horse show honors, with earlier data on her husband, John Carpenter, a real-estate developer and oil magnate who dabbled in athletic teams, notably the up and coming Houston Rougnecks. Now that was news to me. I thought I knew something about Major League Baseball. He must have been a dummy owner, because it wasn't in any of the sports news I'd ever read.

Again, though, not much was gleaned from my searches. I entered what there was into my case notes anyway. Sooner or later I'd connect a dot or two, or something seemingly innocuous would leap into prominence.

At last I thought I'd finished for the evening. It was past eleven. With a sigh, I climbed into my queen bed with the brown, Texas-star trimmed linens, fresh and crisp from the dryer. They smelled of the lavender sachet I'd tossed in at the last minute. Lavender always relaxed me.

I was somewhere in Dreamland when the dogs stirred and growled. They came out from under the covers on either side of me, began barking, and rushed to the door.

What the...? Who the...? I turned on my bedside lamp to see the time was one fifteen.

I swung out of bed, slipped into my sheepskin flip-flops and stumbled to the door. I listened a moment as the dogs continued barking. But I noticed they also wiggled their butts, since they had only corkscrews for tails.

There was a knock at the door. With a glance at my shotgun to the left of the hinges, and feeling more than a tingle of nervousness, I pulled back the drapes and looked out the window.

A tall familiar figure stood in the porch light's yellow glare.

My heart jumped.

Sonny Chief!

I'd almost forgotten he might come. I certainly did not expect him so soon.

I unlocked the deadbolt and slowly opened the door.

"Hey," he said, melting me with his wide white grin. His eyes flashed through half-closed lids. A black braid tied with a red strip lay across one shoulder. He wore a black tee shirt, black jeans and black cowboy boots. As usual.

Before I could answer or invite him in, he swept me against his chest, bent down and pressed his lips hard against mine.

I gave a helpless squeak. I didn't want to fall under his dangerous spell, again. There was nothing in it for me. Sonny had lady friends everywhere. Maybe a wife, or five, like Sitting Bull. Sonny claimed that powerful Sioux men, like powerful men of every race, seemed to require many women, even thrive on it.

Oddly, I accepted that in Sonny, though I accepted it in no other man. Maybe it was because I accepted him exactly as he was. Unconditionally. As I accepted my children and dogs, flaws and all.

Besides. I so craved his touch, his attention. Craved it down to my marrow.

At his lingering kiss, with his tongue tip probing mine, a warm feeling trembled through my core. My toes tingled. I almost fainted.

Finally Sonny let me go. He had to catch me to keep me from falling.

"Hey," I sputtered, my heart beating fast. "That felt amazing. As always. Wow. Didn't expect you so soon."

"I was in Montana," he said, stooping to tussle with the dogs. "Only took twelve hours. Easy."

His black pickup at the end of the path looked dust-covered and road weary. What looked like blood spatters and a tuft of hair dotted the lower left fender.

"Hit a deer?" I said.

"Already dead," he said.

"You hungry? Mom gave me a peach pie today. I'll warm it up, and make coffee."

Sonny nodded and stepped inside.

"Mind if I use the bathroom?" he said.

"Help yourself," I said.

It was only a civility. Sonny already at the door on the side of the living room opposite my bedroom. This Lakota warrior had the ability to vanish from one spot and appear in another without your seeing him actually move. Whether inherited or learned, I never knew, but often puzzled about it.

I went into the kitchen, got a plate and slipped a quarter of the peach pie into the microwave for one minute. I scooped vanilla bean ice cream on top. Meanwhile I made fresh coffee. Sonny did love him some coffee. Any time, day or night. It was a love he shared with the other Indians I knew.

When I took the treats into the living room, Sonny was lying flat out on the long yellow leather couch. One arm was flung over his eyes, and I could see that part of his hairline was wet. He must have splashed his face when he washed up.

"Here's your pejuta sapa and pie," I said, setting the French roast and dessert on the coffee table. I was proud I knew a few Lakota words such as "pejuta" for medicine, and "sapa" for black.

"Washte," he said. "Smells good."

"You're exhausted. Bet a shower would feel good."

"If you're in it," he said, opening his eyes to gaze at me.

I laughed.

Pie and coffee weren't the only things Sonny was hungry for. 'Twas ever thus.

He sat up, swung his feet down and attacked the pie. Then he drained half the cup of coffee, and it was a big cup.

"So what's the deal with the horse that was killed?" he said. His brow lowered, hooding his eyes even more.

I filled Sonny in on the events of the past twenty-eight hours. He interrupted with a brief question from time to time. But I could see him processing every detail and nuance. His eyes moved from side to side as he stared into the near distance.

"Huh," he finally said, looking at me directly. "Lotta bad stuff. You better ease off, Pepper. Bad people around. Might hurt you. Let me do the checking."

"Nobody will tell you anything," I said. "I've raised enough suspicions, and they already know me. You're a stranger. Besides, if the sheriff finds out you're messing in his investigation, with your being a tribal officer, not even from this state, we're done."

"Uh-huh." He nodded but looked as if my words blew right past him.

What did "uh-huh" mean? Was Sonny being dismissive? Appeasing?

My voice trailed off. I felt a little annoyed, even offended. It was beyond me what he thought he could do that I couldn't. Was he implying I was incapable? Or in some kind of danger that I couldn't handle?

He sat, swaying, elbows on his knees, looking innocent, and handsome as hell, I relaxed an iota. Here Sonny was, only trying to help, while stirring up all kinds of ill-advised but absolutely thrilling feelings in me. Feelings I had not felt in years.

I picked up his empty cup and plate, trying to keep moving as I worked things out. "I am glad you are here, Sonny," I said. "I'll be busy the next two days preparing for the show, doing my own research. But it's good to see you. And I do appreciate your concern, your offer of help."

"Help in ways you don't know," he whispered matter-of-factly, studying me.

I was sure he meant that as a double-entendre. But I tried to let it pass.

"Possibly," I said. "But look, Sonny. I have to go through with this, as much as I can, on my own, for my friends and for myself. Fast. Get a clearer idea of motives and suspects. Target or eliminate locals. Then, with myself and most in our barn leaving Sunday night for a horse show in California, I'll concentrate on them and their competitors down there, if need be."

Sonny just looked at me, smiled, and shook his head. He half-stood, and reached out to stroke my cheek and the side of my head. As if I were a kitten.

"Won't even know I'm around," he said. "Most of the time, pretty lady." He tugged on a lock of my hair.

I pulled away.

"Careful. Just had my hair done."

"I love it. The color of sun, the earth, and streaked red. Like blood."

"Sonny!" I was exasperated. He was like a child that won't listen.

"Pepper."

He grabbed one of my hands and pulled me down to sit beside him on the couch. He kissed my lips softly. Then he caressed my ears and touched his mouth to my cheek and neck, working his way around my face.

I sighed and ran my fingers under his tee shirt to his warm, hairless chest. I traced around the tiny hard scars left after a South Dakota Sun Dance. Praying for his people, Sonny had dragged four buffalo skulls tied by rawhide strips to eagle bones piercing the skin on his chest. A sacrifice that some likened to that of Christ on the cross.

Sonny had been to many Sun Dances, prancing from sunup to sundown around a cottonwood in a field encircled by a shade trellis for family and friends. Dancing to the beat of a buffalo-hide drum and haunting voices of singers, he had fasted, sweated, and thirsted to purify himself as he asked the Creator for visions and healing.

I had been to a Sun Dance myself, years ago, before meeting Sonny. I found it challenging beyond belief in windy heat and lightning storms. I had camped on the perimeter, and, shaded by the trellis, prayed and sang along with the dancers.

Now, I reflected, Sonny and I were having a Moon Dance. The opposite of a Sun Dance, to the drum of our heartbeats. We were setting aside our earthly worries, joining together in a kind of prayer, that spoke of joy and thanks

Yes, I could get a little spiritual, from time to time. I had no problem with that.

I did, however, regret giving in so easily to Sonny Chief's passion. Part of me felt annoyed with myself for letting it all go without a word of protest.

But in that long loving moment, Sonny was all I knew, and all I needed to know.

12

I was later than usual arriving at Brassbottom Barn the next morning. It was closer to eight, than to seven. I might not have a chance to ride. But I'd had a worthwhile excuse. Two words: Sonny Chief.

I had sent that loving Lakota on his way after a kiss, coffee and a bacon croissant. We'd meet up for dinner. Sonny had other business in the area, and other friends to catch up with including Boo George, a distant cousin who was a semi-retired sheriff's deputy. Sonny had promised to stay out of my way, and just, as he said, "do a little digging."

Dutch Grandeen was in the barn aisle saddling a horse, a gray three-year-old filly. Donna was somewhere in back, cleaning stalls next to Jody on one side of the aisle as Carlos worked on the other side. Three wheelbarrows stood in the aisle. Soft Spanish singing came from the stall where Carlos worked.

Dutch and I greeted each other as I slipped past his cross-tied gray horse at the beginning of the aisle.

"What's up, Miss Marple?" he said with a grin. He looked snappy in his straw hat, white tee and faded jeans. But his eyes had dark circles under them.

"How do you know about Miss Marple? Do you read old English mysteries?"

"No, but Donna does. Has a few dozen stashed in the office at the house. I read one once, and they're pretty good. 'Murder of Roger Something'."

"Ackroyd."

"Pardon?"

"Roger Ackroyd, almost like in the former 'Saturday Night Live' star, Dan Aykroyd."

Dutch nodded, and changed the subject. He cocked his head and gave me the once-over. I'd added extra mascara and blush, and worn especially tight jeans with heavily crystalled pockets

"You look positively glowing this morning," he said. "New boyfriend?" Dutch's eyes lit up. He was always eager for juicy gossip. Like all good Brassbottom people.

I thought that ironic, as, according to Lana last night on the phone, Dutch himself would now be at the center of some pretty steamy talk.

"Nope," I said. "Old boyfriend." I didn't want to elaborate. I had to get a move on, to do more investigating before I gave my horse a quick longe, and then hit the Horsehouse to pack Patsy Ann's tack, plus stuff I'd have for sale at the California show.

Dutch raised his eyebrows.

"Oh? Old boyfriend?" he said. "How old?" His eyes sparkled.

If I didn't know better, I'd think Dutch was flirting with me. But then I always thought that. Thus far his flirting, interested friendliness or whatever, had come to nothing. I knew better. I was the kind who'd fall in love, then crash, if dumped.

"A fling from ten years ago," I said. "Knew him in Seattle."

"A midnight visitor," Dutch said. "The best kind."

"Hey, I heard you had unexpected visitors yourself yesterday."

Dutch stiffened. His flirtacious manner dissolved.

"We had a lot of traffic at the barn," he said, guarded now but still smiling.

"Patsy Ann Carpenter and her daughter?" I said. Keeping it unexpected and brief, then waiting him out, should produce a reaction or answer I might use.

"Oh, yes, I believe they did stop by," Dutch said, eyes wary. "Who told you?"

"Stewie," I said. "He texted me. I was just checking with everyone about Vader, doing my investigation thing. Donna told you about it, right?"

"She said something about your looking into it. Doc Givens says we won't know the cause for a few more days, until results from the samples come back."

"Why did the Carpenters stop by, Dutch?"

"Oh, guess they were in the area for a reunion or something," he said, his cheek starting to twitch. "They own a Vader relative, you know, and are good friends with Marietta. They wanted to check in to see if we'd heard anything."

Judging by his "questions done" tone, that would have to satisfy me, for now. But it still seemed odd Patsy Ann had taken the time to stop by when she and her daughter were on their way to have dinner with the governor of the great state of California.

"I know you're busy, Dutch," I said. "But what time did they come?"

"I don't know, Pepper." Exasperation filled his voice. "After lunch."

"They went down to look at Vader before you buried him?"

"They wanted to see him, see how he looked."

"Did you think that odd?" I said.

"No," he said, turning back to cinch up his horse.

I knew I'd get little more out of him. But I tried anyway.

"So when do you expect to see the insurance investigator?"

Dutch turned to lay the gray filly's reins over her neck as he prepared to mount.

"Later today. Or tomorrow." He put his left foot in the stirrup.

"What company did the Von Susterns have Vader insured with?"

I figured I'd hit two birds with one stone. Learn not only which company, but whether Vader was insured at death, and who held the policy.

Dutch turned to stare at me. There was fire back of those blue-gray eyes. He was tired of questions. He needed to get on with his work day.

"Sterling," he said.

"One more thing," I said. "The sheriff heard I was here first yesterday and tried to imply I might have been in Vader's stall. You and I got here about the same time, right?"

Dutch narrowed his eyes.

"Far as I know," he said.

I felt relief. Dutch probably would have said more if he had seen me in the stall.

"I also heard Victoria might be moving her horse after the show."

Dutch's face froze. His tics started again.

"Where'd you hear that?" he said.

"The Barn drums," I said.

"As you know," he said, "we sometimes disagree with owners who think they are trainers."

"True," I said, watching the gray filly start to chew on her tie rope. "I might know something about that, myself." I thought back to a few arguments we'd had over the years, concerning Chocolate Waterfall's training.

"Besides," Dutch said, yanking the rope from the filly's mouth. "Drums can be wrong." With that he unsnapped the horse, mounted and rode away.

As hoofbeats receded down the aisle toward the arena, I was left knowing little more than when I'd started questioning Dutch. I knew the insurance company, but not who'd paid the premium. I was pretty sure Richard Von Sustern, because he'd been so proactive and defensive. But I was not convinced.

Dutch also had confirmed Patsy Ann had visited Brassbottom, looked at Vader and asked questions. But he had not given a reason beyond morbid curiosity why Patsy Ann had stopped when she had to make Sacramento by dinnertime.

I hoped to have better luck questioning the barn cleaners, Jody and Carlos.

***

"Hey, Jody," I said, watching the sturdy blond in cutoff jeans and boots sling the last bit of horse poop into her green wheelbarrow. "Got a minute?"

Her dark blue eyes looked surprised to see me. But she kept moving, rolling the barrow out of the stall and locking the door.

"Sure," she said. "If it don't take too long."

My eyes ran over the piercings in her nose and eyebrows, and took in the rose and skull tattoo above the scoop neck of her tank top. Such things used to bother me. But I had long ago given up my judgments on that issue, especially after leading artists, musicians and actors – and some business execs -- started sporting body art.

"The sheriff interviewed you about the dead horse, right?" I said.

"Me and everyone else," she said, shaking her head. She squinted at me as she brushed back a blond hank that had fallen over her face.

"Ask anything unusual?" I said.

"Not really," she said.

"Did you tell him anything unusual?" I said.

"Not really. Depends what you mean unusual." She coughed and spat to the side.

"Well, like, if you saw or heard anything about any of us, or anyone connected with the barn? Or saw any strange people or cars at the barn the night Vader died?"

"Not really," she said.

This was going nowhere fast.

"He thinks I went into Vader's stall yesterday before anyone was here," I said.

"Really? Why would you do that?" she said.

"That's what he thinks," I said. "Why would he think that?"

She hesitated, looking unsure of the question and how she should answer.

"Maybe he thought one of us saw you?" she said.

"What I'm thinking." I said.

"Me and Carlos didn't see nothing," she said.

"You both came in with Donna," I said. "A little after I came in."

She nodded.

"And no one else was here before me. Or here last night. No other cars out front?"

"Not really."

Back to the "not really's." I felt exasperated, but more or less had an answer. It would have to do.

"Okay, Jody, thanks," I said, moving across the aisle to speak to Carlos.

The handsome squat man in a red tee shirt and worn jeans looked up from his work, as a dun gelding drank from an automatic waterer in the corner.

"Hola," he said. "Comme esta?"

"Muy bien," I said. "Have a quick question about the Vader investigation?"

"Si?"

"The sheriff is bugging me about somebody thinking I was in Vader's stall yesterday because I was here early. Know of anyone who might think that?"

It was as oblique a way as I knew of asking if he knew anything.

"Not really."

"Any idea why he'd think it was me?"

"Not really." Carlos went back to cleaning the stall.

"Gracias," I said. "By the way, Carlos, thank you for your great stall cleaning." And I meant it. Cleanliness kept the horses from staining the white of their coats, and from contracting respiratory diseases.

So the stall cleaners had "not really" seen me or anyone else at the barn Thursday night or before it got busy yesterday. Their two-word answer, though not as exact as I wanted, had to suffice. I hoped it could be taken as a "no."

***

Hysterical barking erupted outside. The barn dog was going nuts. A stranger must be driving in. It couldn't be one of the Barn buddies or workers, as the dog knew them. In response or support, horses started whinnying.

At that moment Donna jogged past, shooting me a smile and nod. She looked tan and well rested. In fact, freshly coiffed and more carefully made up than usual.

"Hopefully it's the insurance people."

Looking after her, I felt sympathy roll through me. Donna not only had to deal with the dead horse case and its ramifications, but also the travails of getting people, horses and their live-aboard trailer ready for the California trip.

I really hoped that what Lana had said about Victoria and Dutch was merely gossip or speculation. Hopefully Lana misheard the "two-timing" statement, and that it referred not to another woman, but to his spending more time on another owner's horse than on her two. That kind of jealousy was a recurring issue at any show barn.

I was thinking that was the case, anyway. About all Dutch and Donna, not to mention we—their dependent extended family—needed was a murdered marriage.

13

I peered through the double doors as Donna, shadowed by the barn dog, walked across the parking lot to a dark green, top-of-the line Buick.

A slim man resembling a cave newt with a briefcase slithered out of the car as dust hung in the air around it. He wore spectacles, had skin as blah as his tan suit and sported a puffy combed-up hairdo that Donald Trump would envy.

Had to be the insurance dude.

A spoken name that sounded like "Filmore" or "Filbert" drifted to me. Plus the word, "Sterling."

My heart beat a little faster as I walked to a tree near the barn, kneeled in its shade and called the dog over to me. I pretended to be busy petting her as I eavesdropped on Donna and the insurance dude's conversation.

The horses still whinnied in the barn, and overgrown bushes and vines on each side of the house rustled as a breeze came up, so I only caught parts of the talk. But I caught enough to make the effort worthwhile.

"We can go into the house," said Donna. I couldn't hear the next bit, but figured from her gestures and mouth shapes that she also said, "where it's cooler."

Filbert or Filmore nodded, raised a white forefinger and set his briefcase on the hood of the car. He pulled a handkerchief from his jacket pocket and dabbed his face. Then he carefully inserted it back in his pocket.

Please say more, I thought, *before you go in the house.* He did.

"There," he said. "That's better." I thought he also said, "-- ice water, if you've got any."

The barn dog strained at her collar, but I held tight. She wanted to go to Donna, to guard her from this intruder. But I tensed my muscles and braced myself.

"Stay," I commanded. The dog relaxed a little. She let out a whine. I stroked and scratched her harder, concentrating on her butt at the base of her stub tail. She sagged with pleasure as I massaged her itchiest spot.

I inched a few feet closer to where Donna and Filmore, or Filbert, or whoever, started to move.

" – out of the heat?" Donna said.

" – be great," said "Fil."

They began to walk toward the house. The last words I heard as they passed under a rose-draped arch leading to the patio and back door, came from Fil.

" – any changes to the policy regarding medical and show records," he said. "I've also already talked with the vet, the sheriff and the deceased horse's owners."

"I expected so," Donna said.

Bingo. Fil had already talked to Vader's official owners. Since he was here to talk with the Grandeens, that meant Vader was owned by the Von Susterns at his time of death. A transfer of ownership and insurance had been signed and sealed.

One vital question of mine, down. A few more to go. Well, more than a few. But I stood to gain a lot here, if I could hear more.

He and Donna were at the house. She turned the handle and pushed open the door, gesturing at Fil to enter. He wiped his shoes, more a formality than a necessity, and stepped into the dim interior.

Doggone it. Was this all I'd be able to hear? I just might have to collar Fil after he talked with Donna, ask a few questions myself, after he was done with this meeting. But he doubtless would be reticent to share business details with a stranger. I'd do a whole bunch better if I could overhear a few more tidbits here.

Luck was with me. Fil paused in the doorway. He turned back to look at Donna. A final chunk of conversation floated to my ears.

"– see for myself where he was found, talk to who found him and to anyone else who could possibly carry a grudge against you and your husband, or against his owners."

"Absolutely," Donna said. "Remember to ask about 'Mad' Mattie Henderson, a former barn assistant. She still carries a grudge for our firing her."

Fil nodded.

That was the end of what I could hear. They went inside and closed the door.

At that moment the dog lunged free from my hand. She ran whining to the house. She looked at the door a long time, turning her head sideways. Then she trotted around the corner and disappeared into a narrow tunnel in the shrubbery beside the house.

I looked around. No one was in the parking lot. No one was anywhere else outside that I could see. Excellent.

Keeping near the fence line, I approached the house. I stopped to one side of the arch to the patio, and spied an opening in the roses. The opening led to the path the dog had taken, around to the formal front of the house, which faced the road. The side with the living room. Where Donna and Fil might settle for the rest of the conversation.

Twigs snapped as I crept forward. I ducked through the maze of shrubs and small trees. A spiky plant raked my bare arms. As I made my slow way, greenery bent back, then whipped my face. The smell of dog poop and mashed evergreen rose to my nose.

Two flies began to buzz and whine around my eyes, nose and mouth. They darted in and out. They stayed maddeningly beyond reach, trying again and again to bite me or suck the moisture from my facial openings.

I batted at them as I pushed aside branches, then stumbled as I caught a toe on a rock or root. Hitting the ground hard, I yelped. Then I lay there, hoping no one had heard. I lay a little longer, to make sure I hadn't been discovered.

I saw my right foot wrapped in the thickest bunch of periwinkle vines I had ever seen. The determined mat of spaghetti-like vines with spear shaped leaves covered the ground and grew three feet up the side of the house, with only a smattering of blue flowers to show for all its effort.

Those plants were desperately seeking full sun and had found only a spot of it.

Same with me. Seeking light and space, as well as answers. Plus I worried about being discovered, and also how I'd get the flake out of there without arousing suspicion. What had I been thinking? Or drinking?

My gaze swept the parking lot. Took in the front and sides of the barn, and over where trailers and tractors were parked. Unpeopled and empty except for Fil's, the Grandeens' and my vehicle. All good.

I struggled up and pulled my foot free of vines, only to feel a sharp stinging pain on my left shin. Looking down I saw a reddish spot stain the blue of my jeans.

Nice. Now I had drawn blood.

What in screaming heck was I doing creeping through shrubbery and sneaking around in broad daylight? I was behaving like a caricature of an amateur sleuth. Miss Marple as a Twenty-First Century rock and roll cowgirl. Miss Marple braving deadly bugs and Amazonian jungles. For what? To solve a mystery involving not a beloved mistress, heir apparent or rich aristocrat, but a common, hay burning, poop dumping horse? An overpriced horse, to be sure. But a horse just the same.

Mom was right. I should have left this to the professionals.

So not!

I stopped that thought train when I heard voices.

They sounded faint. As if coming from a distance. But voices. Donna and Fil's. I pushed aside more branches and inched around the corner. The voices were louder. They came from a slightly open window in the dining room next to the living room.

Sucking in my breath, I went for it.

I tried to be as quiet as possible as I settled on my haunches next to the window. I heard papers shuffling. No one spoke for a moment.

Then Fil cleared his throat.

"Their policy is essentially the same as yours, only at a higher value," he said. "In your opinion as a trainer, and buyer and seller of horses, does the value look reasonable?"

"Wow," Donna said. "A hundred fifty thousand. That's three times what we had Vader insured for."

Man, I thought. There's a twist. Three times more. I wondered what it meant.

My knees were beginning to cramp. I shifted my weight as I huddled near the open window, and leaned my cheek against the house siding.

"Is that value out of line?" Fil said. "I need your opinion because the new insured value was pending until verified by you and our professional assessors. Was there a reason for the bump-up? New winnings or standings in the show records?"

"We probably had him valued too low," said Donna, ever the businesswoman, and protective of clients past, present and future.

"All right," said Fil. "Any other reason for the new value?"

"Look," said Donna. "The situation is this. Any horse's value is extremely hard to establish. It fluctuates even if established by, say, its sale price. We sold Vader for fifty thousand, as you know. We might have got more, but needed the money. And anyway, value is whatever a buyer will pay. If a similar horse sold for a hundred fifty, if there were a similar horse, I suppose it would be reasonable to price Vader in that range."

"I see," said Fil. "So one-fifty could be a reasonable price, then."

"Possibly," said Donna. "One or two other horses could approach that price."

The barn dog began whimpering on the front porch. She stared at the door. Why was she doing that? She never went into the house. She was a barn dog, for Pete's sake.

"Shhhh," I hissed, shooting her an angry look. She shushed. I hoped she wouldn't start up again and have me discovered, or blot out the rest of this telling conversation.

"Good," said Fil. "The Von Susterns, with their financial situation, clearly would not need insurance money from their dead horse. Did they ask for any unusual options or conditions when they bought Vader? And what is your general opinion of them?"

"Oh," said Donna, changing her tone to one of surprise. "Well, no. And they seem like good, sincere people. We've only met the one time, when she tried the horse. They had Vader vetted, he passed, and the transaction was pretty straightforward."

"Good," said Fil. "I guess that's all I need for now. I'll check in with Dutch, talk to the man who leased Vader, Freddie Uff … Uffenpinscher? And be on my way."

"If I can be of further help, let me know," said Donna.

I took that as a cue to make my getaway. Slick as a garter snake, I slithered back through the shrubs, already having forged a convenient path. I popped up on the other side of the rose arch and brushed myself off, no one the wiser.

Or so I thought.

14

A red rose petal clung to one of my eyelashes as I stood near the arbor and stared straight into the startled blue eyes of Tulip, my bosom buddy. With my mad dash back through the bushes, I hadn't heard her drive in. Lucky it was only her.

"Why, I do declare!" she said, one hand to her breast. "Y'all scared me silly. Don't pop out of the brush like that. I coulda had a coronary."

"Sorry, Tule." I sighed, blowing the rose petal off my eyelash. We started walking to the barn. "Lots on my mind. Gotta go work horses and start packing for the show."

She strode alongside me.

"Hey," she said. "What were you doin' in the bushes?"

"You'll never guess," I said.

"Try me," she said.

"Reconnoitering," I said. "Paid off, too."

"All right," she said with a fist pump. "Don't hold back. Details, please."

I told her the story of my sneaking around the house to eavesdrop on Donna and the insurance man's conversation. As I talked, I looked back to see them exit the house.

"And that's all I got, for now, Tule."

Barn buddies were starting to arrive for the day's riding and show prep. I headed for Choc's stall. I knew I shouldn't take the time to ride, and planned only to longe him, get him exercised. The day had been crazy so far, and it was just getting started. I had to remain calm and focused. A headache began to nibble at my temples. I recognized it at once as a "tired" headache.

"Oh, have another bit of news," I said to Tulip as she headed for her horse's stall. "Actually, two bits. You'll never guess. Well, maybe one you'll guess."

"I'm a pretty good guesser," she said. "Though you had me with that Miss Marple caper in the bushes."

"I spent the night with Sonny Chief," I said. "He just dropped in from nowhere. Wants to work on the Vader case behind the scenes. Offer his muscle, if needed."

"Whoa," she said, raising her eyebrows. "That elusive but adorable hound dog, Sonny Chief? So how was it? I mean how is he?"

"Elusive, but adorable," I said. "As always. I told him to leave this case to me. But you know Sonny. He's persistent. Though not always in ways I want."

"Or maybe in ways you do want," Tulip said, letting loose with her famous raucous laugh.

Two of our newer, less well-known barn buddies stared as they walked past us to take out their horses. Suzy and Jill. Two peas in the pod. Younger, well coiffed, pedi'd and mani'd forty somethings just getting started in the horse showing game. They had been driving Tulip, me and our other old hands crazy with questions the past week.

"Why does everyone bathe their horses three days early, when we have to bathe them anyway at the show?" Suzy had asked me Friday morning.

"Leg and face hair must be clean so Dutch can clip it without dulling the blades," I'd answered. "Blades cost twenty dollars each, and he goes through a ton."

"When do we band the manes?" Jill had asked Tulip, wondering what time during show prep that manes were separated into sixty narrow sections secured along the top of the neck with rubber bands. This row of bands lies flat, making the neck appear long and lean. Banding also eliminates mane-flapping, a distraction to the judges as horses pass before them. Do it when we get to the show, Tulip told Suzy and Jill.

Oh well, I thought. *We should always be ready and happy to help. Not like some showgirls, who could appear distant or snooty.* It only took a minute or two to answer a question, assist a beginner. Tulip and I, in fact all the Brassbottom buddies, had been there once. We'd all been clueless but enthusiastic rookies before earning those coveted silver spurs and belt buckles.

I don't care how long someone has ridden. What mountains, valleys, cows, storms or deserts one has ridden over. Showing is an entirely different ball of hoof wax. Aside from draining your bank account and retirement savings, it demands extreme focus, training and persistence. Oh yes, and a tough hide.

Feelings run high in competition. Divas are abundant, running the control game with steel fists until something goes sideways. Then they vent like a banshee to a partner, trainer or other competitor. Or cry their eyes out in the privacy of a trailer or restroom.

Their alternate trick is to beat you bloody in the show ring.

"Hey, dreamer," Tulip said, startling me as she came up behind me with her horse, Fire Bird, a chestnut and white Paint.

"Jeez," I said. "Don't sneak up like that."

"Gotcha back for sneaking out of the bushes on me," Tulip said. "You zoning out? Sonny keep you up too late?"

"Apparently," I said. "Plus this Vader case. Don't know if I'm coming or going."

"Hey, I have good news and bad news," she said. "I sold some things yesterday at the store. But the landlord called. Said if y'all don't come up with the rent money for the past three months, you're out of there. He wants it by Monday."

"What did you tell him?" I said.

"Not to get his knickers in a twist," she said. "Told him it'll be all right."

"Good girl," I said. "But dang! I already paid the first month. He knows that. He's just being mean. Hey, I sold that saddle and bridle to Patsy Ann. So we're good."

"Yes!" Tulip said. She high fived me. "Now we can tell Mr. Grumpy Pants to go, um, amuse his greedy li'l ole self. Sold them for how much?"

"Fourteen for both," I said. "She talked me down, and Jane needs the money."

"No kidding," Tulip said. "You delivering the saddle to Patsy Ann at the show?"

"That's the plan," I said. "Hey, listen. She stopped by here yesterday to talk to Dutch and see Vader's body. On her way to California. If she went to California."

"What do you mean, 'If she went to California'?"

"When they left the store they had to make Sacramento by dinner."

"Can do, if you burn up some highway and don't take too long gussying up."

"Then," I said, "I heard from Lana that Victoria and Dutch had a shouting match yesterday. Lana thinks they may have been hooking up."

"Nah," Tulip said. "Vic's smarter'n that. Spat probably was about her horses."

"Maybe," I said. "But don't forget. We've been wondering about Vic and Dutch. Love her to death. But she can be loose with the truth when the talk turns to lovers."

"As the hot-walker turns," shrugged Tulip. "Regular soap opera around here."

"Speaking of soap," I said. "I've got a horse to bathe and longe. Then get myself to the Horsehouse. Assume you'll be along later to help pack up the trailer."

"You got it," said Tulip. "And maybe I'll get to see Sonny. What's he's cookin' up today besides you?"

"Ha ha," I said. "Catching up with friends. That translates into renewing contacts in the sheriff's place, sneaking up on all things pertinent to the death of Dark Vader."

"How can Sonny be sneakier than our own Miss Marple?" Tulip said.

"Sonny has his ways," I said. "Believe me. Tricks we white folk, we wasichu, know nothing about."

***

By noon the temperature had risen a good twenty degrees, making it a pleasant eighty. The barn population had risen, too, with every client accounted for as well as a few curious extras. Several teen children texted nonstop from the edges of the scene, along with the odd husband or boyfriend taking time to stick their nose in. I waved to Little Stewie and gave him two thumbs up as he marched to his horse's stall.

Miles outside the city, this part of the valley didn't see much serious crime other than the odd cockfighting operation or drug bust. Brassbottom was curiosity now.

Hovering around Victoria was her estranged husband, Robert Whitfield-Smith III. Togged out in white visor, blue shirt, khaki shorts and sockless boaters, he looked fresh from the golf links.

Months ago Whitfield-Smith III had told Victoria that she had to choose between him or the horses. Hence the tag "estranged husband" on his resume. However it looked like he was still hanging in there, possibly nursing ill will toward Dutch, whom he blamed for keeping his wife hooked on horses. Or something to that effect.

By mid-day I had longed and bathed Choc, along with having done other show prep. I had taken Choc back to his freshly bedded stall. I struggled to pull on his nylon "sleazy," a head and neck sleeve with eye- and ear-holes. The sleazy would keep his mane from fluffing up when it dried.

"Excuse me," said an all-too-familiar male voice at the stall door.

"Oh, oh," I whispered under my breath. I Velcro'd the sleazy's belly band in place, and sidled around my horse to the stall door.

Sheriff Jack Henning stood in the aisle. His arms were folded over his chest. He didn't look happy. I wondered what had put such a scowl on his face, and why he had come to see me for the third time in barely twenty-four hours.

"Well, hello, Sheriff," I said. "What can I do for you now?"

"For starters, you can drop the innocent act," he said.

"I don't know what you mean," I said. "It's no act."

"We'll see about that," he said. "Now I understand you've sent your Indian boyfriend snooping around my deputies for information on the horse case."

"My Indian what?" I said. "I've done no such thing. What my old friend Sonny Chief does with his free time is not my concern."

"Really," said the sheriff. "One of my men was at Katie's Kitchen today. He saw my deputy, Boo George, having coffee with another Indian who Katie says is your boyfriend. She said you two came in all the time a couple years ago. My man overheard them discussing the Vader case. Whaddya know about that, Miss Kane?"

I closed my stall door. I took my time sliding the bolt. Then I turned back to Sheriff Jack, and flashed him my most guileless look.

"Less than nothing," I said. "The Vader case is general knowledge. It was on the news last night, in the paper this morning, and I imagine everyone's talking about it."

Sheriff Jack frowned, jutted out his chin and looked around. Most of the horse washing, clipping and grooming was happening at the front end of the aisle.

"Katie told me something else, Miss Kane," he said. "Remember that little talk we had in the squad car yesterday?"

"How could I forget?" I said, feeling my face grow hot.

"About your going into Vader's stall before anyone else was here yesterday?"

"I remember what you were implying, and trying to get me to falsely admit. Pure bluff and supposition. And a fair amount of harassment."

"Really," he said. "Then why did you pull aside barn cleaners today and try to intimidate them?"

My heart thudded. Did the sheriff really, finally, have something on me? If so, who squealed? Or was he still bluffing, acting on circumstance and supposition?

"I just told them they were doing a great job cleaning my stall," I said, mostly telling the truth. "That's about it."

"Really," he said, taking a spread-legged stance, one hand on his sheathed Glock.

"Really," I echoed with all the conviction I could muster. I folded my arms.

So Sheriff Jack had been at them again, just as he was relentless at prodding me. I changed my impression of him. He was not a grizzly but a pit bull, mean and stubborn. Had I crossed him some way? Embarrassed him? But I couldn't for the life of me think how.

His tiny eyes bored into mine. I detected a flicker of intelligence. The merest flicker, but a flicker, just the same. A little knowledge. That, when paired with stubbornness and a tendency to screw up, could be deadly.

I tried something different. I relaxed. I let my arms drop, looked away and kicked dirt with one toe of my cowboy boot. Corny, I knew. But it just might work.

His aggression ticked down a notch. I felt rather than saw it.

"You need to be aware of something, Miss Kane," he said at last. "I am watching you, your friend Freddie, that Indian whatever he is to you, and everyone else who has tangled themselves in this case. I am keeping meticulous notes. We won't stand for interference of any kind, shape or form."

"I understand," I said. "You have your job to do. It's just that we all are worried, and curious about the case. It's natural to wonder and talk about it."

He pressed his lips together. He looked at his watch, then back at me. His walkie-talkie crackled with unintelligible words. He ignored it.

"All right," he said. "But that had better be as far as it goes. Are you aware, Miss Kane, that investigating by you or anyone else not connected to the case will be considered tampering with possible witnesses or suspects?"

My palms began to sweat. He had me. But I wasn't about to let him see it.

"Yes, I am aware, Sir," I said, lowering my eyes dramatically. Submissive tactics had eased our talk a little already, and this should take the last wind out of his sails.

"But are you really?" he pressed, unwilling to yield his apparent upper hand. "Do you understand the actual consequences of interfering with an active investigation?"

Definitely a bull dog, not a griz. Did Sheriff Jack himself have something to hide?

"I am," I said, raising my head to meet his gaze.

His eyes practically shot sparks. Spittle clung to one side of his mouth. Sheriff Jack seemed to actually enjoy intimidating me.

"Then be warned, Miss Kane. Butt out. Call off all your bloodhounds, too, or you'll regret it." A drop of his saliva hit my cheek. I refused to blink. I stood taller.

"Are you threatening me, Sheriff Henning?" I said. "Because there are laws against that, too."

He wiped his mouth but still held me in his fiery glare.

"Make no mistake, Miss Kane," he said, in a deeper, colder voice. "You go against me, or mess up this case in any way, and no lawyer or court in the world can save you."

15

As I watched the sheriff walk back down the barn aisle, his fists clenched and his arms stiff, I stood flabbergasted at his words and their frightening intensity. Why had he been so angry? It was unprofessional, and gave me the creeps. Could he somehow be involved in Vader's death, or in a cover-up? I wouldn't put it past him.

People and horses drifted down the aisle past me on various pre-show chores. But for another minute I couldn't move.

Sheriff Henning actually had threatened me. Not in as many words. Nothing he'd said, per se, was actionable. But I would have to be super careful now. The bulldog/griz was gunning for me. He was sure he had me on the run, and liked it way too much.

I became aware someone else was standing at my side, trying to get my attention.

"Oh! Sorry," I said. "Hi, Victoria!" I relaxed as I gazed into her violet eyes. Her horse, which she had been leading, nudged her for treats. We weren't supposed to hand-feed treats, as it encouraged nipping. But some riders gave treats anyway.

"Pepper," she cooed, "I saw Sheriff Jack talking to you. He looked mad as hell."

"That's our Sheriff Jack," I said. "Thinks I'm messing with his investigation."

"Well," said Vic. "You are, aren't you? Doing your own investigating?"

"That's not the point," I said. "I am curious, like the rest of us. Might be asking a few questions. The Grandeens are down with that. Of course we would share anything important to the case with the sheriff."

"We?"

"The editorial 'we.' I assume you or anyone else around here who learns anything pertinent would share with me, as well." I watched my friend closely.

"Oh, well, sure," she said, glancing to the front of the barn, where Whitfield-Smith III stood silhouetted in the open barn doorway. "Almost done, honey," she called. She turned back to me. "He's taking me out to lunch at the country club."

"Nice. Well, I have a question for you, Vic."

"Can you make it quick? Robert's already pissed. Says I spend way too much time here. And money. Even thinks I hooked up with Dutch. Can you believe it?"

"Actually I can," I said. "So are you?"

Victoria shook her curly mane.

"That's confidential information," she said with a brittle laugh.

"So you are, or have come close. Is that what you fought about yesterday?"

"Who told you about that?" she said, flushing. "Well, that happened to be about my horses. He isn't riding them as much as I'd like. I'm thinking of sending them to Royce and Rogers in Texas." She fiddled with her rope, and straightened her horse's forelock. He tossed his head as if in agreement.

"Well," I said. "Everyone thinks their horse doesn't get as much of a trainer's attention or riding as they think it should. What did you two really argue about?"

"It was actually about the horses," Victoria insisted. "Though it could have been about me and Dutch, a very long time ago."

"Thought so. How long ago?"

"Long enough. Like it never happened."

"O-kay," I said. "What happens in the barn stays in the barn. Can't believe you'd do that to Donna, though. She's such a friend to us all."

"To some more than others," Victoria said.

I wondered what that meant, but didn't have the time or inclination to go into it.

"It's none of my business," I said, "what or who you do or don't do. It's hearsay anyway. Just please don't leave, and please don't let anything upset the barn balance. We're already under a helluva lot of pressure."

She absorbed this, nodded, and then led her horse back toward his stall.

Victoria still was a friend. I did not betray friends. Even to other friends. I just hoped she was being straight. Was her fling with Dutch really over? Because if their argument was about another woman, I wasn't sure what position I would take. It depended on who that other woman was. And who else was affected.

My thoughts flashed to Patsy Ann Carpenter. What if rumors about Victoria had reached Patsy Ann? Was that the reason Patsy Ann stopped by Brassbottom on her way to California yesterday? To check up on her lover, or would-be lover?

This opened up a can of worms I wasn't eager to deal with. Patsy Ann and Dutch. Was theirs an only-at-the-shows romance, if it was a romance? This was not uncommon, among some trainers and customers. Shadowy figures doing shady things in shadowed stalls. More important, did it have any bearing on who killed Vader?

I tended to want to pin such questions and suspicions to timing and coincidences of the recent days, how events and people aligned. Vader's sale to a competitor, Vader's mysterious death, the surprising appearance of Patsy Ann here before one of the year's biggest shows, the warnings given me from Richard Von Sustern and Sheriff Jack, the hefty bumping up of Vader's insurance.

My mind whirled like the dust devil now spiraling down the aisle, horses snorting in its wake. Likely, because of fatigue and my need to solve this case pronto, I might be connecting dots not meant to be connected.

***

I stopped by Katie's Kitchen to pick up a raspberry lemonade and hot French dip sandwich before settling in for a day of paperwork and packing at the Horsehouse. By some stroke of luck and foresight I already had cleaned and organized my live-aboard trailer behind the store. One less thing to stress about.

As I waited at the counter for my order, Katie herself, balancing lunch platters, paused beside me. She raised her eyebrows and leaned in conspiratorially.

"Saw your old boyfriend here this morning," she grinned. "Lookin' good, too. So you two getting back together?"

"We never really were officially together," I said, hoping to avoid conversation, especially about Sonny. "He's on a quick visit, is all."

"Lucky you. Say, he and some deputy had quite the tête-à-tête over coffee today."

She awaited elucidation from me, but I only shrugged.

"Boo," I said.

Katie drew back. A frown line appeared between her eyebrows.

"Huh?"

"Deputy Boo George. Sonny and he are distant cousins off a rez in South Dakota. Probably catching up on family matters, or something like that."

"Oh. I thought it was about the horse that was killed. Lot of people are buzzing about that. They got the cause figured out?"

"Not that I know of. I'm not in the loop."

Katie looked disappointed, but I offered nothing more.

"Now I have a question for you," I said. "What do you know about Sheriff Jack? Hear anything about gambling debts, favors owed, connections to rich out-of-towners?"

"Oh," said Katie. "I get it. He's been riding you a little too hard, trying to get you to back off the case. You're guessing it may be cuz he might be involved."

"Gotta work all the angles. Katie, you're the queen of the valley when it comes to hot gossip. You must have heard something about him, even if it is only rumor."

Katie pulled herself up importantly, resettling the platters in her arms.

"Well, as a matter of fact," she said, making me wait. "No."

"Too bad." I felt deflated. She saw it and pounced.

"Well, I can't back it up. But I did hear that the sheriff has a little prescription drug problem. Forget who I heard it from."

I nodded, and filed that away. An addict often needed increasing amounts of cash and suppliers than he could gather on his own. Finding another person to confirm it, maybe Sonny via his contact, would help. I subscribed to the smoke-fire connection.

The next minute a waiflike young man, whose blond hair poked out from a chef's toque, stepped from the kitchen. He plopped a white paper bag on the desk. I paid, took the bag, and left.

When I entered the Horsehouse, I saw Tulip standing, arms akimbo in front of the counter. It was piled with tops, shirts and designer jeans. Boxes of hats and boots surrounded her on the floor. She looked over and gave me a huge smile.

"I knocked off early at the barn," she said. "I knew we'd have our hands full here. But it'll be all right."

"Holy cow," I said, surveying the store's nearly empty shelves. "We can't take everything. Serrano won't have anything to sell."

"We all gotta take the good stuff," Tulip argued. "Horse shows put people in full spending mode, and we can't afford to miss a trick."

'True," I said. "But let's try to be a little more selective. Otherwise won't be any room for us in the trailer."

She and I spent the next few hours slogging through what to take, what to leave. We folded clothes, filled boxes, gathered grooming items and made countless trips to the trailer and back. We stashed Patsy Ann's saddle and bridle last, covered by a quilt on the queen bed that filled the top gooseneck section of trailer.

Luckily Tulip and I had only a half-dozen customers, and those mainly sought easy stuff like fly spray, horse treats and feed supplements.

We got a chuckle from a cute little gal who introduced herself as Cherie. She reminded me of someone but I couldn't think who. Togged out in a hot pink tank that spelled her name in rhinestones, the plump teen also wore tight jeans tucked in high-top turquoise boots. I figured her for a rodeo barrel-racer. Those fast riding ladies did like them some sparkles.

Cherie gave Patsy Ann's new saddle an admiring once-over. She asked its price, then nearly fainted when I told her.

"That costs more than my horse," she said, jerking her hand away as if burned.

Cherie admired several items in the jewelry cases, and finally bought an over-the-top, pink lace-and-rhinestone studded ball cap meant for trendy rodeo-istas like her. It had crosses and crystals plastered on every surface.

"You can never be too thin, too rich or too blinged out," she laughed, pulling the hat deeper over her blond, pigtrailed hair.

"True," I said. "Don't mean a thing if it ain't got that bling." I gave myself a figurative pat on the back for that turn on the title of a Swing Era song.

Tulip gave me a pained look.

"Really, Pepper?" she said.

Who cares, I thought, *if the customer is happy. Flatter them, make them smile, and leave them wanting more. Whether it was fine merchandise or personal attention.* Tulip had no reason to rag on me. She did the same thing herself, laying on a deep Southern drawl and witticisms no matter how corny, if it meant a sale.

We went back to packing and toting, folding and arguing. Bringing some things back in, taking new ones out. Stacking metal towers and rounders. I had designated piles for each kind of merchandise, and prioritized them in the order in which they went into the trailer. That'd make things so easy when it was time to set up at the show.

Tulip left the shop midway through for a hot dog. Then it was back to the grind. The phone rang several times, with people wanting to know if we carried this or that. I was relieved for a chance to sit down and rest my aching feet during the calls.

Finally it was nearing our five o'clock closing time. We might actually be ready to go, I marveled. That would be a first. That meant I could devote most of Sunday to getting things ready at my house, while I did a little more digging on the Vader case.

We were both beyond exhausted. Tulip wondered if Sonny would come "home" for dinner that night. I told her that I welcomed him, but at the same time it would have been nice to be alone, to rest up for the trip.

"I certainly don't feel like cooking," I said. "He might have to take me to dinner."

"I hear you," said Tulip. "But wouldn't it feel nice just to stay home and watch him barbecue something?"

"Hey," I said. "I do have hamburger in the fridge. And tomatoes from the garden."

* * *

As Tulip and I prepared to leave the store, with me wrapping up some last-minute paperwork including a fat check for the landlord, I gave my old laptop one final peek You never could tell when an Internet order might come in.

My email inbox showed a message from my daughter, Chili. Dear, smart Chili. I envisioned her gingersnap eyes under her frothy red hair caught in a high ponytail.

"R. Von Sustern in trouble last year for selling a Lamborghini with altered VIN," she wrote. "Obscure ref in Nevada paper. See attachment. All I could find. Have fun in Cal. Talk to you later. Love you."

I read the attached article. It was only a few paragraphs, mentioning Von Sustern had been sued by the man who'd bought the car, only to have Von Sustern countersue that buyer for defamation of character. The story briefly mentioned two other alleged shady deals that involved Von Sustern and luxury goods, but neither example was supported enough to have him prosecuted. In other words, he was a slick one.

So, now a better, though tarnished, picture of Marietta's husband was beginning to emerge. It wasn't much. But it was better than nothing. It suggested the man might be capable of breaking a law, and that he had no problem retaliating when wronged. Aggressive countersuits come in handy as smokescreen, when hanky panky is afoot.

I hoped to meet Von Sustern, and learn more about him, at the horse show. What if he'd had his wife's horse killed after raising its insurance, so he could make good on a bad debt? Pay off a too-talkative tongue in one of his shady deals?

***

Before wrapping up at the store I ran through my other possible suspects. Freddie, of course, had found the body. But he was so distressed by Vader's death, somewhat of a coward and so enamored of the Brassbottom gang, equines included, that the likelihood of his being the killer seemed remote.

Mad Mattie, the former employee with her grudge against the Grandeens, seemed remote, as well. However she could have been an accessory if the real killer had learned about her. She knew the barn routines and gossip. But she'd been neither seen nor heard from in months. Supposedly still in California.

Not so remote as persons of interest were Patsy Ann and even Sheriff Jack. I definitely needed to know more about the latter. Sonny could help with that.

But I kept coming back to Von Sustern. The dude had been so mean with me on the phone. Threatening. Scary, even, with that slick refined demeanor masking his control-freak persona and checkered business history. What did he have to be so defensive about? Something had set him against me.

I just couldn't shake the notion that he was involved in Vader's death. He may even have been the one paying Sheriff Jack.

Events the next day convinced me I might be on the right track.

16

Sonny's pickup, windows down, stood in front of the house. It was parked under branches of the hickory tree in my shade garden. But even that sheltered area was no match for the heat of a midsummer's eve in southern Oregon.

When I pushed open the door, the dogs jumped wildly, licking my hands, running for toys. As my eyes adjusted to the dimness, Sonny clicked off the TV, rose from the couch and took my measure. He looked concerned and did not approach me.

"Hey," he said. "You look like you ran a marathon."

"I'm beyond beat," I said. "Not even the strength to make dinner. Hope your day went better."

"Got some leads to check tomorrow but nothing major," he said. "You go shower and I'll rustle us up something."

I smiled and walked over to him. He pulled me into a hug so strong it almost cracked my ribs.

"Ow! I said, stiffening. Sometimes he didn't know his own strength, even when he tried to be tender.

He loosened his hold.

I sighed, comforted by his strong arms holding me, shielding me from the world's evils. I pressed my forehead against his chest, shut my eyes and drank in his intoxicating scent. It was a mixture of clean tee shirt, spicy aftershave and warm-blooded male.

"Mmmm," I said.

"You read my thoughts," he said.

In another moment I slipped free from our embrace and retreated to my master suite for a shower. The water, pounding my chest and shoulders like a million needles, felt divine. I did a one-eighty and stayed there, back to the spray and eyes shut, for what seemed an hour. It was only ten minutes, but did wonders for my energy and morale.

By the time I emerged freshly creamed, combed and coutured, in loose cutoffs, flip flops and a man-size white tee, the aroma of grilling hamburger filled my nostrils. My stomach rumbled in anticipation.

Sonny poked his head through the open sliding door to the deck.

"Found some hamburger in the fridge," he said. "Do you have salad fixings?"

"Think so," I said. "Smells delicious. I forgot what a grill master you are. I am hungry enough to eat a horse."

"I'll go get Bob," Sonny laughed.

"Not that horse," I said. "He's wakan. Sacred."

Sonny nodded, and raised his spatula.

"Oh," he said. "Serrano called. Wanted to know if he should come down here tomorrow, or on Monday."

"That kid," I said, shaking my head. "Has the attention span of a gnat. Probably why he can't hold a job. I thought my folks were forgetful. But Serrano's something else. I told him at least four times to come Sunday."

Sonny said nothing. He had grown kids of his own, who had been known to give him some grief. Sonny ducked back outside to tend the burgers and buns.

I gave Serrano a quick call, left a reprimanding voice mail, then built Sonny and me a fabulous salad, if I do say so. Greens and tomatoes from my garden, with carrots, radishes, green onions and bleu cheese. I topped it with olive oil and wine vinegar.

I was feeling almost human again, what with the long shower, the self-pampering and the prospect of a super intimate outdoor dinner. I stooped to turn on the cobra-shaped water spritzer to cool us as we sat at the wrought-iron dining set.

As I was about to go inside for plates, glasses and utensils, and maybe a cold one to drink, I hesitated. A night like this, a meal like this, the company of a man like this were tailor made for a mug of foamy beer. It'd be frosting on the meal, to mangle a metaphor. Sonny probably would be okay with my enjoying a brew.

But I just couldn't make myself do that in front of him. He'd been ten years clean and sober, and still worked hard to stay there.

I set the table, then set myself down just as Sonny brought the plate of burgers, swimming in juices and topped with sea salt and cracked pepper, to the table.

"Wow," I said. "Looks fantastic."

We started eating, I with a hunger that seemed boundless. Long minutes passed, punctuated by yummy sounds from us and hungry whines from the dogs.

"So," I said, having tucked away half a burger with all the trimmings, as well as much of my salad. "Katie at the Kitchen and Sheriff Jack said you had coffee this morning with your deputy-cousin."

It occurred to me that I was eating as if for two people, lately. But I was well past the years for being pregnant. Two bacon burgers in two days, peach pie, French dip, bacon croissants. Impressive. But knowing that didn't slow me down any. I figured investigating took energy, and burned a lot of blood sugar needed by the brain.

"Yes," Sonny said, wiping his lips with a paper towel. "We relived old times." He grabbed his glass of cola, rattled the ice and gulped some before settling back in his chair.

"What else did you talk about?" I said, dipping the last bite of my bun into the last juices on my plate.

"You mean did we talk about the case?" Sonny's eyes looked playful, teasing. He knew darn well I was starved for any tidbits the sheriff's department might have turned up regarding Vader's death.

"You know that's what I mean."

"Seems that they've been looking into Richard Von Sustern, for one thing," Sonny said, "related to the horse's insurance and all. Checking his financial status, outstanding large debts and such."

"Anything out of the ordinary? My daughter, Chili, turned up some shady dealings regarding luxury cars and lawsuits."

Sonny rolled the salt shaker back and forth between his long fingers.

"Yeah, they had that," he said. "Boo is getting it printed out for me. They're also running checks on his wife, but she's pretty hard to find stuff on. Stays in her husband's shadow a lot, has homes in Dallas and North Tahoe."

"What I've discovered," I said. "Anything on Freddie, or Patsy Ann Carpenter?"

"Freddie is still a person of interest, since he found the horse," Sonny said. "But there's nothing new on him. They were questioning him again today."

"Would've had to do it at his shop," I said. "I think he had appointments all day. What about Patsy Ann? I wondered if she really went to California, as she told me."

"She showed up at the barn yesterday," Sonny said. "Poking around your trainer and going to see the dead horse. They questioned him and her about her business there."

"Someone told me," I said. "Do you know what time? And her business?"

"Apparently Patsy Ann tried to buy that horse, and was chewing out Dutch for not selling it to her. Dutch's words."

"Well, why didn't he sell? Patsy Ann could have afforded it."

"Apparently Patsy Ann thinks he sold the horse to Marietta to spite Patsy Ann. That he might even have killed it."

I sat back and rolled my eyes.

"That's ridiculous," I said. "Plus she and Dutch barely knew each other."

"Not the way Boo tells it," said Sonny.

"Oh?" I said.

"Guess they'd once been more than friends," he said.

I nearly choked on my cola. I began to cough violently. Sonny rose and slapped my back. I felt dizzy, and gripped the table for support.

"You okay?" Sonny said, leaning down.

I nodded and waved him away.

"I … knew … it," I sputtered. "I just knew it. I never saw them together, but our barn buddy, Victoria, had a big fight with Dutch yesterday."

"Hmmm," Sonny said. "Maybe a lover's spat?"

"Something like that," I said, swallowing a few times to make sure my airways were clear. "She said it was over her horses, that he didn't pay them enough attention."

"I see," Sonny said. "Was that the real reason?"

"She kind of suggested they'd had an affair," I said. "But supposedly a long time ago. Ancient history."

"Or not," Sonny said.

"Or not," I echoed. "Oh, next time you talk to Boo, ask if Sheriff Jack has any big debts or addictions."

"He threatened you again, I take it."

"Pretty much. More than you'd expect. Just need him checked out."

Sonny and I sat in silence a moment. Sipping colas, we both looked out over the pasture. The close hills to our right, cloaked in oak and madrone, lay in purple shadow, the sun having dipped below them. Turkey vultures with vee'd black wings and blood red heads rode updrafts as violet-green swallows chirped and swooped after insects.

"The thought plickens," I said at last. "But what does it mean?"

"That the thought has just got even more complicated," Sonny said.

"Ha ha," I said.

We fell silent again, lost in our musing. It was almost dark. The breeze picked up and the wind chimes began to clink and tinkle. I toyed with my last bits of salad, and Sonny slipped the Boston terriers a few crumbs.

I was about to hatch a new theory, when Dolly Parton's bouncy vocals sliced through our evening.

It was my cell phone. Probably Chili or Serrano. I went into the kitchen, catching my baby toe on a chair leg. A sharp pain coursed through my foot. I gritted my teeth.

"Dang!" I yelled limping to pick up the phone. My toe hurt like heck. The same one that had been broken by horses stepping on it. I pressed my lips tight to help me stand the pain. Dolly was nearing the end of her chorus.

The phone's pane lit up with the name of the security firm I used for the store.

Oh, God, what now? I thought. My pulse pounded in my ears, matching the tempo of the pain in my toe.

"Hello?" I said into the phone.

"All America Guardians," said a robotic male voice. "Is this Pepper Kane?"

"It is," I said.

"The Best Little Horsehouse registered to you showed a security breach at nine p.m. Pacific Daylight Time today. Law enforcement has been notified and is en route."

My heart lurched. A break-in at my store? Great. That was all I needed right now. Hopefully my alarms scared whoever it was away before they could take anything. And hopefully there would be no broken windows or doors to repair. Though I doubted it.

"Okay," I said, trying to keep my voice level. "Anything else I should know?"

"We have no further information," said the voice. "But we advise you to go to the store as soon as you can to assess the damage and losses, if any, meet with law enforcement, and re-secure the premises."

I looked at the time. Nine-twenty. Why had they taken so long to call? A burglar would have had the chance to grab a bunch of stuff. Whatever was going on at my shop was likely long over.

Then another thought occurred. Had they broken into my live-aboard trailer, too? Loaded with merchandise for the show?

Then I heard a siren in the distance. It was easy to hear things in the evenings, as sound carried better in the slightly cooler air.

"Hello? Are you still on the line, Miss Kane?"

"Um, yes," I said, my thoughts racing.

"We, of course, will do a full investigation, working with police," said the voice. "We'll contact you in a few days. Your policy is current, so you should be okay."

"That's something," I said. "Thanks." I was stunned, trying to remember if I kept the paperwork at the store or at home. I'd never thought I'd have to consult it.

"That's what we're here for. Call if you have further questions."

I hung up and ran out on the deck, where Sonny was gathering up dirty dishes.

"Let me do that," I said, filling my arms and heading back to the kitchen. "You start your truck. That was the security company. Been a break-in at the Horsehouse."

Sonny ignored my order and carried the dishes into the kitchen himself. Then he strode through the living room, opened the front door, and started his truck. The diesel engine's roar filled the house, as did its diesel fumes.

I ordered the dogs to stay, closed the house doors and threw my purse through the open front window on the truck's passenger side.

"I'll go open the gate," I shouted above the engine noise and crunching gravel as Sonny threw the truck into reverse and turned it around.

Heart beating wildly, legs pumping, bile backing up in my throat from the heavy meal, I chugged down the driveway to the gate. My toe still throbbed so I had a pathetic limp going. Then I had to lift the gate up on hinges I'd been meaning to fix, to get it to clear the gravel as I walked it around to the open position. After Sonny drove out and waited in his truck at the road, I walked the gate closed, cursing under my breath.

It was like the world had slipped into slow motion. Every sight and sound were magnified, each move was executed at a maddening crawl. I felt as if I were in a nightmare where I could barely move.

When I finally pulled my sweaty, desperate body up into the passenger seat and felt the truck rumble down the road, I took a breath down to my belly button.

"Cowgirl up," I said to myself under my breath. "Cowgirl up."

I had the feeling whatever I found at the store could change my life for the worse, if not forever. A bad enough loss could put me flat out of business.

17

The ten minutes it normally took to drive the roads to the store seemed a whole lot longer. A jogger, a bicyclist, and a truck and trailer slowed Sonny's and my progress on the two-lane blacktop. I had my window down, sweating it out until the AC kicked in.

I was about to shout at the cyclist ahead to ride in his lane instead of atop the white line at the edge of the car lane. But on he pedaled, oblivious or uncaring, elbows out, forcing us against the center double line that was illegal to cross. The shovel-chinned man looked so darn arrogant in his striped helmet, yellow jersey and Spandex pants.

My fists clenched. My cheeks flushed hotter as my blood pressure rose.

I looked over at Sonny. Both hands gripped the wheel. His chiseled profile set off by that black braid over his shoulder looked intimidating, but told me nothing of his feelings. Maybe I'd urge him to just cross that center line to pass the bicyclist.

As if our thoughts were in sync, he floored the gas pedal, swerved the truck out and dove back into our lane mere feet in front of the cyclist.

Lance Armstrong spewed obscenities and flipped us off as we passed. The horn of an oncoming hybrid car the size of a goat bleated in protest.

I looked over at Sonny, whose face still revealed nothing in the deep twilight.

"Attaboy, Crazy Horse," I said. My invincible Sioux warrior.

Further along toward town and my store, I analyzed each car, pedestrian and wind-tossed shrub. On the walkway of the narrow bridge over the river a raggedy man with a bulging backpack hurried along, a pit bull glued to his side. The man glanced from side to side. Our eyes met as we passed.

Could he be the burglar, trying to act casual as he made a cool getaway on this darkening summer night?

Out front of the Nugget tavern stood the usual half-dozen Harleys and riders, men with bare chests beneath their leather vests. White beards and mustaches caught the last of the light. A gold earring glinted here, tattoos dotted white flesh there. A blonde in a purple bandanna and tight leathers boogied onto the sidewalk to ancient rock rhythms thumping through the doorway. Laughs erupted. Saturday Night Fever, Gold Hill style.

Sonny finally turned his truck down the street where the Horsehouse stood. A few onlookers hovered near the sheriff's official green-and-white SUV.

Somewhere a dog barked repeatedly. Another answered with a soulful howl.

The SUV's door hung open, and its lightbar threw blue and red flashes around the neighborhood. The radio blurted words from dispatchers and officers speaking some outer-space lingo made up of blips, numbers and choppy syllables.

Someone a few doors down shouted at the dog to stop barking. That morphed into a spirited shouting and barking match that made my head throb.

All the store lights were on. The door stood open. The windows showed someone moving around inside that looked like Sheriff Henning. No mistaking that grizzly bear profile and Smokey hat.

I flashed back to our interview the previous day. He'd asked how my security was at the store, and if I'd ever had any trouble. I'd found his questions peculiar, wondering why he was concerned about that. Odd, how things had turned out.

He had reminded me that this part of the Valley was more active than other parts, when it came to illegal drug activity, as it was near the freeway and lacking a police presence.

"At least the sheriff's here already," I said, jumping from the truck.

"Pretty fast, eh?" Sonny said. "Almost like he expected trouble."

I looked at my watch. It read nine-thirty. The law had arrived in less than a half-hour since their call from All America Guardians. Some kind of record, for a reported non-violent activity. With law-enforcement budgets in these parts stretched threadbare, officers took awhile to respond, if they responded at all, unless lives were at stake. I guessed that with my involvement in the Vader case, my store and I were special.

We approached the store. The door and windows looked fine. The burglar either picked the front door lock, or entered through the back.

As I went through the doorway, the sheriff looked up. He stood at the counter, writing in a pad and talking into the walkie-talkie on his shoulder.

Around him the Horsehouse had an empty, violated air. Part of the emptiness was because Tulip and I had packed so much into the trailer already. Random merchandise littered the floor.

"Miss Kane," he said. "Don't touch anything. But take a look around and give me an idea what's missing. You can work up a full list after I leave. You'll want to anyway, for the insurance people."

"Okay," I said, feeling Sonny step up behind me. "This is my friend, Sonny Chief. He's a cousin of your deputy, Boo George."

"Mr. Chief and I have met," he said with a scowl. But he nodded at Sonny.

"The shelves look a little bare," I said, "because we'd put a lot of merchandise in the trailer out back, to take down to the horse show in California."

"Too bad," said the sheriff. "Cuz they hit the trailer, too. So take a look in there but don't touch anything."

My heart sank even lower. Not the trailer, too. This was bad. Really bad.

"How did the burglar get in?" I said. "Someone searching the area for him?"

"That's handled," the sheriff said. "My deputy's checking with neighbors. The perp appears to have used a key or picked the lock on the front door. Try your key and see whether the lock's been damaged."

I fished my keys out of my purse and tried the Horsehouse key in the door lock. It slid in and out without protest.

"Seems fine," I said.

"Try the back one, too," said the sheriff.

"I just can't believe this," I said, looking at him, then at Sonny. I rubbed my arms even though it was warm in the store. Glancing around, I saw a few spurs, shirts and bridles on the floor, or catawampus on their hangers, but I really couldn't tell for sure what was missing. I'd have to do a thorough walk-through in the morning, when my brain was back in full gear.

"Before you check the trailer," said the sheriff, "tell me what day and time you last were in the store, if you were with anyone, and who locked up."

"Tulip Clemmons, my friend who helps me here, was with me today, packing the trailer," I said. "We left a little after five. I locked up."

The sheriff nodded and wrote in his pad.

"You two the only ones with a key, or access to one?" he said.

"Yes," I said. "That's correct."

"How about Mr. Chief?"

I glanced at Sonny, over by the counter. He shrugged. I shook my head.

Then I remembered something. Freddie knew where I hid the spare key, under the flower pot to the right of the front door. I'd told Freddie last fall when I called one night and asked him on his way home from Brassbottom to check that I'd shut off the lights and armed the security. I'd been called to my folks' for some emergency, and left the store in a hurry, thinking I'd be right back. The crisis took way more time than I had expected, and Tulip was at the Coast for a fling with a man from dance class.

I wondered if I should tell the sheriff about Freddie's knowledge of the hidden key. I decided not to. It had been a one-time key use, I trusted Freddie's honesty in such things, and he was under enough suspicion. As I pondered, the sheriff broke in on my thoughts.

"Have you recently had any suspicious visitors or customers, or odd behavior by familiar ones?" said the sheriff, tapping his notepad with his pen.

"Not really," I said, trying to remember.

"Then I need descriptions of everyone who came here the past couple days."

Before answering, I glanced again at Sonny, who now stood on the other side of the counter studying the cash register without touching it. It hadn't even been opened, although it looked as if it had been dusted for prints.

I looked back at the sheriff, whose notepad tapping had gained speed. Patches of sweat shone on his brow and upper lip. But I assumed he didn't want me to close the door or mess with the air conditioning at this point.

"Let's see," I said. "I don't know if I can remember everyone who came in. We get all types."

The sheriff gave me an exasperated look. But his voice stayed even. He enunciated each word, as if I were retarded, or hard of hearing. Or both.

"Those you can remember," he said. "As many as you can remember. Particularly anyone out of the ordinary. Not your typical shopper, or perhaps someone a little too interested in your merchandise or operation."

"A few days ago, I said, "there was this hog farmer looking for pig grooming gear that he easily could have found at The Grange. Yesterday there was a lady from out of town, whom we know from the horse shows. She bought a saddle. Then there was a glitzy barrel racing girl this afternoon. But not one was unusual."

"Give me descriptions, names, anything else you remember."

As I did so, my thoughts lingered on Patsy Ann Carpenter. That expensive saddle and bridle she'd bought. The ones I'd put in the trailer, under a quilt on the gooseneck's queen sized bed? Were they still there? If they, too, had been ripped off, what in holy heck was I going to tell Patsy Ann and her daughter, Honey? They counted on these singular tack pieces to help them stand out at the up-coming horse show.

More important, what would I tell Jane Pardee, the tack consignor, who counted on the money from the sale of the tack? Insurance probably would cover the theft. The question was, how long would that take?

Worst of all, how was I going to pay the landlord, for this month and the next? He had told Tulip he needed the money by Monday, or would throw us out. My main source of income, and a great way to snag my own tack and clothing at wholesale prices, would disappear like fly spray on a windy day.

I dashed to the back door. It stood ajar to the now black night. I took the two back steps in one jump and sprinted across the steamy asphalt to my long silver trailer.

I felt Sonny right behind me, his footfalls lighter than mine despite his superior height and weight.

The forty-foot-long trailer's side door stood open, partially torn off the top hinge. I took the three steps up, covered my fingers with the bottom of my tee shirt, and turned on the light. I stood there a moment, sweating heavily. A jumble of equipment and clothes littered the floor. But it didn't look like much, if anything, was taken.

That, coupled with the store's cash register still having been closed, made me wonder about the burglar's motive.

Then, with a sudden chilling realization, I knew what it was.

Turning right, I stepped from the long, former horse compartment that was now a traveling tack shop, into the living compartment. It contained a sink and stovetop, a tiny bathroom and a table-bench combo that converted to a double bed. Up a few more steps lay a comfortable queen bed.

I...I was afraid to look, but I had to.

The bed's quilt and pillows were tossed aside, revealing only clean white sheets. Empty white sheets.

Sheets pulled into neat corners top and bottom, as I always made them. As I took pride in making them.

Patsy Ann and Honey's saddle and bridle were nowhere in sight. There was only a slight dent and sheet ripple where they had been.

I felt dizzy. A sick feeling filled my stomach. I jerked forward, gulped a few times and tried to back down the steps to the tack compartment. My foot caught a tossed bridle, so I kicked to free it. As I did so, I reached toward the doorframe to steady myself.

Somehow I lost my balance and missed the frame. My bridle-caught foot slipped back down the steps as my hand clawed the air. I threw an elbow into the stairway wall, hoping to break my fall. But I fell anyway, at a right angle, tumbling backward and half through the exterior doorway. A clang rang out as the back of my head slammed the metal stairs. The last thing I saw was a black sky riddled with stars.

18

"Pepper! Pepper! Wake up."

A felt someone shake my shoulders. Sonny's voice came to me as if down a long dark tunnel.

I was angry. I wanted to sleep some more. I felt so tired. Why did I have to wake up so early? I needed my sleep. I had a horse show to go to.

As I drifted up through the layers of consciousness, I opened my eyes to see my Lakota boyfriend's worried face. It was lit on one side by my store's back porch light. Sonny knelt beside me, holding me by one shoulder. He gently shook me again.

Sheriff Henning stood a few yards away near the back door. His expression looked neutral. He held his notepad but wasn't tapping it with the pen any more.

My back felt cool and damp. I looked up to see the trailer standing in front of me, one of my legs still on its pull-down steps. I lay on a small patch of grass and weeds that grew under and around the steps.

The back right side of my head hurt like blazes. I touched the sore spot with my fingers. Good. No blood. But a big lump.

"Wow," I said. "What the – ." I still felt a little dizzy.

"Get a cold towel," Sonny told the sheriff. "From the store bathroom."

The sheriff grunted, turned and disappeared into the store. He came out a moment later with a white towel dripping water.

Sonny squeezed my shoulder, then grabbed the wet towel and held it to the hurt side of my head. With his other hand he reached into his jeans pocket and drew out a leather pouch. He pried it open and produced a two-inch piece of black root.

"Pejuta," he said, touching it to my lips. "Medicine. Chew it."

I did as directed. The taste was horrible. Bitter and sour at the same time. But I chewed and he watched. My mouth flooded with saliva. As I swallowed the remaining shreds of snake root I almost gagged, but kept them down.

Sonny nodded. He turned to the sheriff.

"Get some water," he said, motioning with his head toward the Horsehouse.

The sheriff, meek for once, went back inside, returning with a bottle of water.

Helped by Sonny's steadying hand, I lifted my head. It felt heavy. Drinking took effort. Some of the cool liquid ran down my neck, but most entered my mouth. It tasted like plastic. However it felt pretty soothing. I sucked down half the bottle.

I looked up into Sonny's eyes again. Despite his hold on me, I worked my elbows under my body and tried to rise. Sonny's grip tightened.

"Wait a little," he said. "Let the medicine work."

I blinked and fell back.

"What hap'n'd?" I mumbled.

"You fell and hit your head on the trailer step," he said. "You'll be fine, you're a tough one. But lie now, rest. It's wise not to get up too soon."

I vaguely remembered entering the trailer. Turning on the lights. Seeing a mess on the floor. That was all.

Then it hit me. I sat up, breaking Sonny's grip. My eyes widened as I recalled what had happened before I fainted.

"The saddle and bridle," I gasped. "Gone. Got to get up."

This time Sonny let me go. I staggered upward, pushing off the ground with one hand, finally regaining my feet. A feeling of sadness and loss weighed down my heart. That saddle and bridle had been my ticket back from the brink of bankruptcy.

Sheriff Henning stepped forward.

"You okay?" he said. "I can call the EMTs. Or Mr. Chief can take you to the ER. A concussion's nothing to mess with."

"I'm fine," I said, tempted to add, "Sweet of you to care." Instead I said, "How long was I out? Has the deputy turned up anything?"

I refolded the towel and again pressed it to my head. The pain began to lessen.

"A minute or two," said the sheriff. "No, nothing yet."

Sonny took my hand and squeezed it. It felt good to have him here. Really good.

"Gotta call Tulip," I said, wiping my mouth and looking around for my phone.

"Already did," said the sheriff. "She wanted to come. I said it's under control."

"Not really," I said, wondering why Tulip didn't call me.

The sheriff gave me a stern but questioning look. Then he shrugged.

"Tell me anything more you remember about recent days, he said. "If anyone was mad at you or Tulip."

"Mad at us?" I said.

"The cash register wasn't touched," he said. "Things are thrown around, racks and shelves are busted. Pretty obvious theft may not have been the main motive. Have to look at all possibilities. I'm sure Mr. Chief will agree with me on that." He looked at Sonny.

Sonny looked right back, his face giving away nothing.

"Look, Sheriff," I said. "All due respect, but a saddle and bridle worth at least fifteen grand were stolen here. I was to deliver them to Patsy Ann Carpenter, at the show on Monday. I hid them well. The thief had to have been looking for them."

"Not necessarily," he said. "Ever heard of a crime of opportunity? Could have been the thief was high on drugs or alcohol, trying to get back at you or Tulip for something, when he uncovered the saddle and went for it."

"No," I said. "It's someone who had knowledge of the saddle and bridle. Why else look in the bed compartment. That narrows the suspects to someone we know in the horse community. Our customers or maybe even someone at Brassbottom Barn. That's what you should be looking at."

"Really," said the sheriff. A statement, not a question. He closed his bear button eyes and spat to the side.

***

Sonny and I didn't get back to my house until almost midnight. I heated us some almond milk to soothe our frazzled minds, or at least my frazzled mind, since Sonny managed to stay calm through it all. Then I took a Tylenol. I tried Tulip's number, but it went to voice mail. Then Sonny and I hit the hay.

There was no hanky panky that night. Just endless tossing and turning followed by comfort hugs with Sonny every hour or two. I'd been pulling long days and late nights, and it had begun to tell. There would be late nights at the horse show, plus extremely early mornings. And that was only for the showing portion of the week.

It appeared I also now had two investigations to work on. For the life of me, I couldn't come up with any possible common thread between the horse killing and the break-in. Yet there had to be one. The crimes were close together, and it was widely known I was investigating the first one.

I had gravitated toward Patsy Ann as Vader's killer, for various reasons. I still held to that, and only had to prove it. Only. Small word, big problem.

There were also Richard and Marietta Von Sustern to consider. Or at least Richard, angry as he had been about my investigating Vader's death. Was this an escalation of his warning to me to back off?

Or had someone else known about the tack, and maybe Patsy Ann's purchasing it? Had he or she timed the theft of the saddle and bridle from the Horsehouse right before the show, to put her off her game?

***

The smell of fresh ground and brewed coffee filled my kitchen when I stumbled in, rumpled as an unmade bed, but my face washed and my hair combed, at seven the next morning. Sonny sat finishing biscuits and gravy that he'd found in the freezer, then defrosted and nuked. He was perusing the Sunday circulars.

Even though my mind still whirled, and my head ached like blazes from the night before, it was so comfortable to have him there, to see him like that. We seemed like an old established couple, an illusion that wouldn't last but one worth savoring that moment.

At the stable the horses were neighing. I was late with their feed. I gulped down a giant jolt of java before getting up to do chores. But then Sonny rose, stretched those amazing arms and wandered over. He stroked my hair, gave me an affectionate peck and went out the deck door.

Without exchanging words I knew he was going out to feed the horses for me. Sonny came from a ranch family in South Dakota. He knew about things like hungry livestock. Besides, no one could miss that whinny-fest down at the barn.

Twenty minutes later, with coffee and breakfast in me and the kitchen somewhat decluttered, I stood on the deck to watch Sonny top off the horses' water troughs, then drag the hose to my whiskey tubs full of petunias.

The Boston terriers suddenly jumped out from under the patio table to run barking through the open front door behind me. Their toenails rattled over the front porch. I went through the living room and peeked out the doorway to see the cause of the commotion.

Tulip's pink pickup stood outside the closed gates. The woman herself, all blond skinny tallness of her, walked purposefully toward my front porch as the dogs leaped and barked around her.

"I'd kill for a cup of coffee," she said, worry lines pleating her forehead.

"People have killed for less," I said, taking the hint and bringing her one.

She had plunked herself down in one of two Adirondack chairs facing the lawn, driveway and front field.

"Horrible about the store," she said, shaking her head.

"We were up pretty late dealing with it."

"Well, I swung by, looked through the window, then came here. What a mess. Would've called, but I dropped my phone in the toilet after I took the sheriff's call."

"Say, what?".

"I was out cuttin' a rug last night with this guy from class," she said. "So tell me about the burglary."

"As you said, everything's a mess. Apparently after Patsy Ann's tack, he didn't touch the cash register or take a whole lot else. Picked the door lock or had a key, and pried open the trailer door."

"Any leads?"

"Not yet, but could be connected to my Vader investigation. Ow!"

"What?" Tulip said.

"I was searching the trailer," I said, "but fell and hit my head when I saw Patsy Ann's saddle and bridle were gone."

"No," breathed Tulip. "Sorry you hurt yourself. But who all would know about the tack, then go looking for it?"

"That's the question. I have ideas, but nothing solid."

"Insurance should cover it."

"Assume so. Gotta call them."

"And the landlord," she said.

"Him, too," I said. "Hope he understands."

"Or else he's a heartless jerk."

"He's already that," I said, rolling my eyes.

"Did you call Patsy Ann? Or Jane Pardee?"

"Wanted to talk to you first. What do you think?"

"That we, but mainly you, are in double deep doo-doo," Tulip said.

"Tell me something new," I said. "Like why that sheriff thinks the burglary is the work of drugheads, and a crime of opportunity, or a spite thing, someone pissed at us."

"That jackass. You sure it wasn't Sheriff Jack who hit his head?"

I stared out at the field where two crows screamed at each other from fence rails. Their spat seemed pointless. But then, a lot of things seemed pointless at that moment.

"Earth to Pepper," said Tulip, touching my arm. "Come in, Pepper."

"I'm here," I said. "Just woolgathering. The fall rearranged my brain."

"It'll be all right," Tulip said. "So woolgather this. Patsy Ann never went to sunny California. She kept track of your whereabouts Saturday. Then stole her own saddle."

I sat up, snapping to attention. Lucky I didn't still have hot coffee in my hand, or I'd be contending with scalded digits as well as a bruised head.

"Now whose brain is rearranged?" I said. "Actually, you might have something."

"Okay," Tulip said. "She killed Vader both to spite Dutch for two-timing her and also for selling Vader to Marietta. Plus to get the horse out of her way at the show. Then she bought that saddle, made up the going-to-California story, hung around, and did the burglary to keep the attention off her."

I ran that through my brain a few times. This was complicated but possible.

"Know what?" I said.

"What's that?" she said.

"No possibility is too bizarre to contemplate."

"Correct. So what do you plan to do about it?"

"I'm calling Patsy Ann right now. Shock her, get the truth. Clear this up once and for all. I just don't need this pressure on top of the coming show."

"Okay," Tulip said. "But you won't get the straight story from that be-etch."

"It's a start," I said. "I'll get some kind of story."

"Know what I think you should do?" Tulip said.

I thought a moment as I drained my coffee mug. The sharp staccato sounds of another bird fight, sparrows this time, broke through my thoughts. I reflected that my thinking lately was like that fight. Noisy, distracting, desperate.

"Let's hear it," I said.

"Call Marietta," said Tulip. "Say that Patsy Ann claimed she was meeting Marietta in Reno this weekend, that you can't reach Patsy Ann, but need to tell her something. Say it's an emergency. Which it is."

"The indirect approach," I said. "Marietta might say where Patsy Ann was or is, as she likely knows nothing about the stolen saddle. I may actually get a straight story."

"You might," said Tulip. "That's what I'm saying."

"Marietta has no reason to know why I am calling or asking about her friend. Then I can call Patsy Ann and see whether their stories and reactions match up."

Tulip gulped down the last of her coffee, licked her lips and tilted her head.

"So what are you waiting for, a written invitation. Call already."

19

I immediately checked my recent calls list on the cell phone, showed my crossed fingers to Tulip and hit Marietta Von Sustern's number.

It rang three times.

A stern male voice said, "Richard."

Dang! Somehow I'd punched in the wrong number. Maybe Marietta's husband's number. I braced for a tongue lashing.

"Oh! Mr. Von Sustern," I said, putting some purr in my voice. "I am so sorry to bother you. I was trying to reach Marietta, um, about the show. Patsy Ann told me you two are in Reno with her and her husband for R&R before coming to the show?"

A beat of silence. Then I heard a woman's voice faintly calling in the background. A "Who is it?" A muffled male voice saying, "That Pepper person," as if Von Sustern put the phone to his chest while talking to his wife.

"I distinctly told you not to call again," he said to me. "You seem to have a problem with that. Don't make it a big problem."

What was the deal with this dude? Or was he always an iron fist in a velvet glove?

"You asked me not to call you," I said, fumbling for the right tone and words. "I respect that, Mr. Von Sustern. I just need a quick word with your wife."

"Then make it quick. She's very tired."

I waited. Looked over at Tulip, and shrugged.

"Is this Pepper?" said Marietta's breathless voice. "Why are you calling? Have you turned up anything new regarding Vader?"

Finally. A voice of civility and reason, if it did sound a bit anxious. She'd been cordially cooperative on the phone Friday. I hoped she saw me as a person concerned with her best interests, despite my prying ways.

Again I conjured up her image, though I had encountered her up close at a slight distance only the one time she tried out Vader. A tiny, stocky brunette with a steely spine, exotic face and long but strong looking neck. No wonder she was a top equestrian. The neck made her look tall in the saddle, and her square back gave her unshakable stability atop a horse's rocking, rolling gaits.

"No," I said, fibbing only a bit. "However I do have a problem, Marietta."

"Oh, no," she said, pausing. "Not another horse, I hope?"

"No, nothing as bad as that," I said. "But I need to talk with Patsy Ann. Like right now. It's kind of an emergency. She said she and her husband were meeting up with you and Richard for a Reno weekend before the show. Will you have her call me?"

"Can't you call her yourself?" she said.

I thought fast, deciding against the "lost number" excuse I'd used when I called Mason De Young to learn if Patsy Ann really had been in Southern Oregon for a family reunion. If Patsy Ann got wind that I'd used it again, she might put her guard up.

"I tried," I said. "But I kept getting the 'out of service' message."

"Oh," said Marietta. "I can ask her to call. I see your number on my phone."

"When will you see her?" I said.

"We planned to have lunch together, then hit the tables," she said.

"Great," I said. "Good luck, then, and thank you for your help."

"What is the emergency?" said Marietta. "I hope it isn't about that fabulous new saddle and bridle she bought. Honey was so excited about it."

That stopped me. Why would Marietta think of the saddle? But then, I reasoned, Patsy Ann as a friend would have told her of the purchase. Besides, it was probably the only connection between Patsy Ann and me that Marietta could come up with.

"Just have her call me," I said. "See you at the show."

"Are you driving down with your trailer?" said Marietta.

"We're leaving in a few hours," I said.

"Smart," she said. "Air will be cooler then." She clicked off.

I turned to Tulip just as Sonny came out onto the porch and bent down to give Tulip a bear hug.

"The great and mighty Sonny Chief," Tulip said. "All hail the chief."

"And the bloomin' Tulip," he grinned, leaning back against the porch rail.

I smiled, and tapped my fingers on my chair. Time was a-wasting.

"I'm calling Patsy Ann directly," I said. "Marietta won't have had time to tip her off, or mention our emergency, and I might get an interesting reaction."

"No," Tulip said. "Don't call Patsy Ann. Let it play out."

"It's hard to be patient. I need answers so I can concentrate at the show. I'm like the cartoon lady

Maxine, in that card where the cover reads, 'God grant me patience'."

"Where inside the card she says, 'And hurry it up'. I do love me some Maxine."

"Hey, Tule, let's get a move on. We need to clean up the store. Maybe we'll turn up a clue."

***

Sonny followed us in his black truck. He was going to spend a few hours helping us clean the store and repair the damaged trailer door before heading out for his own investigating. He would talk with hay and shavings suppliers, neighbors and farriers, to see if animosities were afoot, and learn people's whereabouts the night of Vader's death.

I felt deep gratitude for his help. These were things I would have done myself, had I not been knee-deep in show preparations and my own investigations. I felt confident that he would be as stealthy and thorough as I, perhaps more so.

Sonny also would shake down his Cousin Boo again, this time for any news or clues about the store break-in. Hopefully he would not rattle any critical cages.

He parked his truck out front of the Horsehouse. Tulip parked her truck, in which I'd hitched a ride so we could gab, behind the store. We gathered empty boxes from the storage room and began cleaning up the trailer. I held a pen and clipboard, taking inventory, while she sorted things into boxes. Sonny worked in the main store.

About halfway through I called my insurance agent, got a recording, gave a brief report of the burglary, and said I'd fax my inventory report later. It was possible other things were missing, although we hadn't discovered any as yet.

Tulip and I talked little, just giving bar codes on merchandise as it got folded into boxes and trailer shelves. It was hot, mind-numbing work. We guzzled bottled water, lay briefly on shaded grass, then returned to our labors.

At one o'clock Sonny left to do his own digging. He had made shelves usable again, and jerry-rigged the trailer door so it would close and lock.

Tulip and I found half a brick of cream cheese in the fridge. We smeared it on old plain donut holes, and called it lunch.

I kept looking at my cell phone to see if Patsy Ann had called. Maybe I'd missed the ring, or the phone had malfunctioned. I began to worry. I sat on the store's back step and checked that I had full service. Four bars. Good enough.

"I can't understand why she hasn't called," I told Tulip, who sat next to me.

"Maybe Marietta hasn't had a chance to see her or call her," Tulip said.

"Or maybe Patsy Ann just doesn't want to talk to me," I said. "Maybe she is in fact guilty of the store break-in, and is getting her story together."

"And maybe my theory about Patsy Ann is horse pucky," Tulip said.

"I beg your pardon?" I said, blinking in disbelief. Tulip rarely, no never, admitted error. If she did misstep, she dismissed it with her favorite phrase.

"It'll be all right," she said then, not disappointing me.

"Hope that's true," I said. "I'd better get home, fax my reports and do a final pack. Gotta run the dually through the carwash, and tank up. We're still set to leave at six, right? From the store?"

"I'll be here," said Tulip. "Got some packing of my own to do."

"Dutch and Donna planned to leave at six, or maybe five, to arrive at the show grounds before midnight."

***

I ran the red truck through the carwash ten miles down the road, tanked up with diesel, and drove home to park in the shade with the truck bed facing the garage.

The day had developed into another screaming hot one. I had to stay hydrated, so I went up to the house and chugged a full pitcher of ice water.

My cell phone sounded as I leaned over the sink to let the last streams of cold H_2O slide down my gullet. I wiped my mouth with my arm and dashed to pick up the phone from the bathroom counter, where I'd set my purse.

I saw Marietta's number on the viewing pane. I expected it to be Patsy Ann.

"Marietta?" I said. "Did you see Patsy Ann?"

"Not yet," said Marietta. "We were to lunch at one o'clock at their new casino and townhome development? She's almost an hour late, and I can't reach her."

Marietta's voice had a slight slur. Had she been drinking?

"Well, it's one-fifty now," I said. "Did you try her husband?"

"He's here with Richard and me," Marietta said. "He hasn't heard from her, either. She was supposed to meet him here yesterday."

"I see." I held my breath, awaiting further explanation. Was Patsy Ann not there in Reno at all, then? If not, where was she and what had she been doing? Tulip's wild idea that she had stolen her own saddle didn't seem so wild after all.

"Apparently they dined with the governor Friday in Sacramento," said Marietta. "But she had some last-minute business to attend to, and stayed on while Carson came here to see the opening of his development. I drove in from Tahoe."

"But you were to meet Patsy Ann for lunch today," I said.

"Yes, I told you that," she said, annoyance hardening her voice. "She better make it soon. Richard wants me to try to recoup some losses here before heading to the show."

I thought a moment. Maybe I could gather a bit more information while I had the unsuspecting Marietta on the line. It was out of left field, but I had to try.

"What do you know, Marietta, about Patsy Ann's trying to buy Vader at one time, and Dutch not selling to her?"

There was a pause. Then a fit of rough coughing.

"Excuse me," Marietta said. "I really should quit smoking. What was it you said?"

"Patsy Ann had tried to buy Vader once, but Dutch sold him to you?"

"Oh," she said. "Yes. My, you do ask a lot of questions. I guess he thought I could do more with the horse. Who can understand what's in a trainer's mind at any given time? There's so much jealousy and pettiness in this crazy horse show world."

"You're right about that," I said.

Boy, was she right. Trainers and owners often did the most unexpected things, such as swapping clients and selling horses for no apparent reason. Yet rumored reasons swirled like tornadoes among the horsey set. Most rumors turned out to be unfounded. But some had at least a grain of truth caught up in them.

My questioning of Marietta hadn't opened up anything except defensiveness, and deepened the mystery of Patsy Ann's whereabouts.

"So," I said, "you and Richard, along with Carson, have been in Reno how long?"

"Since Friday night. My birthday. I was in Tahoe, read that the Carpenters would be in Reno for their condo opening, and called Patsy Ann. We hatched a plan to party and win some money this weekend before the show, and I popped over to Reno."

"I thought your husband was in Europe," I said.

"Oh," she said. "He had clients cancel there, so he flew in yesterday for other business and to ready our motor home for me to drive to the show."

"Well, let me know when you see Patsy Ann. As I say, it's important. You were right. It is about her saddle. My store was broken into, and her tack was stolen."

"No-o-o!" Marietta said, a little too loudly. "No, really? How horrible. For you, and for Honey. She was counting on having that for the show."

"I know," I said.

"But of course you do."

We signed off. With a hesitant and fearful heart, I made my calls. The insurance folks were positive that my policy was in order. Jane Pardee was shaken that she wouldn't get her saddle money right away, but she understood. What a trooper.

Calls done and a peanut butter sandwich inhaled, I felt my cheeks begin to heat up as I shifted my attention to packing gear and clothes for the show. I desperately wanted to wonder, to figure out, where in heck Patsy Ann was, and what she'd been up to. I craved to know. I wasn't buying the "other business to attend to in Sacramento" explainer.

But I had to prioritize. I had my own work to do for the trip and the show. I had to set one foot ahead of the other.

Investigating Vader's death, and now saddled with the Horsehouse break-in and theft, I was bled of energy and focus. But the show had to be in my sights for the moment. I couldn't afford to mess up.

This show was such a big deal. A do or die deal that I'd been working toward all year. I had a lot of money, a lot of sweat and tears, riding on the outcome of Choc's and my performance in several classes.

A lot riding on it. Good one. At least I still had my sense of humor. But that was soon to change.

20

I felt happy to focus on something besides murder and mayhem. I gathered up my zippered black binder, labeled "Horse Papers" in my office file cabinet, and lay it open to the "Horse Show" section on my dining table.

The first pages noted all the items I needed to pack for a horse show. One page for my things, one page for the horse's, as well as sequential "To Do's" once I was at the show. Yes, I am a bit obsessive-compulsive. I have no problem with that. I enjoy believing it's what makes me good at showing … and investigating.

I clunked ice cubes into a mug of Ginger Ale and stared at the page titled, "Horse Show Stuff To Take."

Silver halter and lead
Silver bridles (2)
Show saddle
Show pads (3 – black, red, Navajo)

The list was long, with every contingency covered. Over the years I'd forgotten at least one item per show, and repeatedly retyped my list. Now it was virtually mistake proof. One less thing to stress over during a show week.

I began to systematically pack things in the crew cab of my dually. On one of my endless trips from house to truck, with the Bostons dogging every step, I dropped my longe line. That was one of a horsewoman's important tools.

"Don't put butt in saddle without it," as Donna Grandeen advised. Five years ago her ride on an unlonged, too-fit horse had landed her in the ER. Five healed ribs and a crinked collarbone later, she stood less erect but never complained. Instead, Donna cowgirled up each day with a sincere smile and professional demeanor.

I fretted over which outfits to take to California. For English, I chose the tailored black hunt coat and khaki breeches, plus a white dickey printed with my initials on a priestlike collar. Also the tall black boots and black velvet hunt cap.

Dressing for Western classes was not as easy. More bling for human and horse was allowed in events inspired by, but barely resembling, moves of working cowboys and pleasure riders. Such as the Scotch-smooth jog of the American Quarter Horse.

"Here you come again," sang Dolly as I folded my crystal-studded red-and-white Western show jacket. This jacket cost me several thousand dollars from my retirement account. These were pauper's rags compared to togs worn by Patsy Ann, Marietta and their ilk. But I did the best with what I had. Just being in the game stoked my fire.

"Hi, Serrano," I said into the phone. I'd forgotten all about my son. It was three o'clock. He should be here soon. In fact his leaving Seattle at nine a.m. as usual, then driving like a bat out of hell as usual, should have put him here by three.

"Hey," he said. "Big semi accident south of Portland. Two hours to get around. But don't worry. I'll make up the lost time. Be there in a flash."

"Not too much of a flash," I warned. He'd already hung up.

I hurried into the guest room to put fresh sheets on the bed and fresh towels on the chest of drawers. As a last love token for Serrano's staying at my ranchita and looking in on his grandparents, while I was away, I mounded a bowl with chocolate chip cookies and put it on the nightstand.

For all his flaws, Serrano was turning out to be a pretty good kid, or adult, at least in the thoughtfulness department. Eventually, the second time around the altar, he might make some gal a fairly decent husband.

I went back to lugging tack and checking it off my horse-show checklist. With only a few items to go, I went into the master bath, stripped to the waist and wiped my face with a wet washcloth. It was way too hot even in the house. I really should have done my packing in the morning. But of course I had more pressing business. Like a cleanup after a burglary.

I turned the water full on and began swabbing my upper half before replacing my sweat-soaked tee for a dry one. When I turned off the taps, I heard the front door open and close. Right when the grandfather clock chimed five times.

Patting myself dry, I wondered if Serrano could be here already. I doubted it. But why else weren't the dogs barking?

"Serrano?" I called through the half closed bathroom door. "That you?"

The floorboards creaked in my bedroom. The dogs began barking on the front porch. Clearly the front door had been closed to keep them out. Were they barking for this intruder? Who was it, anyway? Sonny or Serrano would have spoken by now.

Then Sonny's dark hand and forearm sliced through the opening, pushing the door toward me to reveal the man himself. The lights clicked off and the room went semi-dark.

Next thing I knew I was pulled into Sonny's crushing embrace. He bent me back over the counter as he pressed his lips onto mine. I was intoxicated by his warm, manly scent. But distracted as the arched sink faucet dug into my spine and the mirror met the painful lump on the back of my head.

"Ow!" I squeaked between pulsing, searching kisses. I pushed back as hard as I could. "You're – hurting – me."

Sonny finally eased his grip. I caught my breath and rose to a standing position.

"Sorry," he said. He held my head between his hands. Then he bent until his face nearly touched mine. His breath smelled sweet as a baby's. His lips parted in what I imagined was that wide, pearl-white smile I so loved. But it was too dark to see.

"Serrano will be here any minute," I said. "We can't –"

Sonny pressed one hand over my mouth, raised the other to catch my forearm, and led me into the bedroom. Without a word he fell backward onto the bed and pulled me down with him My breasts smashed against his chest and my nipples stood up. My feet dangled helplessly between his calves over the edge of the neatly made bed.

Thoughts came to me as fast and furious as Sonny's kisses. We shouldn't. I'm too tired. There's too much to think about and to do. Serrano's coming.

But now Sonny's lips brushed down my neck. They skipped along my collarbone, darted across my chest, took in every inch of skin. Dancing from freckle to freckle, as he said. He couldn't see my sun dots in the bedroom's dimness, but he knew them by heart.

As his hands flicked across my back and buttocks I sighed, deeply, several times. I caressed his high cheekbones and the satin skin over his hard biceps. My tongue found the pulsing hollow at the base of his throat.

I craved this man so much. Too much.

No, not too much. Never too much.

My thoughts dissolved in a flush of longing. Again all there was to life was Sonny and me, our souls and our bodies hopelessly entangled.

His loving felt at once trapping and freeing. I floated over him like a goddess with wings. Watched myself from above, as if I were dying. Waves of passion filled my belly. Delight filled every crevice and swelling.

I hung breathless in the air. My eyes stared, as if lifeless. Then I folded in a heap onto his sweaty chest. His arms held me tight. His heart beat as if it would burst.

Neither of us spoke for several long moments. Then I became aware of his knees bending and his toes, the nails a little long, rubbing against my ankles and calves.

I raised up and looked into his face, though in the dim bedroom I could see little but the black pools where his eyes would be.

He closed his lids and shook his head slowly. Then he looked at me. I felt rather than saw it.

"You're the best," he said.

"Because you are," I said.

"No one comes close," he said.

"No one else would dare," I said.

We lay there a few more minutes. Maybe I could make this moment last forever.

Sonny finally rolled me to the side and climbed off the bed. I sat up and followed him into the shower. We let the warm spray wash us clean and pure, soaping each other and splashing like playing children. I still felt warm and tingly in all the right places.

Without talking we toweled each other off, and then dressed, He went out to the sofa while I got us some cold drinks from the fridge.

"At least I'm almost done packing," I said.

"Well," he said, "I've got a little going-away present for you."

"I thought I already had it," I said, giving him an air kiss and a naughty look.

"Then you'll get two presents," he said.

"So where are you hiding it?" I said.

"Here," he said, pointing at his head.

"Don't make me wait," I pouted, distracted by the sound of tires on gravel out front. I looked at the door. "Sounds like Serrano's here. What's my other present?"

"Talked to a lot of people today," Sonny said.

"Yes," I said. "And?"

"You know, Boo, the suppliers, the horseshoer," he said.

"Hurry up," I said. "You're killing me."

"I also talked with neighbors around Brassbottom," he said. "That little yellow house behind the fence around the back pasture?"

"The broodmare pasture," I said, nodding.

"Boo canvassed that house, among others in the area, yesterday after he and I had coffee at Katie's. She told him that when she went on her porch to water her baskets the night Vader was killed, she saw a Jeep parked where the road ends by her house. Didn't think much of it then, as teenagers park there often to drink and neck."

"And?" I said.

"She went indoors for a bullhorn to shoo them away."

"And, and?"

"And when she came back, the Jeep was gone."

"So?"

"That was all," Sonny said. "Boo took notes and left."

"Okay."

"So today," said Sonny, "she told me she was out back filling her wading pool for the grandkids, when she found this piece of black fabric stuck on the barbed wire fence facing the Grandeens' pasture. Wires bent, like someone opened them to go through."

"Whoa!" I said.

I examined the piece, roughly an inch square. I took it and turned it about in my fingers. It was thin, synthetic, probably water resistant. There was something vaguely familiar about it, but I drew a blank.

"Did she call the sheriff to report it?" I said.

"No," Sonny said. "She seemed spaced out. Her grandkids were still there, and bouncing off the walls, so she'd forgot all about it until I stopped by today."

I looked at the fabric again. It wasn't landscape fabric, but like landscape fabric without the holes. And shinier.

Then it came to me. I felt a jolt of recognition. No wonder it seemed familiar. It looked and felt exactly like a piece of a black protective cape from the Manes 'N Tales. One of the stylish new capes I'd worn at Freddie's salon the day before yesterday.

21

"Oh, my God," I said, holding up the piece of black fabric. "I can't believe this. Poor Freddie!"

Sonny tilted his head.

"I don't get it."

"Freddie has protective capes made of fabric like this all over his salon," I said. My mind swirled with possibilities, none of which looked good for my Brassbottom buddy. I had to keep hold of this clue until I figured out its meaning.

At that moment the dogs raised a ruckus as Serrano and his duffle bag stumbled through the front door. He was having a tough time making his way through the sea of Bostons. Well, the pair of Bostons, who nevertheless had a way of rolling. cresting and retreating like the sea.

"Serrano!" I said. "You made it!"

"Said I would," he said, grinning. We hugged in the middle of the living room.

"Hey Sonny," Serrano said over my shoulder as I turned around. "Whatup?"

"Hey," said Sonny with a cordial nod. "How you doing?"

"Great, except for one long-ass drive," Serrano said.

His dark red hair fell over one hazel eye and his skin glowed beneath the freckles. Taller than me by several heads, but skinny as a beanpole in his hot orange tank and low slung cutoffs, he made a beeline for the kitchen. His flip flops slapped the linoleum as he banked around the corner toward the fridge.

"What's to eat?" he shouted. "I'm half starved."

That was Serrano. Like mother, like son. Chili was like that, as well. Metabolism of a hummingbird, or a perennially active teen. We had to eat our weight in calories something like all day long, or pay the price in jitters and poor concentration.

"Your grandmother's peach pie is in the fridge," I called. "And fruit juice, milk, leftover hamburger. Buns in the breadbox, if you want a sandwich. Stocked up for you."

I still held the piece of black fabric in my fingers. I looked at it while Serrano rummaged around. Finally I stuffed the fabric into my jeans pocket.

"So," said Sonny. "You think your buddy, Freddie, could be the horse killer?"

"Don't want to think it," I said. "At least not yet. It's too much to take in. Gotta let it roll around in my head awhile. Something to occupy me on the six-hour drive."

I looked at my watch. Dang! Six o'clock. Had to pack my suitcase and shoehorn it into the dually's crew cab, kiss Sonny goodbye and go meet Tulip at the Horsehouse. She was running late, she told me in a quick phone call. We agreed to meet in an hour.

I sat with Serrano at the table as he wolfed down milk, a nuked hamburger, and the rest of the peach pie. He filled me in on his latest paintings, his outings to Safeco Field to see the luckless Seattle Mariners, and his sad attempts to find a real job.

"Everything sucks, except my paintings," he said. "I've started a baseball series, though. They're pretty decent. I have an appointment to show them to the Mariners PR person after I get home. If she gives them a thumbs up, I show them to the general manager and score a one-man show in the Diamond Club. Could be my big break."

"That sounds wonderful, Serrano," I said.

"I put them online," he said. "Check my Web site, hotserranoart dot com, when you get a chance. "Chili designed it. I'm pretty good at design, but she's crazy good."

"No doubt," I said, patting his arm. "We do have a talented family."

"Good looking, too," he said with a grin. "So what times do I go work at the Horsehouse?" He picked burger tidbits off his plate and tucked them into his mouth.

"Ten to five," I said. "Give or take. Just make sure the 'Open' or 'Closed' signs are up at the right times, and the alarm is on. Speaking of, we had a burglary last night."

"Wha-at?" he said. "Bummer. You weren't there, I hope." He looked anxious.

I filled him in on the burglary, and on our subsequent report and cleanup.

"Dang!" he said. "Should I be taking any extra precautions? Like a gun?"

"No," I said, "just call the law, and me, if there's suspicious activity. Patrols will swing by regularly, and the thieves only seemed to have wanted that saddle and bridle Patsy Ann bought. Still trying to sort it all out."

That satisfied Serrano for the time being.

"Oh," I said," Grandma and Grandpa expect you for dinner at least tomorrow, if not all week. Make sure they don't leave stoves on and water running. Their forgetfulness really worries me."

"Maybe time they moved to a nice retirement home?"

"Not yet, but soon. Tho' I doubt they'd agree. Anyway you know the drill here at the ranchita. I'll text you when I get to the show grounds. It'll be past midnight."

I left him and Sonny chatting at the table, and went into the bedroom to finish my packing. I had done it so often, I finished in record time. Heading for the door with my clothes and toiletries, I paused and returned to my nightstand. I opened the drawer, pushed aside earplugs and tissues, and stared down at the stubby but powerful .38 Smith & Wesson revolver with the two-and-a-half-inch barrel. Butt ugly but reliably deadly.

That was what I put in my saddlebag when I went out trail riding. It was what I now tucked into my purse, with difficulty, as the purse was choc-a-block with a wallet, glasses, cosmetics and cell phone. Plus a pouch with the earring segment and fabric patch. I was taking my investigations on the road, and had to be ready for anything.

Serrano went down to the barn to give the horses carrots.

Sonny carried my stuff to the truck, where I laid them atop my show clothes, just beneath the headliner. He tucked the snack bag on the floor next to the driver's seat.

"You watch out, now." Sonny said, holding my face between his hands. "I'll keep digging here a day or so, and bring you up to date. Then be on my way."

His eyes searched mine. The concern in them was clear. His mouth hung a little open, as if he wanted to say more. But no words came. He kissed me instead. A long, deep, surprisingly tender kiss.

When we pulled apart, I licked my lips. They tasted good. I wanted to say more. Such as if he would be here when I returned, or when I might see him again.

But I stopped myself. We'd had such talks when we began dating, soon after we'd met at a reservation crime scene near Seattle. Such talks always ended badly. Sonny professed his need for the proverbial "space," man-speak for "don't pressure me." Usually after we were together a night or a week, he would then just vanish.

Sonny claimed this was typical of a true Indian man. On the hunt for buffalo or for women, yet eventually returning to the place where his heart truly belonged. I now enjoyed a rich life, independent of him, knowing he'd be back.

Besides. When he was around he took me out like a regular girlfriend, and did special things for me. Like now, with his sleuthing.

We were an odd couple, infrequent but steadfast partners. I used to worry my love for him would prevent my loving another. But I had enjoyed several romances in the years I'd known him. I loved Sonny and the others in wholly different ways, and accepted what each offered without making demands.

As it turned out, I liked my space, too. More than I cared to admit. Sonny and I didn't have a needy or draining relationship. We had something better, much better. It worked famously.

Now as the space between us vibrated with energy, I stood on tiptoes, grabbed Sonny's face with my hands and kissed him back. It was a hard, bruising, penetrating kiss. It made my head spin and my knees buckle.

When Sonny pulled back, he had a surprised look in his eyes.

"Oh, Lady," he said. "What you do." He whistled.

"No," I said, shaking my head. "What you do."

***

Tulip and I were three hours into the drive. It was going well despite the evening heat. We'd met, hitched up the trailer, loaded in her stuff, and left the Horsehouse without further ado.

It was pitch dark outside. The red dually pulling the long trailer had made it over the forty-three-hundred-foot Siskiyou Summit without incident. I feathered the brakes a little on the long way down into California. I was glad I was obsessive compulsive when it came to vehicle maintenance. Although the truck was pushing ten years young, she rarely presented a problem.

We had navigated the narrow, twisting road down along Shasta Lake as easily, although I drove well below the truck speed limit of fifty-five just to be sure. Drivers unfamiliar with pulling a trailer were as sure to cut you off, or brake without warning before you, as night follows day. So I always left lots of room.

As I drove I kept one eye on the road ahead for erratic traffic, and the other eye on the shoulder for errant deer. All I needed was to hit wildlife, to bring to a "lucky" three my recent string of woes.

Lost in such thought, I saw a movement from the edge of my left eye. I glanced over to see a yearling buck leap the center barrier on his way to the truck bed where the gooseneck hitch sat. I heard a loud "bang!" Heart pounding madly, I checked the side mirror. The dead buck spun sideways to the center barrier.

Bile rose in my throat. I began to shake. I slowed down, rounded a curve, found a wide spot and pulled the truck and trailer over.

"Damn it!" I said, pounding the steering wheel. "I was just thinking about something like that, and then it happened."

"Bet he didn't feel a thing," Tulip said. "It'll be all right."

"Just hope my rig's all right," I said.

Turning on the four-way flashers, I waited until a few vehicles had sped by, then walked back to inspect the damage. Lucky for me, the yearling on its way to deer heaven had hit the heavy-duty iron hitch neck, left merely traces of fur and blood, and slid back dead across the highway.

I finished the drive in mourning for all the wildlife humans crushed on their way to somewhere. But I finally figured this was part of natural selection, and thinning. Deer dumb enough to forage near and run across roads would be less likely to reproduce. And their loss would leave more forage for the living deer, which always seemed on the verge of starvation anyway, what with hunting restrictions on the cougar and wolf, predators that kept deer populations under control.

We humans in heavy vehicles on highways were the new wolf and cougar.

"Penny for y'all's thoughts," said Tulip, an open box of Wheat Thins and a tall can of Squeeze Cheese on her lap. She slouched on the driver's side of the bench seat, fanning herself and fiddling with the air conditioning. It was either too hot or too cool.

"I am, after all, a delicate Southern Belle," she'd said, several times, when I shot her an annoyed glance.

Oh well, I figured. You can't pick your best friends any more than you can pick family. They pick you, or just kind of happen.

"You're about as delicate as a steel magnolia," I said.

She snorted, and popped a couple more cheese-topped Wheat Thins.

"We all going to have that meal stop pretty soon?" she said.

"I see you're having some whine with that cheese," I said. "Yeah. Red Bluff, as usual. Twenty minutes. Thirty, tops."

"I still can't see Freddie killing Vader," Tulip said, out of the navy-blue dark, and continuing a talk we'd had earlier after I told her about Sonny's finding the bit of black fabric on the Brassbottom neighbor's fence. "Doesn't have it in him. Besides if he was riding in the arena that night, he simply could have gone into Vader's stall and done it quickly, with no one the wiser. Wouldn't have to go over the fence, wear a cape."

"I agree," I said. "But we have to consider every possibility, even our friends. So. Say it was him, just for the moment. Say he was riding in the arena, his usual practice that everyone knows about, and slipped out to leave the cape bit on the fence, as if someone else came in disguised as him. In case anyone saw something."

"But," said Tulip, "what about the Jeep parked at the neighbor's end of the road?"

"Could've been teenagers," I said. "Neighbor said they park there a lot. Possibly a lucky coincidence the killer took advantage of."

Tulip reached for more Wheat Thins and cheese. The box rustled, the cheese can squirted, making a rude sound. She munched thoughtfully for a few moments.

"Okay," she finally said. "That's an interesting theory. But I still think it was a killer who wanted to resemble Freddie, if anyone saw. And he or she came in over the fence wearing the cape, which probably smelled like Freddie, which explains why it didn't alarm the barn dog."

"Sounds plausible," I said, tapping my thumbs on the steering wheel. "I'm still not convinced, though. Don't forget the burglary at the Horsehouse. Whoever killed Vader might've tried to make it look as if someone else was involved in both crimes. Marietta's been popping into my mind lately."

"Marietta?" said Tulip. "Why would she kill her own horse? Besides. She was in Tahoe and Reno."

"So it appeared," I said. "Now I am not so sure. As to why she might kill her own horse, there are several possibilities, including for the insurance money."

"Hmmm," said Tulip. "Anything is possible, I reckon." She closed the cracker box and put it away with the cheese can in a sack at her feet.

My eyes began to burn with all that anxious staring into the dark punctuated by bright lights from oncoming vehicles. The road was rough, as usual, along these populated areas where there always seemed to be construction.

I also had to pee. Desperately. Yet road signs said I had to wait awhile longer. I was glad to have tucked some cranberry extract pills into my bag to ward off urinary infections. Which Tulip and I always attributed to hot sex and too-tight jeans.

When we arrived at Red Bluff's Pussycat Café and Lounge, we could see through brightly lit café windows that Dutch and Donna, as well as a few Brassbottom buddies, were having dinner. The Grandeens and the others who had caravanned in their own vehicles, probably left the Rogue Valley at least an hour before us.

I thought I glimpsed another pair of show competitors inside, as well, though these women hailed from the Portland area. The Pussycat was a well known stop for horse show travelers.

The Grandeen's white rig, a six-horse trailer with living quarters up front, stood near poplars bordering the parking lot. The drop-down feed windows on the trailer lay open against the left side to let the horses stick out their heads. Choc's head hung out the first window. Two smaller trailers owned by our buddies flanked the bigger one.

Across the parking lot lurked a few minivans, a couple of compacts, and three highly polished sports cars. A closer look revealed one as a red low-slung Italian job. Possibly a Lamborghini. I'd never met one in person before, so I wasn't sure. But it reminded me of Richard Von Sustern's shady car deal Chili found on the Internet.

"Those cars could belong to Mafia," I said. "Some like their rides fast and flashy."

"Maybe like their women?" Tulip said.

Donna spotted us as we entered the Pussycat. She waved a tan, manicured hand to motion us over.

The foyer, refreshingly cool and daylight bright, buzzed with muted chatter from café patrons. It smelled of fresh-brewed restaurant coffee. And it looked like a veritable Toys-R-Us for tourists, with postcard kiosks, shelves of souvenir mugs and caps, and a near-empty pie tower housing half a marionberry pie with a vaulted criss-cross crust.

It seemed that pies and pie towers followed me wherever I went. It was the Fates' idea of a cosmic joke. They seemed bent on sabotaging my ongoing efforts to stay reasonably buff.

Tulip and I made our way to the Brassbottom Barn table. Around it lingered a half-dozen barn buddies with empty coffee mugs and nearly empty plates. We greeted Dutch and Donna, Barbara, Lana, Suzy and Jill. Our Victoria, as well as Freddie and Little Stewie with his mom, were all supposed to drive down in the early morning.

Tulip and I dragged two chairs from another table over to Brassbottom table's open end. A waitress gave us menus and laid two more place settings. I drank a few slugs of ice water, and nibbled a breadstick.

As I sat there, I felt strange eyes boring into my back. The feeling was so strong that I looked back over my shoulder into the half-filled dining room. I nearly fainted when I saw who was returning my gaze.

22

Looking back at me across the tables, and set atop a compact male body in a pearl-snap shirt, was a familiar face, one that I'd sometimes dreamed about. He had unblinking black eyes and long eyebrows under a thinning cap of dark hair. Two companions sat with him, but only that one man came into focus.

I gave him a small smile back before I hunkered down on my elbows at the end of the Brassbottom table. The other women there, and Dutch, chatted up Tulip and me as they finished their meals. I responded with suitable replies as my cheeks heated up. I leaned into Tulip.

"Don't look now," I rasped. "But Tommy Lee Jones is sitting back there."

Of course Tulip immediately turned to look.

"I said not to look!" I hissed.

She shrugged as she turned back to me.

"Appears to be him," Tulip said, raising her eyebrows and scanning her menu.

"I have every movie he ever made," I whispered. "Except 'Emperor'. Did you know he graduated from Harvard? Has polo ponies, rides, and has a ranch in Texas?"

"And a wife," Tulip said. "His third, I do believe. Who's counting? But it's not Tommy Lee Jones. It's a ringer. Y'all always think people look like movie stars. You once said I was a blond Susan Sarandon."

"You are," I said. "And I see he has bodyguards. But what could he possibly be doing in this out of the way place?"

"Not a clue," Tulip said.

"Maybe scouting a location," I continued. "And maybe driving one of the fancy cars out front. He gets ten million a film. He's a quarter Cherokee. Rich, educated, dry sense of humor and loves horses. My dream come true."

"Ain't him," Tulip said, shaking her head. "But don't let me stop y'all from enjoying the ride."

A random idea floated into my mind. Or maybe not so random.

"Oh, no," I said. "It can't be."

"Can't be what?" she said.

"The Lamborghini," I said. "In the parking lot. Richard von Sustern was involved with a luxury car delivery scheme involving just such a car. Red, too. What if it's him? He didn't come with Marietta to try out Vader, so I have no idea what he looks like."

Tulip sighed, and stared off into the space above her menu. Closing the folder, she turned with dramatic slowness to favor me with her most indulgent look.

"Girl," she said. "I will be having the spinach-pecan salad, and you all are having delusions. Listen. You're beat. Running on fumes. Not right in the head. Snap out of it."

"It was just a thought," I said, feeling pouty at her put-down. "But really, that's quite a coincidence. The Von Susterns knew we were driving down tonight. And this place is always a popular stop for horse show people headed south to California."

"He's not Marietta's husband," Tulip said. "Dude's in Reno with her, remember?"

"Maybe yes, maybe no," I said. "We don't really know where he and Marietta were when we talked on the phone. They might have made a side trip for who knows what reason, possibly not good."

Tulip grunted, clearly in no mood for further discussion.

Donna and the other Brassbottom buddies were looking at us now.

"Pepper," Donna said, leaning in. "What gives? You resemble a starstruck schoolgirl." Her eyes darted behind me to the Tommy Lee lookalike.

I shrugged and pretended to be seriously studying the menu.

"She thinks Tommy Lee Jones has the hots for her," Dutch said, giving me a grin and wink from beneath his cowboy hat.

"Something like that," I said. "Whoever he is, the dude is seriously cute." I shut my eyes and shook my head as if to clear out cobwebs. "But a new man I don't need."

"What?" Donna said. "That doesn't sound like the Pepper we know and love. Line dancing, baseball games, scouting the Valley for warm male bodies."

The others at the table laughed, and whispered behind their hands.

"If you don't want him," Suzy said, "can I have him? I like mature men." She stroked her long blond hair and fluttered her heavily made up eyes.

"Immature ones last longer," Jill said, shaking her shoulder-length brown bob.

More laughter, with talk of which ages of man offered the best attractions. Lana put in her two cents' worth about the attractions of women.

Dutch gave me a pointed look. But he kept mum for once. Probably because he was outnumbered by sassy females. Estrogen poisoning, as he often liked to joke.

"Well." Donna said, "when it comes to squeezes, there's always room for one more. In case your current one doesn't work out."

Dutch shot her a sideways glance and sat back, palms upward in a "Whatya gonna do?" gesture.

Donna rose and gathered her purse as the waitress came and took Tulip's and my orders. I was having a turkey-and cranberry sandwich. Health food, for once. Dutch and the other barn buddies got up and stretched.

"Don't you girls stay out too late now," Dutch said, looking from me to Tulip. "We've got us a horse show to go to. Lots on the line."

The Brassbottom gang left in a clatter of laughter. They glanced back at us a time or two. Then Tulip and I were on our own.

We slid into chairs facing each other on the table's long sides. I gulped more ice water. It was a sin for which I'd pay on the rest of the drive. Also I studied the dessert menu, since my overtaxed brain apparently had left the building. Tulip excused herself and moseyed off to the ladies' room.

I was alone, and then not alone. I became aware of someone at my left elbow. I looked up to see Tommy Lee give me a tight-lipped appraising look. Up close he didn't look so much like the actor. More hair, smaller ears, longer neck.

His buddies, a tall slender one with spiky gray hair, and a short balding Buddha, wore expensive watches, designer polos and pressed chinos. They nodded congenially.

Tommy Lee dropped a business card in front of me. Amazingly, it read, "Tommy Lee Jaymes, CEO, Lookalike Luxury To Go, LLC." There was other information in tiny printing as well as contact info. But I focused on the name. Unbelievable.

"Tommy Lee Jaymes, Ma'am," he said with a twinkle in his eyes and traces of a Texas drawl in his voice. He held out a hand, but dropped it when mine stayed in my lap.

Though I was in a relationship, at least for now, I liked a flirtation as much as the next Saddle Tramp. But on my own terms. This gentleman's bold approach had ruffled my comfort.

"Hello," I said, partly fascinated, partly nonplussed. Despite the temptation, I sure wasn't giving out my name to a stranger, no matter how good looking. What was taking Tulip so long, anyway?

"Don't mean to disturb you," Tommy Lee said, "But you gave me a start when you walked in. Look just like my wife."

His name really was Tommy Lee. He actually had a Texas drawl, like the real Tommy Lee, who was born in Texas. And he did have a wife.

"Your – wife?" I sputtered, unsure what to say, or what his dropping the business card meant. All I needed now was to get tangled with some married man. A stranger, besides. A handsome stranger with a killer car and questionable sidekicks.

"My deceased wife," he said, unblinking. "Amazing resemblance. You both look like Reba McIntire. Do y'all by any chance sing? Or do lookalike acting work?"

"Dancin's more my line," I quipped, instantly wishing I hadn't. Part of me wanted this conversation to continue, and another part wanted to hit the brakes. Obviously my mouth took orders from the first part.

"No kidding," said Tommy Lee, his face wreathing in a smile. "Do like me some Texas two-step."

Blessedly at that moment Tulip wheeled around the corner from the foyer. Her stride hitched a half second when she saw the three amigos by our table. But she pulled herself together, walked on and sat down across from me. Her eyebrows rose as she looked at the men, then at me.

"Tommy Lee …. Jaymes," I said, emphasizing the first names. "My friend Tulip Clemmons. Sorry, I didn't catch your friends' names."

Tulip's mouth dropped open.

"Beanpole goes by Clint Yates," said Tommy Lee, "but does gigs as Eastwood."

"Okay," I said. Now that he mentioned it, I saw the resemblance.

"One on my left answers to Carl," said Tommy Lee. "As in the children's book, 'You're a Good Dog, Carl,' which I read to my kids a hundred times. AKA his richer twin, Danny De Vito."

So they really were lookalike actors. That still didn't explain the cars. Perhaps they were fabulous fakes, as well.

"Nice to meet you ladies," said Clint in a reedy whisper.

"Yeah," rumbled Carl, sliding Tommy Lee a "Thanks, Pal" look for the dog reference. Carl glanced at a humongous gold watch on his wrist. "Better get crackin', TLJ. Time's money."

"Pleasure to meet you all," said Tulip. She had her eyes glued to Clint Eastwood.

He did have a pretty good set of shoulders on him, and carried himself with the lanky elegance of a tall young pitcher. His sunglasses returned Tulip's unabashed gaze. Sunglasses at night. Only for actors, and those with iffy identities.

I wished Victoria were there. She might have tumbled for Carl. She always did have a thing for shorter guys. Claimed they tried harder.

Tommy Lee reached down to tap his business card, which still lay in front of me.

"So, Reba, where all you all headed?" he said.

"Horse show, Rancho del Cielo," Tulip said.

I shot her a glare. But she merely shot me a "What?" look.

"Saw you with that horsey bunch," Tommy Lee said. "Figured you all might be headed to Rancho. Middle o' nowhere, but big show, high rollers. Those cars out front? We're delivering one in that area. Gimme a shout, get the chance. Stake you to dinner. You interested in making a few bucks in lookalike work?"

Yeah, I wondered. Dinner, lookalike work and what else? Sounded like a double proposition to me. I'd probably just ashcan the card. His gesture was flattering. I'd been told more than once that I resembled Reba. But she stood a lot taller, had a way better bust, and flashed dimples I could only dream about. Plus, could sing a little.

"So are you driving the Lambo?" I said to Tommy Lee. Might as well glean a little more info, see if there were some kind of Von Sustern connection.

"That would be me," he said.

"Yours, or a client's?" I said.

"Potential client" said Tommy Lee.

"I know someone involved with Lambos. Is it Von Sustern? Wife shows horses.?"

"Can't say," he said without emotion or acknowledgement. "Confidential. Business."

"Sure," I said. "Well, have a safe trip."

Before turning to leave, he made the "call me" phone gesture with one hand. Then he and the other gentlemen left to start their engines, and drive off into the moonset. Tulip looked a little longingly after them, then at me.

"Wow," I said. "That was different. Bet he is delivering to the Von Susterns. Not that many Lambos on the road."

"I can't believe his real name was Tommy Lee," said Tulip. "And that his friends looked like they did, and that he came over, and pretty much asked you out."

"He didn't exactly ask me out, Tulip. Just said to call. Supposedly I remind him of his dead wife. And of course the live Reba. Whatever. But maybe we can score a double dinner. I saw you checking out Clint."

"And they're also going to Rancho, or somewhere around there," Tulip said. "Will wonders never cease? Just when I was about to abandon hope of hooking up."

I sat back as my turkey-Swiss sandwich and Tulip's spinach-pecan salad arrived.

"Hooking up's not the problem," I said when the waitress left. "Finding one that will more or less stay hooked, now that's the sixty-four-thousand dollar challenge."

She was about to say something, but instead favored me with a long hard look. I knew we both were thinking the same thing, the same name.

Sonny Chief.

My heart truly belonged to Sonny, and it probably always would. But ours would never be a permanent, traditional, live together kind of deal. So I had to date others, keep my options open.

Or so I forced myself to think.

***

The show grounds at Rancho del Cielo Equestrian Center looked impressive even after midnight, even from a quarter-mile down the road. One glance at the lit-up campus offered skeleton views of fencing, low stall rows and the big covered arena. Scattered along the edge were shade trees, outbuildings and parking lots jammed with vehicles. Flags and greenery hung motionless in the still, heavy night.

The main parking lot was chock-a-block with silver and white semi tractors, multi-horse trailers and dually pickups bearing barn logos. Close to the arenas stood impressive white motor homes or live-aboard horse trailers of every spelling, as long as it started with a dollar sign. I spotted one 40-foot RV with more popups, slideouts and striped awnings than a three-ring circus.

At any horse show of note, white seemed to be the preferred color for vehicles. It must be because many major equine events are held in warmer states, white being a sun-reflecting color. But I liked to think horse owners and trainers drove white vehicles because they believed black was for hearses, pimps, prostitutes and politicians.

I felt a flicker of excitement as I guided the truck and trailer through the gate and turned toward the exhibitor parking area. The show looked well-attended. I was thrilled to be a part of it, even if I'd had to raid my retirement account to pay for it. It'd cost at least two grand, with fees for everything from entries to RV parking and vendoring.

But this was an important show to attend. Competition would be first-rate, and I'd earn enough points to qualify for the World Open Western Show in Texas that fall. Maybe I'd sell some high-end clothing and tack, to boot. Which made me wonder, and wonder again, why I'd not heard from either Patsy Ann or Marietta.

At the same time, seeing all the vehicles and horses, I was pee-ohed at myself for not asking Tommy Lee when he was delivering the Lambo to this area. More important, exactly to whom. I'd press again anyway, when and if I called him. His customer could be a rich neighbor down the road. But likely it was one of these extravagantly horsed people at the show. More than likely a Von Sustern.

I piloted my rig between trailers parked across from the portable stalls and toward Brassbottom's trailer near the end of the trailer row. Its inside lights were out. The Grandeens already had fed, watered and bedded their animals and themselves.

While passing the Grandeen and Brassbottom buddy trailers, bound for the end of the row of forty-foot-long parking slots where I usually parked the Horsehouse, I spotted something. My high beams picked out two tall orange traffic cones, one with a white, block-lettered sign taped to it: "Reserved for Pepper Kane."

"There's our spot," I said. "Bless 'em. Somebody saved it for us, and right where we want to be, between the arenas." I depressed the gas pedal and got ready to slide my rig into the opening between the cones thirty feet away.

"Whoa!" shouted Tulip as I gave the steering wheel a mighty crank to enter our parking slot. "Pepper, STOP!"

I jammed my right foot on the brake pedal. The tires squealed and the hitch clunked in protest as we lurched in slow motion to a stop.

"What?" I said, unnerved by her urgency.

As the truck came to a stop it thunked over something, bouncing me on my seat and sending Tulip into the instrument panel. Luckily she had her hands out to stop her trajectory. Now she gripped the panel and slowly turned to look at me. Her mouth hung open. Her eyes practically bugged from her head.

"What?" I said. "What?"

"I think we just ran over a body," she said, hyperventilating slightly. She swallowed. "At least it looked like a person."

I stopped breathing. Shifting the truck into park, I dropped my forehead to the steering wheel, and gulped. A chill flashed through me.

"You sure?" I whispered, trying to wrap my mind around her horrific words.

"Thought I saw a head," she whispered back.

My heart raced. A body. Out in the road in front of our parking space. A place we'd parked many times before. It couldn't be.

In the glow of the dashlights, Tulip's eyes seemed enormous. The diesel engine throbbed. Her blond curls vibrated. Tulip shook, too, and not from the truck vibrations.

"I hope to heaven you're wrong," I said.

23

Scared out of my gourd, I left the truck idling and slammed out into a blameless balmy night at the show grounds. I squatted, twisting my head to check out what awful thing lay beneath the wheels.

Tulip jumped from the passenger side and ran around to squat beside me.

"See anything?" she yelled above the rattle-bang of the engine.

"Not yet," I shouted, my pulse pounding like pistons.

I kneeled deeper and stared into the shadows. By the poplars a small dog began barking. A woman's voice shushed him. On the other side of the lot, a horse whinnied. Nearby horses answered and hooves banged walls.

Diesel exhaust filled my nose as I let my eyes adjust to the darkness beneath the truck. Back of the front wheels I made out the lump we'd run over. It looked like a long bundle of clothing. Lumpy but flat. Hard to tell if a person was in there.

One thing was certain. Chillingly so. If it were a person, he or she wasn't moving, and probably never would again.

That would be beyond horrible. My mind ran with it. *Why had this happened? What did it mean? What in flaming heck was I going to do?*

Tulip fidgeted at my side. She lay a hand on my shoulder.

"Do y'all think it's an actual person?" she said under her breath.

"I can't really tell," I said. "I sure hope it's not. Grab the flashlight. Glove box."

As she brought me the flashlight, lights flashed on in the Grandeen trailer down the row. Donna poked her tousled blond head out the door.

"Hey, I see you made it," she called softly.

"Thanks for saving us our spot," I said.

"What spot?" she said. "Oh, the parking spot? It wasn't us."

"These cones?" I gestured toward the parking spot bracketed by orange cones.

"You got me," she said. "Why are you stopped in the road?"

"I'm afraid we ran over something," I said. "Or somebody."

"What?" yelped Donna. She turned back to speak to Dutch in their trailer.

Lights in other RVs and live-aboard trailers flicked on and heads poked outdoors.

I swept the flashlight beam under the truck. The bundle of clothing appeared to have a head. At least a roundish thing at one end. I drew in a sharp breath.

"Crap," I said to Tulip. "I'm going in. Keep the light on me."

She took the flashlight as I flattened my body to the pavement. It was still hot, and I winced as I pulled myself under the truck using my hands, elbows and legs.

I reached out and poked the bundle. There was no hardness and little resistance. Relief flooded me. So it was only a bundle of fabric, maybe clothes.

My fingers touched and felt the round object that looked like a head. It was warm, but had a hard, artificial surface. What the heck?

"So weird," I said. "Feels like just a bunch of fabric, clothes, and something that looks like a head, but isn't."

"OK," she said, straightening up and letting out a long breath. "Definitely not a body. It'll be all right."

"I don't think so, Tule." I scrambled on my belly and knees to gather up whatever it was, and backtrack out from under the truck. "All right that it's not a body, uhh, but not all right that it looked like a body." I stood up and sighed.

"Pepper, what's going on?" called Donna from her trailer. "What is it?"

"Just clothes or something, maybe a doll," I said. "Probably dropped by a kid. Nothing to worry about. See you in the morning."

"Oh," said Donna. "Well, thank goodness. Okay. See you then."

Tulip turned to me and shook her head. Her shoulders drooped.

"What a freakin' way to start a horse show," she said. "Weird."

"No kidding," I said. "And we were ready to believe the worst."

"Guess we've been under a lot of strain lately," she said with a weak grin.

"That's putting it lightly," I said. "Here, take this stuff, and I'll park the truck. Probably a kid's, or someone's clothes they dropped on the way to their dressing stall."

I slipped the truck back into gear and maneuvered our rig into our parking spot, still pondering who would have put out signs and cones for us.

Probably a barn buddy. But I basically was too tired to think much more about it.

"Oh, oh," Tulip shouted when I shut off the engine.

"Jees, what now?" I said, stepping from the cab.

She launched toward me, lugging the clothing.

"Slap yo' grandma," she said. "Y'all not gonna believe it."

"Believe what?" I said, staring down at the bundle she carried in both arms.

Tulip put one hand to her chest. With the other, she held out the pile of dark show clothes topped by the pale, head-like object.

"What won't I believe?" I said, taking the object in both hands and turning it.

Two painted blue eyes with black lashes and penciled brows stared up at me. The head indeed was bald, and made of fiberglass or hard plastic, the old fashioned kind used to hold wigs or display hats. Its most distinguishing feature was a wide crack right down the forehead, probably where the truck wheel had rolled over it. Its cheeks blushed pink, and its lips were covered in duct tape. Stuck to the tape was a red-lettered note:

"Back off or you're next, D.R."

What the what? I thought. A "D" and an "R"?

"Is that the abbreviation for 'doctor'?" I asked Tulip.

I showed her the note. She held it out and squinted.

"Could be," she said. "Letters messed up, though."

I took back the head and opened the truck door to study the "D" and the "R" under the dome light. Two fat, squarish capitals, bright as new blood and folded on themselves like graffiti, at first looked like a "D" and an "R."

But the more I studied, the more the letters appeared to be a "P" and a "K". The thought made me suck in my breath.

Of course they were a "P' and a "K," for Pepper Kane. The more I stared at the letters, the surer I became that they stood for, and the note was meant for, yours truly.

I looked at Tulip, over at our "reserved" parking sign, and back at Tulip.

"It's a 'P' and a 'K'," I said. "Definitely a 'P' and 'K'. I'm sure of it."

"Oh, no," she said, taking the note and looking closer. "Damn right!"

"This is the same block lettering used in the parking sign," I said. "Same color, too. Red Magic Marker. I oughtta know. Used it enough on sale signs."

"It does look the same," she said, drawing back. "And they clearly both were meant for you, Pepper Kane. Pretty creepy." She rubbed her arms.

I let this discovery sink in. Then I looked around us. All the trailer lights had gone out, and the vocalizing animals had gone back to sleep or whatever they did in the wee hours before a show. I wished I were safely tucked into a nice cozy bed, instead of standing in this strange, artificially lit lot in the middle of the night. In my safe bed instead of here, knowing that somebody knew when I'd arrive and that this was my favorite parking place near the big arena.

The idea of a setup, and that someone was now officially threatening me, maybe watching me and Tulip that exact moment, made my arms and thighs break out in goose bumps. I shivered.

"It's beyond creepy," I said. "Actually kind of Stephen King-y. With the head and all." I dropped my face into my hands, and rubbed my eyes. What was happening?

Tulip grabbed me by the upper arms. She shook me a little.

"Hey," she said. "Don't let it get to you. Probably just a prank. Or some coward with no balls trying to scare you a little."

"And succeeding a lot," I said. "Someone who wants me off this Vader case."

"Listen," Tulip said. "Don't let the bastards win. It's probably a bluff. Get a good night's rest, shift into show mode tomorrow with friends around, and it'll be all right."

I pulled away from her grip and stroked my arms.

"God, I hope so," I said. "I can't be any good at the show, always looking over my shoulder, let alone stay focused on this case."

"There y'all go," she said, turning her palms upward.

"Still," I said, "part of me doesn't buy it, doesn't believe 'It'll be all right'."

"So, make it believe," she said. "Fake it 'til you make it. Just don't cave."

"I still have to keep my radar on all the time," I said. "That goes for you, too, Tule. They probably figure you know what I know."

"True," she said. "Just be aware. Be very aware."

It took only a few minutes for Tulip and I to drop the trailer onto its gooseneck stand and park the truck nearby so we'd have use of the truck for runs into town or whatever. We chocked the trailer wheels and hooked up to the power box nearby.

Keeping a wary eye, I found Chocolate Waterfall's stall. I gave him an oat-molasses treat and a goodnight pat. The Grandeens were so good at settling in clients' horses, I regretted not being there to give them a hand. Doggone Tommy Lee.

I fingered his business card in my jeans pocket. Would I call him? Should I call him? I wasn't sure, in that tired time of night, after all I'd been through. I'd have to see how I felt the next day.

Tulip and I showered in record time, tanked down iced herbal tea from the mini-fridge and hit the hay. She, as usual, commandeered the pullout couch by of the dining table. I burrowed into the crisp sheets on the queen bed up in the gooseneck.

The queen bed where Patsy Ann's saddle and bridle had been stashed, then stolen. First thing in the morning I had to reach Patsy Ann and tell her about her stolen tack.

Either that or find out from Marietta where in holy heck Patsy Ann was, and what she'd been up to. Maybe learn, too, what Marietta's husband had been up to. I wouldn't put it past him to put a little scare in me. To put parking cones for me along with a body-shaped pile of clothes and a cute little head with an un-cute note attached to it.

Who, what, when, where, why. Classic reporting.

I had a ton of questions for a ton of people, and vowed to have most if not all answered tomorrow. Get answers, crack the case, as I'd cracked the mannequin head. Hopefully I wouldn't have my own head cracked in the process.

24

"Pepper! Y'all dead, or what?"

Tulip's voice harangued me up through thick layers of sleep, freeing me from being chased by cloaked figures with split mannequin heads.

"If I were dead, would I be talking to you?" I pulled the pillow over my head.

"Past eight. Thought you were with your horse or would've woken you sooner."

I threw my pillow at her, but she ducked. Smelling fresh coffee, I dragged my carcass out of bed. My stomach gave a mighty rumble.

"Whoa!" I said. "Gotta feed the tapeworm. Stressing over weird stuff drains you."

Tulip tossed a paper plate into the trashcan under the tiny sink.

"That staged warning was super weird," she said on her way to see her horse. "Be careful today."

"You too."

I jumped into a clean tee, jeans and my trusty boots, and nuked a bagel with cream cheese into edible rubber as I sipped coffee.

While munching, I pulled back the curtains to see a hive of activity. Stocky little Barbara struggled with garment bags of show clothes toward the Grandeen dressing room in their stall row. Suzy and Jill walked giggling alongside my trailer, and stopped to wave when they looked up and saw my face in the window.

I slid the window open.

"Pepper?" said Suzy, smoothing back her blond hair. "When you opening the Horsehouse? We need some things." She looked resplendent in a tangerine crystal bedecked tank top with pointy elongated sides over a shorter white camisole.

"After I longe my horse and get set up," I said. "Ten-ish."

They strode off, chattering about the biggest horse show they'd attended.

As I stepped out of the trailer and I heard neighs, shouts and clopping hooves. Pungent smells of a horse show wafted past. Essence of pine shavings, diesel exhaust, hot asphalt, horse sweat, poop and pee. I never tired of it. The sensual overload was energizing. It promised high emotions, Herculean efforts and plain hard labor to come.

Nearing our stalls I passed horse owners, barn helpers, small dogs off leash, and children trying to look grown up. Little girls sported pony tails or buns, sparkly earrings, lip gloss, mascara. Shows were as much beauty contests for riders as for horses.

Everything and everyone was on a mission. Wheelbarrows, electric scooters and golf carts rolled by, to or from the show office beside the main outdoor arena, or to and from the shavings bin on the edge of the stables.

I waved or said hello to pals and passing acquaintances from other shows, other times. Eva Gray excitedly told me about her new horse, and Sandy Fitzgerald sadly relayed news of the one she'd finally had to retire.

"We'll give you and Choc a run for your money in the showmanship," Eva said, pulling herself up to her full five foot height. "This new one's a showmanship machine."

"I'm happy for you," I said. "But we've been practicing extra hard this summer."

"Gunner's out to pasture now," Sandy said, spraying her horse at the wash rack where a male competitor flashed a million dollar smile at us. "Gave me twenty good years. Just couldn't keep his joints comfortable anymore."

"I know what you mean," I said. "We make such demands on our horses, trying for perfection, and then the show committees redefine the word upward."

"How's Chocolate Waterfall?" Sandy said, brushing back a shock of silver hair.

"Thanks," I said. "He's doing great, seems really tuned in to me."

"Horrible news about Vader," Sandy said, acknowledging the elephant in the arena. "Word is he may have been killed. Possibly by fatal injection."

"Whoa," I said, surprised. "The barn drums work fast. The state lab's processing his tissues and fluids now."

"They got any idea who did it?" said Sandy in a lower voice as she moved closer.

"Working on that," I said. "They're looking at Freddie, and the rest of us, too."

"Freddie?" she said. "Why would that be? How is he taking it?"

"Vader'd just been sold to Marietta Von Sustern," I said. "So he was hurting and of course he feels terrible now. So do the Grandeens,"

"Oh," said Sandy. "The gossip mill didn't say she'd bought the horse."

"He was supposed to be her next world champion."

"Who's investigating the case? Insurance company, police?"

"Yes, and me, unofficially," I said. "Freddie asked me to. I used to be a reporter, you know. So if you see or hear anything from the gossip mill here, let me know."

That seemed to satisfy Sandy, and we went our separate ways. I was bugged by her questions. I hadn't formulated clear enough ideas in my own head about the case. I also had a feeling this wasn't the last time this week I'd be put on the spot about Vader. That didn't thrill me. It would distract me from the show business at hand and pull me off the mystery trail. I decided to defer any other questions to the Grandeens.

Garth Gunderson really put me on the spot.

I literally ran into that lean, tan and toned Adonis as I rounded the stall-row's end after making sure Choc had fresh shavings and full water buckets in his stall. Dutch and Donna were setting up a hospitality canopy with chairs and refreshments. Their stall-curtain, a six-by-eight green banner with gold lettering that read "Brassbottom Barn" above dGd initials, was already stapled up on the outer stall wall.

"Garth!" I said, nearly losing my balance, then feeling his hand steady me.

"Hello, Pepper Kane, ex-newspaper ace." His blue-green eyes widened, more than ever giving him the look of a genial teen, and him well past the half-century mark. Garth wore a jaunty black-and-white woven straw hat. His faded chambray shirt matched his form-fitting starched Wranglers. He was always a looker. This was why his gorgeous blond wife, Jada, a specialist in

English events, kept an eye on him without being too obvious. It's tough being a trainer's wife.

"Long time no see," Garth said, sizing me up. I'd had a horse in training with him when I lived in Seattle. Despite our age difference, I'd always felt there was something special between us. Something neither of us would take further, but something we savored at arm's length. Much like my relationship with Dutch.

"Haven't seen you since the last show here," I said. "Can it really be that long?"

"Did you bring your cute Chocolate What's-His-Name horse?"

"Chocolate Waterfall, yes," I said. "We need to earn a few points here to qualify "

"Got time for a frappe?" Garth said, nodding toward the ice-cream stand, which already had a line of customers. The morning was hot and lunch wouldn't be on our list until we had worked, watered, and mucked up after our horses. They always came first, before we even thought of taking care of ourselves.

"A quick one," I said. I followed Garth toward the red-and-white bunting bedecked window of the white cold-treats truck.

In line, we talked of the eight horses he'd brought here. We also chatted of how his customers were doing with their horses. I was saddened to hear Garth's biggest client, Shari Jean, had euthanized Armed and Dangerous. The great western-pleasure gelding, whose hock joint was regularly injected with joint fluid to stave off pain, had contracted an incurable infection.

"That's horrible," I said, shaking my head. I hoped Choc wouldn't too soon need maintenance injections in joints stressed by show-level gaits and maneuvers. But injections, whether in joint or muscle, were a fact of a show horse's life.

When the line cleared, we gave our orders for double frozen frappes. Garth and I sat down at a shaded picnic table. His eyes burned nearly green under his hat brim.

"Now," he said. "I heard what happened with Vader. Any idea who's to blame?"

"So that's why you're treating me," I said. "No one knows. I have ideas, nothing concrete. Freddie and even us other Grandeen clients are persons of interest."

"I'd focus on Dutch and Donna," Garth said. "Seriously."

I felt a needles of worry prick my forearms.

"Why do you say that?" I asked. It was unimaginable that Dutch or Donna could be guilty or conspirators in Vader's death. And yet ...

"I can't see Freddie doing the deed," Garth said. "The rest, either."

"Patsy Ann Carpenter had tried to buy Vader," I offered, "and Dutch refused."

"Hmmm," Garth said. "Didn't hear that. Maybe Dutch wasn't ready to sell."

"Or he had a problem with her," I said.

"Consider this," Garth said, between sips of his frappe. "Say they had a financial crisis and Marietta's offer came in right then. What if they struck a deal to be cut in on insurance money if anything happened to Vader. Maybe they got the Von Susterns to raise the horse's value on the insurance."

"Whoa. That's a pretty wild theory. I shouldn't even consider it."

"But, being a good reporter, you should and you will."

"I guess it's possible. The Von Susterns did raise the insurance after buying Vader. And the Grandeens have had money problems from the trouble caused by that fired barn helper, Mad Mattie Henderson. She sicced the Oregon Department of Labor on the Grandeens for their employee compensation."

"So," Garth said. "Check it out." He finished his treat, wiped his mouth with a pristine napkin and rose to leave.

"I will. But the Grandeens are horsemen. They don't have a killing in them. They bought Vader for fifteen hundred as a clunky yearling. They made him a champion, and champion sire. They truly loved him."

"Listen, Sweetie. Everyone has it in them. Besides. Dutch and Donna's troubles are about to get a whole lot worse."

"What do you mean, 'worse

"You didn't hear?"

25

"Hear what, Garth?" I said, facing the handsome Seattle trainer. My heart skipped a beat as I wondered what new tragedy had struck the Grandeens.

"I know how you love your barn buddies," he said. "But a client of mine's husband is an attorney, and has a brother who's an attorney in Medford."

"O-kay," I said. "And?"

"Seems Freddie filed a suit against your sheriff for harassment, and another suit against the Grandeens for selling Vader before Freddie's lease was up."

"What?" I said, "Freddie suing people? That's not like him. Are you sure?"

"Well, ask him. He just got out of his truck over in the parking lot." Garth stared over my shoulder and nodded.

I looked where he indicated. Freddie, in crisp jeans and summer plaid Western shirt, stood by his white truck tapping his phone.

I said goodbye to Garth and started toward Freddie. I had a horse to exercise and a store to set up in my trailer. But now I had to talk to my friend, Freddie. I hadn't thought him the suing type. Bad things had happened to him over the years, but he had never been involved in legal action that I knew of. Hadn't been that sad or angry about anything. Hadn't, that is, until Vader's death.

Yet Garth's words, and the trainer surely was telling the truth, made me wonder. Did I really know Freddie?

I also flashed on whether I really knew the Grandeens. I had to feel them out about anything that may have sparked a sudden need for big money.

Glancing at my watch, I saw it was nine-fifteen.

"You must have left at o'dark thirty," I said to Freddie. "And then driven like a bat shot from a cannon to get it here so fast."

He hugged me as if we hadn't seen each other in ages. Freddie seemed to be his same lean, smiling self. But bags hung under his eyes, bags he'd dabbed with skin-tone concealer. He fetched a white straw from the cab and settled it onto his shiny head.

"Left the motel moments ago," he grinned, enjoying the joke.

"What?" I said. "You said you were driving down today."

"Got antsy, couldn't sleep, and said, 'What the heck?' Drove down last night."

"That sounds smart. You're more rested."

I slid my arm around his waist and started walking with him to the stalls. It already was hot as blazes in the parking lot, and getting hotter.

As we passed the row of luxury motor homes, we caught a little shade. Many people had unfolded or were unfolding their awnings, and now lounged with bloody Marys or mimosas in their outdoor furniture.

"Easy drive?" I said, not wanting to hit Freddie for info right away.

"Little truck traffic around Lake Shasta. Can't complain. But I will, anyway."

"That's the spirit," I said. "Speaking of complaining, I heard you're suing Sheriff Jack, and maybe the Grandeens."

He stopped, licked his lips ad blinked rapidly.

"Where'd you hear that?"

"Word gets around."

"Who actually told you?"

"Garth," I said. "The Seattle trainer? A client of his is married to an attorney whose attorney brother lives in Southern Oregon. The one you allegedly hired."

"Well, crap," Freddie said, starting to walk again. "You can't even pee without the world knowing."

"So it's true?"

"You are such a reporter." His words had an accusatory tone.

"Hey, that's not a crime," I said. "But you know I have to dig into every rumor, even if I don't want to."

"That's just what it is, Pepper," he said. "Rumor and innuendo. People love them some drama. There's no lawsuit. Nothing. Nada."

"Well, rumors don't start over nothing. What do you think sparked it?"

"No idea," he said with a shrug. "Except I guess I did have a consultation call with a lawyer Friday. Real short. Ten minutes, tops."

"That was it?"

"That was it. He said the sheriff was only doing his job. And that the lease I had with the Grandeens, which I faxed to the lawyer, spelled out their right to sell under extenuating circumstances. In super fine print, of course."

"I see," I said.

"I made that call in the heat of passion, after Vader's death. I was beside myself. I realize you need to solve this. But Vader was my life."

Freddie looked at me, his eyes sad and hollow.

***

Choc's nose pressed against the stall bars.

"Hi, Honey," I said, stroking the velvety pink and white skin.

Choc nickered and lipped my fingers between the vertical bars.

"No!" I warned, tapping his nose smartly. As if offended, he drew back and resumed his never ending search for hay wisps among his shavings.

I noticed he'd left a pee spot and fresh nuggets of manure for me to clean up. But I'd do that after longeing him. I had to longe, as well as ride, more than once that day. It helped him burn extra energy, made him a bit tired, so he'd focus on performing rather than playing at the 8 a.m. show start the next day.

Then I'd band Choc's mane, and bathe him.

Luckily the next day's early classes were "leading" classes. First was halter geldings, a class judged on a horse's conformation. He was led at a walk and trot past a couple of judges, then stood up square in a lineup. He should approximate a breed ideal.

The second class was "masters" amateur showmanship. That's where handlers over 45 are judged on how well they lead horses in backups, curves, lines and pivots. Grooming of both horse and human matters. So does a horse's focus on his handler instead of on people walking by the arena or doves fluttering in the rafters.

While I rummaged through the tack stall for my twelve foot whip and thirty foot longe line, Tulip called out from the aisle.

"Pepper! Where y'all been?" Her tousled blond head poked through the doorway. I held up the longeing tack for her to see what I was about to do with Choc.

"I ran into Garth. He bought me a frappe in exchange for the lowdown on Vader." I looked around to be sure no one else was within earshot. Although at a show even stall walls seem to have ears.

"And?"

I filled her in on Garth's and my conversation including the rumors about Freddie and the Grandeens. I also told her Freddie'd driven down the previous night.

"Whoa," Tulip said, a hand to her chest. "He could have set up the head and sign."

"Or it was meant to look like he did it. "

"Y'all tell anyone about that?"

"Don't want to tip my hand. We know the perpetrator is right here at the show. Maybe watching us now."

Tulip shivered.

"You call Tommy Lee yet? Like to know if he is connected to the Von Susterns, or knows something more about them. You could tease it out of him."

I stopped and drew in my chin, probably creating a few extra ones in the process. I'd been toying with the idea of a face lift, or at least some creative lasering. A lot of ladies our age went for treatments as easily as for booster shots.

"I do have his card in these jeans."

I took out my cell phone and tapped Tommy Lee's number. I'd have time as we waited for a spot to open in the arena. It already was full of horses moving in big circles around their handlers. A cloud of tan dust hung over the space despite its decomposed-granite footing having been sprayed by the water truck an hour ago.

"TLJ," said the high, slightly nasal masculine voice on the other end of the line.

26

"This is not Reba, but close," I said by way of greeting the man from the Pussycat Café. The man driving the hot red Lamborghini. The man who would be Tommy Lee.

"Awright," Tommy Lee said. "Reba! Hey, hold on. Wrapping up another call."

I heard muffled, animated talking in the background. Muffled arguing, A cuss word. Silence.

Tommy Lee came back on.

"Sorry, Reba," he said. "Little misunderstanding here. Hey, I know that's not y'all's real name. Tell me again. Senior moment."

"Pepper Kane," I said.

"God, girl," he said. "I hoped you'd call. I really did." That drawl. Had to love it.

"We barn buddies are having a before-show dinner tonight. Care to join us?"

"What all time?" he said.

"Probably six," I said.

"Where at?"

"The Gilded Bull."

"Gelded Bull?" he chuckled "Wouldn't that be a steer?"

"Right," I said. "A bum one."

"Gilded Bull," he said. "Yeah, I know the place. Got some more business to take care of, though. I'll call to confirm. See your number here."

My chest tightened as I threw a purposely wild pitch.

"Love to see that Lambo up close. Be a first for me. If you haven't delivered it yet to, who was it again, the Von Susterns?"

The line went silent for a beat. Maybe I'd guessed right.

"Somebody like that. You're a pretty good guesser, Miss Pepper."

"No, just an nosy ex-newspaper reporter."

"Hey, hold on. Sorry." More muffled talking in the background. Then a distinct, "All due respect, no can do." Then, to me, "See you at six. Bring your blond friend."

We rang off, and I gave Tulip a thumb up. She smiled and patted her horse.

Two handlers left the longeing arena with their horses, and Tulip and I led our horses in. We sent them out on circles with us at the center.

Hot as it was, with the sun beating hard, Choc's veins soon stood out on his neck and shoulders. Damp spots darkened his flanks. It was quite hot, so he would sweat anyway before tiring. He'd had only ten minutes of longeing. He needed thirty.

Outside the arena spectators drifted along the rail. Dogs barked. A diesel engine ran nonstop, although you weren't supposed to do that in California. Somewhere a desperate horse neighed repeatedly for an absent stable mate. It got on my nerves.

I coughed as dust settled over me. Flies worried my face and arms. Thankfully a breeze kicked up, keeping me from melting into the sand.

By ten o'clock most of the circling horses had been replaced with people riding around the arena. Tulip and I led our horses back to their stalls and put them away.

Tulip headed off to open up our Horsehouse-on-wheels. I lagged behind, planning to pick up Choc's stall. As I searched the stall row for the pitchfork and wheelbarrow, at the end I saw a good-looking Hispanic-looking man in a purple tee bathing a horse at the washing platform. While haphazardly spraying the bay, he alternately shouted and sulked at an even better-looking younger man in a black hat and jeans with fancy white stitching and crystals on the hip pockets. The men exchanged rough words, most of which I couldn't hear. But I caught a few "F" bombs. I hoped no kids were around. The younger cowboy had the final words, flipped Purple Tee a rude gesture, and strode aggressively toward the next stall row. That was fronted by a giant black-and-lavender banner. A gold diamond framed double "Rs" at the banner top.

So those are the stalls rented by famed Texas trainers Royce Ball and Rogers Valentine. The famous, industry dominating Royce-Rogers duo. The very outfit our buddy Victoria threatened to send her horses to, after fighting with Dutch. The same cowboys Patsy Ann rode with.

I filed the location in my mental folder. I'd try to check with Royce and Rogers, or at least their employees or clients, later, regarding how well they knew her as well as Marietta and our Victoria. Maybe they knew meaningful scuttlebutt.

Meanwhile Mr. Purple Tee untied the bay horse from the wash rack bar and jerked its lead shank, making the horse throw its head. He jerked it repeatedly.

I felt a stab of annoyance. Who was this poser? Why did some people punish horses for no reason? Why bring needless pain or fear to these beautiful equines, who basically just want to get along and go with the flow of the herd, whether horse or human. Negative emotions have no place in dealing with horses.

Choc tugged at the lead rope as I put him away. I came out of my trance when my cell phone sang. I pulled it out. Tulip sounded frantic.

"Got the Horsehouse open. We're slammed. Were you kidnapped by aliens?"

I explained the tiff I'd witnessed, and the apparent connection of Purple Tee and Mr. Fancy Pants to the Royce-Rogers training stable.

"Royce and Rogers are gossip kings. Or queens."

"Ha ha," I said. "An oldie but a goodie."

"Wait!" she said, "Here comes your boy now. At least it's some dark good-looker in a purple tee and straw hat."

"I'll be right there," I said, happily setting aside my plans for a stall cleanup. As I rounded the stall row corner I saw Purple Tee walking up the trailer steps. Close behind, chatting animatedly, was ... what? Freddie Uffenpinscher. They clearly knew each other. I had a few more questions for Freddie. And a slew of them for Purple Tee.

As I put my foot on the trailer step, looking around at the tank-tops, saddle-pads and boot displays Tulip had placed outside during her short stint at the Horsehouse, a movement on my left caught my eye.

A ginormous luxury motor home decked out with custom bronze swooshes cruised imperiously toward me. Deluxe chrome wheels, nicely trimmed windows, slideouts and doors galore. That was some piece of machinery.

I tried to see who was driving. It was dark in there. But I squinted hard and finally brought the driver's head and shoulders into focus.

A jolt of excitement shot through me. Talk about lucky breaks. This was exactly the person I most needed to talk to.

It was Patsy Ann Carpenter.

27

The rolling Queen Mary angled toward an open space beside trees at the far side of the lot. Shading my eyes with one hand beneath my cap brim, I saw orange cones marking Patsy Ann's parking spot. She pulled the RV into it with room to spare.

Who'd put those cones out for her? The same one who'd put cones, along with the bizarre warning bundle, out for me the night before? Were these incidents connected? The idea chilled my chest. So it must not have been her, as she was just this moment arriving.

"You made it," Tulip said, leaning out the trailer door through which Freddie and the man in the Purple Tee had entered. "We've been busier in an hour here than we were all last week in Gold Hill."

"The revenue should thrill the landlord," I said. "Shoot! Forgot to call him." I ducked into the shade from our own trailer-mounted awning and called our Gold Hill landlord to explain the burglary, and the coming insurance payoff. He didn't sound happy, which is how he always sounded. But he sighed, and agreed to wait.

As I turned to step into the trailer, the ramp end of which was down to let in breezes as well as customers, the phone rang. Wonder of wonders. Patsy Ann.

"Hello, Pepper," she said with a lilt. "Marietta said you all wanted to talk to me?"

"Yes," I said, steeling myself to deliver the news of her stolen saddle.

"Hey, I see you're at the Horsehouse trailer," she said. "Can the news wait? I've got a few things I need to take care of. Honey had a bad asthsma attack and requires aftercare. We'll come on over to your trailer in a bit."

"Okay," I said. The delay would give me time with Freddie and Purple Tee.

"Thank you," said Patsy Ann. "Marietta and I will be over soon."

I paused to process this.

"Is Marietta here?" I said, trying not to show my surprise. "I thought she was bringing her own rig."

"Actually," said Patsy Ann, "this is her rig. Mine broke down Saturday and she's on some new meds that are fighting each other. She didn't trust herself driving."

"So, are your husbands along, too?" I asked, hoping to be able to soon talk to the key players in my investigation.

"No," said Patsy Ann. "Carson is staying in Reno to get our RV fixed, and then heading to Vegas for other business. Richard is driving their Range Rover over here. Without them, it's girls gone wild. With credit cards at least. Woohoo."

Woohoo? Patsy Ann might have had meds, a drink or both, herself. And it was before noon. Well, as the song says, it's five o'clock somewhere.

I went into the Horsehouse. Tulip sat behind the short counter opposite the door.

She lifted her chin to direct my gaze to the trailer end. Freddie and Purple Tee were examining silky pearl-snap show shirts. These designer tops came in eight laser shades with woven in shadow plaid. I expected these finds of mine to fly off the rack even at $250 a pop. Classic cotton shirts commanded only $80.

"Hey, Freddie," I said, slapping on a smile. "Aren't those shirts fantastic?"

"They are dope," Freddie said. He held up an emerald green one and swished it side to side while looking at his companion. "Pepper, meet my friend, Carlos Guitierrez. He's an assistant trainer for Royce and Rogers."

"Nice to meet you," I said, stepping forward to take Purple Tee's hand.

Carlos shook my hand. He fixed me with smoldering eyes beneath shapely brows. His lips were deep bronze. His muscular forearms were a darker bronze with white showing above the elbow where skin met purple tee. Horse rider's tan.

"How do you and Freddie know each other?" I said, looking from one to the other.

Freddie appeared on the verge of a giggle.

"We met last night," Freddie explained. "When I came in to see if my horse was here yet. Bumped into him on the way back to my car and the rest is history."

"Freddie thinks the new shirts are perfect for Royce and Rogers," said Carlos.

"Royce might like the burgundy," said Freddie. "Go nice with his black saddle and bridle." He held up the shirt and turned it around. It rippled seductively

"Can I take it on approval?" said Carlos. "Maybe a couple more?"

"Of course. By the way, Carlos. One of your customers, Patsy Ann Carpenter, is due here any minute."

"Oh, she's a nice lady," Carlos said. "Rides good horses."

"How long have she and Honey been with Royce and Rogers?"

"Well, let's see," he said. "They bought Dark Victory from us in twenty-twelve, but the daughter had a horse with us before. Old one was a pig."

"I heard they also tried to buy Dark Vader," I said, watching Carlos closely.

His face showed no expression, not even a lifted eyebrow.

"That's the horse at your barn that was killed," he said. "The one Freddie leased."

"Yes," I said.

"So sad he died," he said, looking at his snip-toe lizard boots. "For you, Freddie, but Marietta, too."

"Might've been Patsy Ann, if she'd bought him," I said. "Why didn't she?"

"I guess they weren't ready to sell," said Carlos. "We're not sure why."

Freddie frowned, and tugged at one of his earrings.

"I told you, Carlos," he said in a low, colder voice. "I had a year-long contract."

"You also thought Dutch and Patsy Ann were old show hookups," Carlos hissed. "She'd promised to bring him her horses, but never did and never would."

So I had thought right, thanks to Brassbottom gossip girl, Lana. There had been something between Dutch and Patsy Ann. Was Patsy Ann so angry he had sold Vader to Marietta, that she had killed Vader for spite? And as a side benefit, removed Vader and Marietta as her main, world-title competition?

But if Patsy Ann is guilty, why is she now cozying up to Marietta, partying with her in Reno, then traveling here in Marietta's RV?

Besides. There is the question of who, then, had set up the parking sign, cones and mannequin head, to scare me. The women had just driven onto the show grounds.

Could one of these men have been their accomplice?

Then I had an idea.

"Carlos?" I said.

He looked up.

"Go ahead and take however many shirts for Royce and Rogers." I said. "I'll get a garment bag. You can write the sizes and colors and sign for them."

I hurried to the counter where Tulip pulled a garment bag from under the counter.

"Go for it," she whispered. "At the very least you'll get a sale."

I grabbed a pen and notepad and gave them to Carlos.

"I trust you, but I just need this for inventory, to remember which ones you take in case someone else wants one Royce is looking at."

Carlos noted and signed for three shirts and handed the pen and paper back to me.

I glanced at what he'd written, trying not to be too obvious. I couldn't really get a good look because my hands trembled a little. I hoped that if this handwriting revealed what I thought it might, that Carlos wouldn't guess what I was up to.

"See you later, Pep," Freddie said, leaving the trailer behind Carlos. "I wish I could afford one of those shirts. But am watching my pennies. I've got the Manes 'n Tails owner to a selling price I can live with."

"Oh, I'm so happy for you, Freddie," I said, giving him a hug. "I always thought you'd find a way to buy the salon."

I wondered how he'd suddenly come up with the money to complete the sale, although he had been saving like crazy.

***

Tulip startled me when she rose and stretched. She had such a large wing span she could touch both sides of the trailer at the same time.

"Y'all gonna take a gander at that handwriting?" she said.

I stared at Carlos' writing on the notepad. It looked slanted, and hurriedly written. It was not as blocky as the writing on the parking sign and mannequin-head note. Yet I felt a nervous stir in my stomach. Had I just been talking with the perpetrator? One who could hurl expletives at a colleague and torture a horse?

"Hey," Tulip said, looking over my shoulder. "Writing looks somewhat similar. Let me find that parking sign and note from the living compartment. We can compare."

She disappeared through the dividing door.

***

"Ready or not, here we are," said a familiar female voice at the trailer's open end.

"Warm up the credit card swiper," said another lower, familiar female voice.

I wheeled around. Patsy Ann and Marietta, resplendent in sparkly tops, reptile boots and appliqué jeans, swept into the trailer.

"Hey, Ladies," I said, greeting the women without missing a beat. "While the cats are away, the mice will play, eh?"

Patsy Ann shrugged.

"Our husbands don't really care what we do, Pepper, as long as it's not illegal. We won spare change in Reno. At least I did. Marietta's down a hair. But she'll get it back."

"'I'd better," Marietta said. "My husband's about to divorce me. Seriously."

"So what else is new?" laughed Patsy Ann.

Marietta fingered a crystal pendant on a braided leather cord. Patsy Ann stroked a feather-trimmed tank top on a black display torso, and graced me with a smile that didn't quite reach her shocking turquoise eyes.

"Now," she purred. "What was it y'all wanted to tell me?"

28

"Well, we had a little problem back in Gold Hill," I said, bracing one hand on the glass counter. I returned Patsy Ann's questioning gaze. This was not going to be easy.

Patsy Ann glanced from me to the merchandise-stacked walls of the Horsehouse.

"Where are my new saddle and bridle?" she said. "Honey hopes she recovers enough to use them at the show. It'll give her the edge she needs."

I took a deep breath.

"That's what I wanted to tell you about when I tried to reach you yesterday. Marietta didn't know where you were. I really did try." I glanced at Marietta.

She frowned back at me. Patsy Ann gave her a questioning look.

"Marietta, you knew I took Honey to the clinic," Patsy Ann snapped.

"I knew later," said Marietta. "Then I didn't want to bother you in your crisis. Besides, I did call and you didn't answer."

What was the story with these two? Whatever it was, I had to tell Patsy Ann about the stolen tack, that Honey couldn't use it here, that I'd already run her card with the fourteen-thousand-dollar charge, and that I had no way to make good until my insurance paid me.

"So what were you calling about?" Patsy Ann said with an indulgent smile.

"There was a break-in at our Gold Hill store Saturday night. They got your tack."

"What?" she put a hand to her chest. "How awful! Honey will be devastated."

She slowly lowered her trembling hand, its rings a blur of silver and turquoise. If she were acting, this performance was over the top.

"I had security systems in place," I said. "The cops came, but there was nothing they could do. I am so sorry, Patsy Ann. The insurance won't pay until the investigation is complete. It may take weeks."

Marietta stood stoically by, hands clasped in front of her. Those slanted, coal colored eyes were unreadable. But she put a reassuring hand on Patsy Ann's arm.

"Any idea who did it?" Marietta said, swinging her gaze back to me. "I know how sharp an investigator you are, Pepper." She took a step forward. Her question had a taunting tone. Her second statement dripped sarcasm.

I thought it bold of her to say that, considering her meekness when her husband was near, and her deference to him in many matters. Yet I recalled she'd been tougher when I'd given her my condolences, from our store in Gold Hill. Richard Von Sustern mustn't have been near her then.

Her short square form remained rigid. Her upswept eyes, full red lips and large brunette head on a muscular neck reminded me of a female circus-horse acrobat from Poland I'd interviewed for the paper. An acrobat accused, and then later tried, for the murder of her husband and son. She'd made it look as if they were trampled.

I had never seen Marietta close up before. Not even at Brassbottom. Her magazine photos clearly were PhotoShopped.

"No idea who did it, Marietta," I said, jumping back into the present. "Hopefully they'll find the burglar soon. But, as you suggest, I am investigating. Checking to see if the saddle and bridle will be offered on Amazon or eBay."

Marietta cocked her head and gave me a questioning look.

Patsy Ann squared her shoulders and gave me a weak smile.

"I had some jewelry stolen from our RV at a horse show," said Patsy Ann. "Honey saw it up on eBay the next day. Got it all back."

"You were lucky," said Marietta. "These days thieves can always hide their ID." She stood so close I felt her body heat.

"Well, keep trying," said Patsy Ann. "I wouldn't be surprised if it shows up."

Marietta eyed me critically. "Its sale will pay a lot of bills for somebody."

A thought came to me. It locked my eyes wide open.

Everyone knew Tulip and I were just getting by with the Horsehouse, hit hard by the Great Recession, finding it increasingly difficult to make ends meet. We complained about it to anyone who would listen. Did Marietta think we had staged the burglary to collect the insurance money, or money from selling Patsy Ann's saddle?

Good grief. In the toxic wake of Vader's killing it seemed that everyone suspected everyone of everything. It was just crazy. Or maybe I was crazy.

Tulip startled me when she stepped down out of the trailer's living compartment. She closed the door, and waved the block-lettered papers and note triumphantly.

"Found them," said Tulip. "Wasn't easy. It's a mess back there already and the show hasn't even started." She looked at Patsy Ann and Marietta. "Oh! Hello, Patsy Ann. How are you?"

"Pretty good except for the stolen saddle." She pursed her lips.

"We all are just so sorry about that," said Tulip.

"By the way, Tulip," I said, "this is Marietta Von Sustern."

"I have seen you show your horse, Marietta," Tulip said, pushing the papers under the counter. Nice to meet you in person. Sorry about your loss of Vader."

"Nice to meet you, too," said Marietta. "And thank you." She looked away for a moment. When she looked back, she asked, "Still no clues, then?"

"Have ideas but nothing substantial," I said. "Just keeping our antennae up."

"I still can't believe it," Marietta said, her manner turned slow and sad. "I was so counting on this show, and beating my friend here."

"At least you're moving forward, Marietta," said Patsy Ann. "You're trying that new horse at Royce and Rogers'. Might be even better than Vader."

A beat of silence passed among everyone. Then Patsy Ann started moving down the rows of show vests and blouses. Marietta followed.

"Meanwhile," said Patsy Ann, "try retail therapy. Usually works for me. Look at this aqua vest. Only $400. It has just amazing beadwork, patterned like one of Mama Belmont's vintage Hermes scarves."

While the women started shopping in earnest, Tulip motioned me over.

"Whoa, that was tense," Tulip said under her breath. "Can I take some time to work my horse, and see if the show office is open so I can enter my classes?"

"Go ahead," I said with a wave of my hand. "And bring me a pattern book. I need to memorize the showmanship routine. I can't remember patterns lately. Too much else on my mind."

"I know," Tulip soothed.

"But this show is do or die," I said. "I have to find a way to keep an eye out but also show like there's no tomorrow."

"It's what we gotta do," Tulip said. "Cowgirl up. We have a life or death distraction, literally. But also a lot else on the line."

"We've paid a ton of money to be in this show. Worked all year for it. Every point we earn in a class, counts. I need to earn enough to qualify me for this year's World Show. I don't know if I will be able to afford it next year."

"Amen," said Tulip. "Something will break soon in the Vader case. I just know it. Meanwhile, you have a show to do. And remember, I've got your back. It'll be all right."

Patsy Ann bought the aqua vest, a white silk blouse to go under it, and an aqua and white wool pad to go under the saddle she already owned. The combination would look stunning on her black and white horse. Her mood had changed to all business.

When the women left, I went back to our living quarters for a cold bottle of green tea. I settled at the counter and sipped my tea in a blessed moment of peace.

But it was only a moment. Dolly Parton began warbling her familiar tune. It was starting to bug me. I planned to change it, maybe for something by Reba. My ha-ha lookalike. I loved those classic country voices.

I smiled when I saw the caller ID'd on the phone's pane. *Sonny Chief.*

"So you got there okay?" he said. "A little worried not to hear from you."

"Been crazy busy," I said. "But was about to call. How're things there?"

"Good," Sonny said. "Serrano stopped by your parents' this morning, is at the Horsehouse store now, and plans to go back to Grants Pass for dinner with them."

"Great," I said. "And you? Turn up anything new?"

"Pretty quiet around here," he said. "Miss you."

"Me, too. Miss you."

"We might have a possible lead on the burglary," Sonny said.

"Really?" I said, jumping off the stool. I picked up a pen on the counter and began to roll the pen through my fingers.

"Katie at the Kitchen said a couple came in for dinner last night who hadn't heard about the burglary yet," Sonny said. "They live a block from the store. When they were on their porch Saturday night, they saw a black Jeep or something square like that, with engine running, parked under a streetlamp."

"Really," I said. "And?"

"Wife saw a chunky someone at the wheel," he said. "When they got out they were wearing some kind of superhero cape."

"Bingo!" I said. "That sounds like the get-up we think our horse-killer wore. And the black SUV. Like the Brassbottom neighbor saw before finding that black fabric on her fence. You tell Boo, or Sheriff Jack?"

"All over it," Sonny said. "Trying to locate the car or driver. Not much to go on, though. Keep you posted."

"Well," I said. "Sounds promising. Might be related to the Vader case. Make everything a lot easier. But you never know. Yeah, keep me posted."

"Right," he said.

"So did you find anything worthwhile about the sheriff himself, as a person of interest in the Vader case?"

"Just that Boo thinks Sheriff Jack's never let his problem become a problem," said Sonny. "In treatment years ago, and no scuttlebutt on debts or favors owed."

"Well," I said. "it was just a thought." I was disappointed but not surprised. I could cross the sheriff off my list, for now. "Hey," I said. "I do have news for you." I filled Sonny in on Tulip's and my strange encounter with the cones and cracked mannequin head posed for us to see when we drove in the night before. I also mentioned my encounter with Freddie and Carlos, and the arrival of Patsy Ann with Marietta an hour ago, with Richard Von Sustern due there soon.

"Well, be aware and take care," Sonny said. "Keep Mr. Smith & Wesson close."

"In my purse," I said. "But not when I'm working my horse. Such times there usually are lots of other people around."

"Just can't help worrying about you," Sonny said. "Down there alone with all those people of interest closing in."

I bristled a little at his assumption that I couldn't take care of myself. I had proven I could. But, then, maybe that was just a man thing. Was I also sexist for thinking that? Probably. So mount a demonstration. I couldn't override millennia of evolution. As long as I was aware of my thinking, and didn't use it to offend others or poison relationships, who cared?

What happened the next minute shook me to the spine and blew a chunk of my self-sufficient attitude clean off the counter.

29

I was finishing my up iced tea with cheese crackers when movement outside the trailer's open door caught my eye.

Tulip, long legs pounding and blond curls bouncing, raced across the parking lot. She charged up the steps. She braced her hands on the counter. Her hair was tousled, her blue eyes enormous.

"You – you won't believe this," she said, swallowing hard. She grabbed a cracker and swallowed it whole, coughed, and drained my tea bottle.

"For God's sake, Tulip," I said. "Slow down. What is it?"

"I was bringing my horse back after his bath. Everyone was out with their own horses. Somebody jumped out of Choc's stall and ran away before I got a look."

"No," I growled in disbelief,

"Yes," she hissed.

"I hope it was someone cleaning my stall?" I said, dreading the answer.

"Oh, no. They had no tools, left the door open, dropped this on their way out."

She raised her fist, turned it over and opened her fingers. My breath caught in my throat. I stared down at a full livestock syringe with the needle still attached. A bead of milky liquid hung at the tip.

Words froze in my throat. My hands felt cold, as if plunged in a deep freeze.

"My fingerprints are on it. But I had to get it before Chocolate stepped on it."

I jumped off the stool and took the trailer steps in one move.

"Man or woman," I gasped, now running hard toward the stalls, Tulip at my side.

"Man," she panted as we ran. "I think. Muscular. Shorter. Black flappy windbreaker, tight jeans. Boots clumped on the asphalt as he ran away."

"Did you," I breathed, "look around the corner?"

"Yelled 'stop,' but he just vanished."

"Choe look OK? Why didn't you stay with him, and call me?"

"Left my phone in the trailer, so sorry," she said as we started down the stall row.

"Call security while I check my horse," I said, handing her my phone. "We can't leave the horses alone for a minute now. Can't ever forget our phones either."

Breathing hard, I reached Choc's stall. At least Tulip had closed his door. He shied away when I threw it open. When I saw the brightness of his eyes, the steadiness of his legs, I stepped forward to hug his neck. The solid furry warmth calmed my heart.

"Thank God," I said. "Good boy. You're safe now."

But I didn't believe it. Someone had just tried to inject my precious horse with a dose of something, probably of whatever killed Dark Vader. Someone had targeted me and my horse. I didn't know if I could continue to show. The game had changed. Lives were at stake, now. My horse's, if not my own.

My cell phone rang. I stepped back from Choc and answered, my hand shaking.

The pane lit up with the country sheriff ID. A dispatcher was repeating something.

"Pepper Kane?" said a calm female voice. "Sheriff's office. Is this Pepper Kane?"

"It … it is," I said.

"Show security just called to say a stranger reportedly entered your horse's stall with a syringe with intent to harm, but was interrupted and ran away. Correct?"

"It is," I said. "Are you sending on officer?"

"But your horse appears to be all right," said the dispatcher.

"Seems so," I said, feeling frustration build. "But these things can take time to work. Others could have been effected."

"We've made a note of it. But no crime has been committed."

The reporter in me expected that answer. But the horse owner in me wanted more. "All due respect, a valuable show horse was killed the same way three days ago at our barn in Oregon. I've received threats for looking into that, and most of the people under investigation are down at this show."

"Ma'am?" said the dispatcher. "Calm down. I've recorded the information you gave. That's all I can do. But call if anything else happens, or people are in danger."

"I am in danger," I said, telling her about the threatening tableau Tulip and I found on driving in the night before.

"Making a note of that. We can do nothing unless a crime is committed. But we are here if you need us." The conversation was over. I stepped out of the stall and shut the door. Tulip held up a zippered plastic bag holding the syringe. I nodded.

At the stall row end, Dutch appeared, leading a lathered horse he'd just finished working. He led it into its stall and tied it to a rope attached to a ring atop the wall.

"Dutch!" I said, jogging over to stand in the doorway.

Seeing the look on my face, he stopped what he was doing. "You look like you've seen a ghost," he said. "What's up?"

"Tulip saw someone leave Choc's stall, run away, drop this syringe," I said, showing him the evidence.

He took the bag. He pressed his lips together and gave me a dark look. "Choc okay? You call the show vet? Security?"

"Yes, no, and I think so," I said. "Choc is eating hay. Tulip told security, he called the sheriff. I talked with a dispatcher. Not interested unless a crime was committed."

Dutch frowned. He loosened his horse's cinch, strode to my stall and examined Choc's eyes and gums. "Seems okay. Have the show vet take a look anyway."

"Will do. So glad Tulip interrupted him. But it scares the hell out of me."

Dutch stared at me. "I can imagine. Somebody's targeted your horse, and I think it's because they may be trying to get at you for investigating Vader's death."

"Really."

"We heard about your store burglary, by the way. Sheriff Jack mentioned it when he dropped by Sunday. He wonders if they're connected. Says you do have a tendency to overstep your authority, piss people off." A teasing smile played at the edge of his eyes.

So everyone knew or suspected what I knew or suspected. Could be good or bad.

"You probably heard about the warning setup when we drove in, too."

He hadn't. So I filled him in.

"I don't like it. I'll ask the show office to beef up security. I doubt whoever is doing this would go after you directly."

"I hope you're right," I said. But I wasn't so sure. The threats had been escalating.

"Don't forget, we have the most important show of the year to get through. Just be very careful. Always have somebody around. Do you have a gun? I can lend you mine."

"Thank you," I said. "I have one. Just need to keep it near." As we talked I realized I had only been grasping at straws in thinking Dutch or Donna were somehow involved in their former horse's death. For my longtime trainer to lay out his concerns like this, knowing the reality of his professionalism, his love for horses and concern for their owners, almost made me ashamed for suspecting him.

"I'll sleep in the dressing-room stall for the duration of the show. Or until they find the person behind all this."

As Dutch left to ride Victoria's red roan-and-white mare, I found the wheelbarrow and pitchfork, and cleaned Choc's stall. It was hard, hot, stinky work. Sweat streamed down my scalp and torso, soaking my bra and jeans. Just when I thought I was done picking, tossing and raking, another nugget or pee patch surfaced. So much for the glamorous horse show life.

At least the labor dulled the needle jabs of my nerves. I had to keep busy.

I was putting away the tools when Tulip and a scarecrow of a man in a white shirt, tan shorts, sunglasses and a horse-show logo cap arrived. Following him were Barbara, Lana, Victoria and little Stewie along with Stewie's mother, a kindly looking matron in shorts, sandals and floaty top. All eyes brimmed with curiosity.

"What happened, Pepper?" piped up little Stewie, his freckled face shining under a fringe of buzz-cut red hair. He was a spitting image of Serrano as a kid.

"Let the security man ask the questions, Honey," said his mother.

Stewie had other ideas.

"When I was getting ready to ride my horse," he said to me, "I saw some cranky old person walking around, looking into the stalls."

"Really?" I said. "Did you recognize him? Talk to him?"

"Don't know if it was a man or woman," he said. "Kind of covered up. But talked kind of crabby and mumbly, 'Looking for a friend', he said."

The scarecrow man in the shorts and cap stepped forward and extended a hand.

"Harley Schwartz, show security," he said, shaking my hand.

"Pepper Kane," I said.

"Sorry to hear what happened. Your horse OK?"

"So far."

"The show vet had an emergency, but will come soon as he can. Can we go somewhere to talk?"

I looked around at my Brassbottom buddies. The other women and Stewie looked disappointed they weren't invited to hear more. But Tulip slipped up to stand by me.

"Include me in," she said.

"Let's go to the Horsehouse," I said. "Our trailer's nearby. Cooler there, too."

Finding the trailer's side door unlocked, I felt a prick of worry.

"That's weird," I said, opening the narrow steel door and stepping into the trailer. "I'm sure I locked it."

"Maybe you just thought you locked it," Tulip said.

"Or Sonny's repair after the burglary didn't hold," I said, motioning her and Harley into the seats flanking the table in the living compartment. I gave them cold bottled waters, and sat down next to Tulip.

"So give me your thoughts," Harley said. "Tell me what you think this incident was about."

I told him about happenings at home and at the show, my suspicions, our persons of interest. He sat calmly, sipping water, nodding his head from time to time. When I mentioned the previous night's sign, note and head, he sat up straighter.

"Do you still have the sign and note? The head? I'd like to take a look."

"The papers should be under the counter."

"I'll get them," Tulip said, rising to retrieve the sign and notes.

"Nice rig you've got here," Harley said, looking around. "You're a retired newspaper reporter, Tulip said. Good to have this gig to pay the bills."

"Totally," I said, with a grin. "I have to work to support my lifestyle, retirement."

He chuckled, shaking his head.

"Same here. I used to be a car salesman in Sac. Leases, high end stuff. In fact one of your horse show friends, Marietta Von Sustern, and I used to do some business."

Before I could ask what kind of business, Tulip flung herself into the doorway. Her gaze shot from me to Harley and back to me. Her eyes blazed.

"The papers are gone!" she gasped.

"They can't be," I said.

"Well, they are."

"Did you look on the floor, in the wastebasket."

"Yes. Now y'all read my lips. The sign and notes are gone."

30

"I saw you put the sign and receipt under the counter," I said as Tulip rummaged in the fridge for another bottled water. This one she held against her forehead.

"You saw me put them there," she said. "So, apparently, did someone else."

I looked at Harley Schwartz, the show security officer, and back at Tulip.

"Someone else who probably wanted them back," I said. "One who guessed we'd identify their handwriting from other documents or from a certain receipt."

Tulip and I locked eyes.

"Carlos," we both said.

"Carlos?" said Harley, rising from the table.

"Guy who works for Royce and Rogers," I said. "Came in with our Freddie. Took some shirts on approval. I had him sign for them to compare his writing with that on the sign and note. Not the same, but there were similarities."

"I need to go talk to these people," Harley said. "Don't worry. I'll ask routine questions. Is everything okay at the show? Remind them to report any problems. Just let them know I'm here and watching."

Harley left and Tulip and I went over what we'd told him. We agreed it was all he needed to know, for now. We still had our own investigating to do. And despite all that was going down, despite my worries, I still had riding to do. My horse couldn't be counted on to school himself.

Now it was Tulip's turn to staff the Horsehouse, and my turn to cowgirl up.

***

The sun, having had all day to get its sizzle on, pounded on my bare shoulders and on my hands holding Choc's reins near the saddle horn. A straw hat protected my head, but it, too was heating up.

I'd spent thirty minutes riding in the warm-up arena, open to the sky, and dodging other riders putting their mounts through similar paces. Twenty minutes concentrating on the partnership between me and my horse.

I had made my decision. I was going to go ahead and show, darn it. I had spent fifteen-hundred dollars from my fast-dwindling retirement account, more if you count clothing and tack expenses, plus a whole year of hard work preparing for this.

Yes, my horse's life, and maybe my own, were in danger. Yes I was a nervous wreck. I would lose sleep, and more than a little sanity.

But scratching classes wouldn't save me but a few hundred dollars. And besides, it would not guarantee safety for any of us. Come hell or high water, I was going to cowgirl up, and show. Fear rode the horse beside me. But I would not let it win.

I had to focus. The events started in less than twelve hours. I could not spend every moment speculating on horse killers or people threateners.

Dutch had already tuned up Choc. But nothing would compare to a good, long ride by me. It would strengthen our horse-and-rider bond, to say nothing of my confidence. As the saying goes, wet saddle blankets make good horses.

My show saddle, spotted with silver and carved with rose designs on the caramel colored leather, creaked pleasantly beneath me as I walked, jogged and loped in straight lines and circles. After each maneuver I dropped the reins to Choc's neck, let them flop and encouraged him simply to walk, which made Choc soften and lower his neck.

I breathed dust. I tasted dust. A whole boatload of it. But a good shower would take care of that.

Across the sea of other horses and riders I watched Patsy Ann working her black-and-white horse, Dark Victory, half-brother to Vader. She seemed to be having a good ride, now posting. or rising up and down on alternate beats of the trot.

On the opposite side of the arena, Marietta stood seated on a tall, blood bay with white stockings and a crooked blaze, which reminded me of my Bob, though Bob was shorter and more compact. She seemed to be talking with Royce, the Texas trainer. Probably she was trying out that new horse. It doubtless cost a pretty penny.

"Pardon me," said a young female voice, as a white horse came abreast of my horse's left side and passed me too closely, making Choc pin his ears.

"Oh, hello, Pepper," said the pouty-lipped blonde in pink cap, tan breeches and black tank.

It was Honey Carpenter. She looked hale and healthy as a lady Marine. There was no trace of a cough or short breath, even in all that dust and commotion. No shadow of anger over the stolen saddle, either.

"Hi, Honey," I called after her as she wove through a group of jogging horses. Riding the horses and talking animatedly, probably about our mystery, were

Freddie, Victoria and Lana. Barn buddies forever. In sickness and health. Or death.

Honey subsequently ignored me, and continued posting the high trot several times around the large arena. That young lady didn't look as if she'd suffered an asthma attack and its aftermath the past twenty-four hours.

Maybe her attack had been slight, or a figment of someone's imagination. Maybe her mother, or even Marietta, had used it as an alibi while they attended to other matters. Such as breaking into my Horsehouse in Gold Hill, or contracting out the burglary, say, to someone like Cherie the barrel racer, or otherwise messing with my investigation.

I also thought it odd Honey hadn't mentioned the stolen saddle.

As it turned out, she left the arena before I did and I still had yet to practice my showmanship pattern, leading Choc around in a halter. I rode back to our stalls, found horse feeding and watering in full swing, and decided to practice a bit later. I couldn't deny Choc his evening meal, and it would be cooler after the sun set.

Horses were neighing. Donna dragged a green hose from stall to stall, watering them. Dutch was pushing a dolly stacked with hay flakes, tossing a thick flake of fragrant green alfalfa into each stall.

As I passed Donna, I saw her tan, French-manicured right hand aiming the thick spray from a nozzle through the bars and into a bucket snapped inside a horse's stall.

"Think I'll skip dinner at the Gilded Bull?" I said.

"Don't blame you. I'm bringing Dutch back some 'man meat,' as he calls it. Muscle and bone and all that good stuff. Can bring you some if you like."

"Thanks, but probably will nuke a frozen pizza at the Horsehouse."

"Scary about what almost happened to your horse today."

"It is," I said, unsaddling Choc and putting him in his stall.

"But the show must go on," Donna said. "Pulling out wouldn't change anything. It can also send whomever a message that you won't be intimidated."

"Exactly," I said. "So yes, the show must go on."

Our new Brassbottom buddies, Suzy and Jill, walked up with their sweaty horses. Suzy stopped by Donna, who was outside Choc's stall, and shook back her loose, blond ponytail under a stylishly shredded cadet cap.

"Shouldn't we padlock the stalls?" she asked Donna. "Dutch can't stand watch every minute. Might have to go to the little men's room."

"We can't lock the stalls," Donna said. "If there were a fire or other trouble we might need to get the horses out in a hurry. He had a coffee can. He'll be fine."

The women agreed, and moved on to put away their horses.

Donna started filling Choc's two water buckets as I was closing up his stall.

"Hear from Tommy Lee?" she said, with a sparkle in her eyes.

"We talked," I said, remembering he'd promised to call back about dinner. "He had business to take care of. Wasn't going well, from the sound of it."

"You're quite the man magnet lately,"

"Feast or famine," I shrugged. "Say, I've a quick question related to my investigation. Which, much as someone wants it to stop, shall continue."

"Shoot."

"Any chance the Von Susterns would sue you for negligence in Vader's death?"

"Anyone can sue for anything," Donna said. "As a matter of fact, their attorney did contact us and ask questions along those lines. But our boarding contract should prevent that. Think we're good."

The aisle emptied as people went to dinner or stayed behind to practice for the next day's events. I busied myself tidying Choc's stall, then pulled him out to lead him through our showmanship pattern, a printout of which was stuffed in my pocket.

Seattle trainer Garth Gunderson was in the front part of the arena with a half dozen clients and their horses. His face lit up when he saw me.

"Mind if I play through?" I said.

He nodded his straw hat-and opened his arms in a "be my guest" gesture. I knew he was dying to know the latest in my investigation, but I was keeping my own counsel now. Things were too close to the bone.

Generously, he offered me a few tips to improve my performance. Such as trotting out with energy, stopping smoothly and keeping my toes pointed to Choc when we stood for the judge's inspection. In ten minutes I dripped sweat. It was still hot, and the arena sand was tough going.

"Very good," Garth said. "Use that same calm energy in your class tomorrow."

"I'm just a hair tired," I said. "Too much going on. But I'll try."

"I've given many an Oscar-worthy performance in a show," he fired back. "Showing horses is as much acting as it is leading and riding."

After leading Choc from the arena, I gave him a quick rinse with the hose, blanketed him and tucked him back in his pine-scented stall.

I picked up my purse containing the revolver, my constant buddy now, and headed for the Horsehouse on wheels. Tulip had just nuked the frozen pizza, and we tucked into it like we hadn't eaten for a week.

As I was brushing my teeth, my phone sang out. I saw that it was Sonny.

"Everything all right down there?" he said. "All set for the show tomorrow?"

"Not quite," I said. "Someone tried to inject my horse with something today but Tulip scared them off before they could do it."

Silence at the other end of the line.

"Damn," Sonny said. "Did she get a look at the person?" Sonny said.

"No," I said. "But little Stewie saw an old man or woman wandering around the stalls this afternoon, someone he didn't know and who spoke rudely to him."

"I don't like the sound of that. Is someone guarding the horses tonight?"

"That would be Dutch," I said. "Plus the security man will patrol the stalls."

"Are you done for the night and locked in? Is Tulip with you?"

Yes and yes, Mr. Chief. Don't worry. I'll be fine."

"I don't like this. Your being there, things still happening, me up here. Not good."

"I said I'm fine."

"You still planning to show?"

"Darn right," I said. "Can't let the bastards get you down."

"That's my girl. Just keep carryin', and keep those pretty eyes open."

"Will do, Chief," I said, moving toward my bed. "Now, I need my beauty sleep. Super early wake up." I reached over my bed and pulled back the covers, punching the pillows a few times..

"Got it," he said. "Good luck tomorrow. In all things. Sleep tight. Love you."

I froze in place. What was that? Love you? Love you? That was some kind of first. I don't believe Sonny Chief had ever said anything remotely like that before. Or even hinted at it. I was twitterpated. Tongue tied. What should I say?

"Um, you, too," I stuttered, feeling a need to respond. "Love. You."

It sounded weird on my tongue. Like loose or knocked-out teeth rattling around, minus the pain. Just totally weird.

I didn't remember when I'd last said those words myself, to anyone other than my family. What a way to say and hear some of the most precious words anyone can say or hear. On the phone, late at night, hundreds of miles from home.

But heard them I had, and said them I had. No taking them back.

"Wow," I told myself aloud after Sonny and I hung up. "Double wow."

In a daze I pulled on my sleep shirt, and crawled into bed. I stared toward the dark ceiling for awhile. I began to remember Sonny's and my best times together, times at pow-wows, baseball games, even line dancing, once. He did the dancing under duress, just to please me. But he only did it once.

I was just drifting off when, unbelievably, the phone sang again. I reached over my head to the window shelf for it, knocking down my waterglass.

Great. Now I had to mop up spilled water on my sheets before I could get some badly needed shut eye. I dabbed at the spill with the spare pillow.

As the phone continued its song, I glanced at the caller ID window, expecting to see Sonny's name there again. What else could he possibly have to say?

Instead, the pane read "Tommy Lee Jaymes."

31

"Hey," I said into the phone, where I heard Tommy Lee breathing softly.

I didn't know what I felt. After all, Sonny Chief had just told me he loved me. Or a reasonable facsimile thereof. I was still dizzy with delight.

"Is it too late?" said Tommy Lee. "You're probably tucked in bed, huh?"

"It is a little late," I said, "and I do have an unbelievably early wake up."

"Said I'd call," Tommy Lee said. "Like to keep my word. Sorry I couldn't meet you for dinner. Maybe I can make it up to you tomorrow. How about lunch? And bring your cute blond friend. Redder hair, she could get work as a Sarandon lookalike."

"We'll be pretty tied up showing."

"Y'all got a boyfriend or something? Guess I should have asked."

"Yes and yes," I said, stifling a yawn. Hopefully the conversation would end soon. I was running on fumes now, and precious little of those.

"Drop by after I wrap up the Von Sustern deal."

My eyes flashed open at that. While Tommy Lee was talking I had been lying on my back and testing my eyelids for leaks.

The Von Susterns. Buying another expensive toy. And, a red Lambo, at that. Like one my daughter had turned up connected to them in a questionably legal way, in her Web search days ago. Was it the same one?

"Tell you what," I said, propping up on one elbow, now fully awake. "My class should be over by eleven. We can do coffee then."

"Great, Reba. Y'all sleep tight now. And good luck tomorrow."

His calling me Reba was getting on my nerves. But I might put up with it enough to learn more about him and the Von Susterns.

I hung up and tried to dial down my mind.

"Everything OK up there?" called Tulip from her bed.

"TLJ is delivering the car to the Von Susterns, and wants us to have coffee with him tomorrow."

"Cool. Anything else?"

"Sonny told me he loves me."

Silence. Then, "About time. That'll give you sweet dreams."

"Hopefully."

But I knew that wouldn't happen. Likely I faced a tortured night, worrying about the show, but also about my investigation and the hornet's nest it was poking.

As I began to drift down through the layers of consciousness, first Sonny's words, then Tommy Lee's, kept going through my frazzled brain. What was this TLJ's game? Were the Von Susterns mere clients, or something more? If he dealt in vehicles, did he have some connection to that black Jeep seen outside the Brassbottom fence the night Vader was killed, and the one mere blocks from my store the night of the burglary?

Then there was the fact I was wide-awake and afraid. Not only for my dear horse but also for my life.

Would whoever was threatening me, dare to break in here and try to kill me, and Tulip, too?

I left my bed and stumbled down to triplecheck the door lock. For more security, I wedged both the desk chair and the steel receipts and orders trunk against the door.

Somebody, namely I, better get to the bottom of this ongoing horror, and fast.

32

The tiny Dollar Store alarm clock rattled Reveille at four-forty-five. I stumbled out of sweat-wet sheets. Nightmare remnants hung like cobwebs in my brain. Dream images of caped, needle-wielding weirdos faded reluctantly.

But I'd slept better than I thought. I remembered and savored Sonny's cellphone declaration of love. I wondered if I would hear those words again.

For now I was safe. It would soon be daylight with plenty of people around. Scary scenarios surely would run in the background. But I had to keep them there while I hit the ground running. I had thousands of hours and dollars invested in a horse show that started in three hours, and tons of chores to do before it.

It didn't take long to wash, slap on my makeup and slide into a pair of lightweight sweats over lacy show underwear. I wolfed down a raisin bagel with cream cheese, but took time to savor my hot French roast as I watched CNN on a wall-mount flatscreen in the dining area. Tulip and I dodged each other in the bathroom and kitchenette. Then it was off to the stalls to prepare our horses.

Although dark, the atmosphere was bright with overhead lights. The sound of clopping hooves and barking dogs ran down the aisles. People bustled here and there watering, feeding and grooming horses.

I went through the pre-show routine by rote, lost in thought. I unbraided Choc's tail, longed him, and began the detailed grooming process.

Partway through, Harley Schwartz stopped by.

"Sleep okay?" he said.

"So so," I said, grimacing.

"Just wanted to tell you the show vet sent the syringe out for analysis," he said. "Her guess is some kind of ultra sedative, enough to disable or kill."

I nodded.

"Well, hope you have a good show," he said. "I'll continue swinging by the area every few hours, as I did last night."

"Sure appreciate it," I said. Then my foggy brain remembered something. "Hey, wait. You said you once worked with Marietta Von Sustern at your dealership?"

"Yes?" He folded his arms over his chest and looked puzzled.

"Well, what was your association? What kind of a person was she? I ask because I know she once had a car leasing business that went belly up."

He scowled.

"Funny you ask. She and I weren't close. But as a matter of fact it was my getting tangled in that operation of hers that drove me out of the car business, and left her near bankrupt. If you can believe that, with her money. She had quite the gambling problem, you know, never quite caught up to her debts, always looking for the next score."

My breath caught in my throat. I felt a jolt of recognition. Of course. Marietta's gambling problem. I had heard about it several times the past few days, from different sources, and seen her attempts to maintain a moneyed image by shopping for another expensive horse as well as a certain Italian sports car, and everything was starting to make sense. She surely had killed Vader to collect insurance money, arranged for the stealing of Patsy Ann's tack to turn another profit, and who knew what else was afoot?

"Harley," I said, "I did hear she had a gambling issue. So sad." But I said no more, and returned to prepping my horse. My mind wasn't fully in it. But I kept on anyway. I just had to find a way to prove my new and certain theories.

While the clear lacquer on Choc's hooves dried, I braided ties at the top of a thick false horsehair tail into braids in his own tail, and admired the lush elegance the extension gave him.

Several Brassbottom buddies shared the dressing room with Tulip and me before our first event, Showmanship. I ducked elbows and feet as I stripped out of my work clothes and into my black pantsuit with a crisp white blouse and white felt hat.

I studied myself in the cheap vertical mirror hung from a hook on one wall.

Lookin' good, I thought. *Uh-oh, forgot the earrings.* I scrabbled through my show box and found the plastic container holding assorted earrings. Picking out a cultured pearl pair with crystals, I put them on, and then touched up my makeup.

I almost looked like a movie star. Or a famous redheaded country singer.

"Damn!" I heard Suzy shout as I stepped into the aisle and went to get Choc. I looked over to see she had overturned a jar of hoof black polish, which splashed onto the toe of one of her boots and created a black spot on her bay horse's white stocking.

As I led Choc toward the main indoor arena, where all the other masters amateurs were heading with their shiny horses, I came alongside Freddie. He was leading his new leased horse, Midnight Oasis, a dappled dark gray Quarter Horse with white socks.

"Hey," I said. "Lookin' sharp, Mr. Fred."

"You too, Miss Pepper." He coiled and recoiled his brown leather lead shank as we walked. Nervous habit, or something else?

"How's it going with your new friend, what's his name, Carlos?" I said.

"Carlos," Freddie said. "He's a fox, for sure. Kind of a slick one, though."

"What do you mean?" I said.

"White lies," Freddie said. "Let me think he was single, then I find out he has a little hottie at his own barn."

"That's a shame," I said. I was dying to share my suspicions about Marietta, but I didn't really have the time. Besides, there were ears all around. I felt my blood pressure rise steeply.

Now the speakers crackled with the announced numbers of the last three of fifteen entrants in the event before ours. Freddie and I led our horses around, starting, stopping and circling them to keep them alert and sharp. The present class winners now were lining up head to tail in the arena for awards. Then the announcer was calling our class. I was first to go. I took a deep breath.

Despite my anxiety at going first in a class, I pasted a big smile on my face, lifted my chins and held my body erect, a skill I had taken countless years and tears to perfect. I stepped in cadence with my horse's strides through the gate into the brightly lit arena.

Small groups of onlookers sat on bleachers rising above the arena walls. A toddler shrieked. A few doves courted and flapped in the rafters.

Harrowed Zen-garden sand stretched ahead for what seemed miles. Five judges in navy blazers and tan slacks and western hats sat in folding chairs beside clipboard-holding stewards on the left side of the arena. A sixth judge, a short woman with a steward behind her, stood about thirty feet in front of them.

I clucked to Choc and led him to the starting cone. Ten other competitors with horses followed me and lined up to my right.

Game on!

When the front judge nodded, I walked forward with my arms positioned as if carrying a tray, with Choc's nose in front of my hands. Two horse lengths beyond the next cone, I turned around and clucked, making Choc back up so his hips were on a straight line to the judge forty feet away.

I made kissing sounds and walked Choc in a clockwise three-quarter turn. Then we jogged to a halt eight feet from the judge. I brought my feet smartly together, squared up Choc's feet and looked over my left shoulder at the judge.

"How are you today?" she said with a nod. All business, no smile.

"Very well, thank you," I said. All business, slight smile, heart racing.

The judge walked around Choc to inspect him. My job was to keep Choc square and looking ahead as I passed in front of his face, staying clear of the judge's sight line. It was like showing off a horse as best I could to a prospective buyer. Hence the class title, "Showmanship."

When the judge stopped behind me, I nodded at her, and then backed a few steps while pulling Choc toward me in a quarter-turn. Then I trotted him in a small, counter clockwise arc away from the judge and toward the far wall.

As I stood there, still showing off my horse while watching the other contestants, I breathed a sigh of relief. My back began to ache with the artificially erect pose I had to maintain. I subtly shifted my weight. A few times I scanned the bleachers, where more people had settled with their maple bars and coffee cups, provided free at a hospitality table near the show office.

I was surprised and a bit shocked to see Marietta Von Sustern. She stood near the bottom bleachers above the arena's open end. I was surprised not only to see her, as she usually took little interest in the showmanship, but also to see who stood near her.

Tommy Lee Jaymes. So he had come after all. Had he delivered that red Lambo to her, or for her? They stood five or six feet apart and weren't talking.

I snapped back to the business at hand. I couldn't let distractions and speculation about outside events spoil what I considered a near flawless performance inside the ring. My head had to stay in the game until awards were announced. Even in this lineup I had to stay militarily straight and watchful of both judge and horse, if I wanted to stay alive.

In the end it all paid off. My heart filled with pride as four judges placed Choc and me first. I was over the top with joy as the other two judges placed us second. Approaching the gate to take the champion-buckle box from a grinning young girl with braces, I saw Donna just outside. She beamed with happiness.

"Good job," she said, patting my shoulder as I led Choc by. "Very good job."

Other spectators congratulated me. I patted Choc. I had my glow on. I had done well. And I would qualify for the World show. That was what it was all about.

The win, yes. But more important, the payoff and recognition for hard work and steely thought control. During the precious few minutes of a class, keeping a positive attitude and your focus in the moment, made all the difference.

Leading Choc to the stall I glanced down Royce and Rogers' aisle. There Honey Carpenter, in tan breeches with black hunt boots, cadet cap and tank top, stepped off a mounting block onto her near-white roan gelding. He was tall, nearly seventeen hands.

"Hi, Honey," I said, halting Choc down the aisle from the willowy teen. "How are you feeling?"

She gathered her reins in black-gloved hands, and swung into the flat saddle.

"K," she said, giving me a curious look. "Why?"

"Your mom said you had to go to the ER Sunday with an asthma attack. I've been meaning to ask about that."

"It wasn't that bad," she said. "My mom can be a drama queen." She reined her horse around to ride off.

"Wait," I said. "I'm sorry about your saddle and bridle. We'll either get it back, or you'll be well compensated."

"I hope so," she said with her back to me.

I'd bent over backward trying to be nice. I, myself, was becoming annoyed. Sweet sixteen didn't apply to all girls that age, apparently. Then I recalled Chili's growing pains, and had to admit even well-bred chicks can at times bloody a keeper's hand.

"Well, good luck in the English," I said. "Oh, by the way, I know you're close to Marietta. Is she buying that horse of Royce and Rogers' she was trying yesterday?"

"Who knows?" Honey said, fiddling with her reins. "Maybe. She's been looking at it long enough."

"How long is that?" I said.

"Maybe a month," she said.

"Sometimes it takes that long," I said. "You have to be sure the horse is right, with good ones priced so high nowadays."

I led Choc back to his stall to eat, drink and pee. Standard procedure after a class or workout. When the next class rolls around, a horse shouldn't fret about necessities.

While putting away my show clothes in our dressing stall, avoiding other buddies doing the same, I thought about Honey's words. She'd pretty much made light of her so-called asthma attack the other day, making me wonder again if it was a story Patsy Ann had fabricated to cover for being elsewhere. I still had to look at all possibilities.

Then I reflected on Marietta's looking at the new horse, for what Honey said was "Maybe a month." Was she looking at it before Vader had been killed? If so, why? You didn't get more show-perfect than Vader.

Of course, I reasoned, many riders always are on the lookout for the even more perfect horse, and try other horses out without a hope of buying.

Meanwhile, expecting to see Tommy Lee Jaymes any minute for our coffee date, if you could call it that, I concentrated on my coiffure and makeup. They were pretty decent except for a little flat "hat hair" up top, and the red line the hat left across my forehead. I fluffed up my crown, and combed wispy bangs above my eyebrows.

"Knock, knock," came a familiar male voice.

I turned to see Tommy Lee's deeply dimpled face peering into the dressing stall. I certainly was glad I'd already dressed. But modesty wasn't really possible at a horse show, where dressing stall doors either stood open to the world all the time, or were veiled by carelessly draped curtains.

"Hey," I said. "You made it."

"Hey, congratulations on your win, Reba. You looked great out there."

"Thanks," I said. "Did you deliver the Lambo?"

"Having it detailed in town," he said with a grin. "Road trip took a toll."

"Saw you with Marietta in the bleachers," I said. "Her husband here?"

"Will be later," he said.

"So are they buying the Lambo?" I said as casually as possible.

"Trying to git 'er done," he said. "Price still the issue."

"So how much does a Lambo bring these days?"

"Real ones, half a mill up to ten or twelve mill," he said, folding his arms and leaning against the door frame. "Depends if it's new or resale. Or a replica."

"A replica?" I said, for the first time noticing his intensely dark eyes resembled those of a snake. A little too closely set, and more than a shade cold.

"Another form of the lookalike game," he said. "That's what this one here is. We provide fabulous fakes for special occasions. Big demand. Like for a golf resort opening in Southern Oregon wine country last weekend. I not only provide lookalike actors, but also lookalike cars a buddy of mine puts together. That fake Lambo body sports a Chevrolet engine under the hood."

"What?" I said. "That's amazing." I now knew it was not this Lambo that landed Von Sustern in court years ago, as per Chili's research. "So, what's a replica cost?"

"Fifty, sixty K, whatever the market will bear," said TLJ, uncrossing his arms and looking back out the doorway. "Say, where's your friend?"

I found it fascinating, the work this guy was into. But could there be anything else fake about him? Was it possible that TLJ may be with his Von Sustern connection had hired out for other jobs, such as staging a warning tableau or injecting a horse? He might even have given Vader that fatal dose. He had mentioned he was in Southern Oregon the past weekend.

And there was Tommy Lee himself, bold as brass, courting me to the Nth degree while possibly setting me up for some more sinister business ordered by his employer.

Tommy Lee was an actor, after all. Paid to pretend to be someone he was not. Probably paid extremely well. Was I part of his job, too?

33

"Pepper!" shrieked Tulip from a corner table in the horse show café that smelled of brewing coffee and sizzling oil. Tommy Lee and I had just burst through the door of the noisy, crowded room.

I nodded, held up a "one-minute" finger, and led Tommy Lee to the counter. I ordered a taco salad, extra salsa, peppers and cheese. Just the ticket for a stomach that jumped around now like taters in the fryer. But somehow the Tec-Mex dish appealed. Maybe I liked dangerous living. I was here with the questionable Tommy Lee, right?

Tommy Lee ordered a bacon cheeseburger with fries.

We poured ourselves drinks at the serve-yourself machine. Then we sat at Tulip's white plastic table. Before her lay a platter with the remains of biscuits and gravy, plus a scatter of napkins suggesting an explosion in an origami factory.

"What?" said Tulip, seeing me stare at the napkins. She swept them into her arms, and ran them over to a trash can. "Little accident," she said, reseating herself. "It'll be all right. Hey, Tommy Lee. Long time no see." She smiled extra big.

He flashed a quick, pure Tommy Lee smile.

"Miss Tulip," he said.

"Hey Pep, congrats on your showmanship placing," Tulip said.

"Thanks. "I thought you had a good run, too. Until you only walked your horse into our lineup along the far wall, when you were supposed to trot."

"Rub it in," she said. "Pilot error. As usual."

They called our names at the pickup counter. TLJ and I got our food, and dove in. At least I dove, eating like a famished ranch hand. Tommy Lee took his time, wiping his mouth with his napkin.

"I usually eat like a bird," I said.

"Yeah," Tulip said. "A California condor." She winked at Tommy Lee.

I gave her a look that said, "Don't push it, Sister."

"Tommy Lee works for Richard Von Sustern," I said casually, watching Tulip for a reaction. "Tell her about it, TLJ. Tell me more, too."

"Ferrying cars like that red Lambo we saw to the new owners?"

That was the impression TLJ had given up the road. Or at least the one we had come up with ourselves, in our highly active imaginations.

"Well, not exactly," said Tommy Lee. "We just did this one job he arranged for us in Oregon. Terms sucked. But we're actors. Always can use the work."

"Got it," I said. "So just the one job?"

"Yeah," he said. "But Mr. V's wife wants to buy this replica – yes, Miss Tulip, it's a fabulous fake, kinda like me. Offering a cut-rate fleet price for it and two other cars from our fabricator friend in Seattle. He's been leasing them to us for our work. She claims if she owns them we'll have more jobs at higher pay, with the Von Sustern connections. She's really trying to undercut us."

"Really," Tulip said, giving me a knowing nod.

"Pretty interesting," I said, keeping my own counsel with the present company in the crowded cafe.

I'd fill her in later on my suspicions. But at least for now, it sounded as if our Tommy Lee might not have been involved in certain disturbing crimes.

"We've been fighting for better terms," Tommy Lee was saying, "We think maybe our friend should just ditch the deal. We'd lose control of what jobs we take, acting and driving fees, all of it. But now she's got her husband coming in today, and he can be pretty persuasive, from what I hear."

Tulip gave Tommy Lee an appraising look. I began to think, with our reservations about him somewhat lessened, that she was developing a crush.

"So what else do you know about the Von Susterns?" Tulip said. My partner in crime solving, bless her heart.

He looked at his hands lying aside his now-empty burger basket. He picked up a napkin and wiped his mouth and fingers. Then he sighed, and smoothed out the napkin.

"Don't know a lot about the Von Susterns," he said. "Mr. V's successful in a buncha ventures, but they have some serious debt. Mrs. V does like the dice."

"Yes," I said. "Any idea how much they, or she, owes?"

"Don't know, don't care," he said. "Couple hundred K, maybe more. But I hear they all can afford it."

"Yet they're out shopping for cars and horses," I said. "Do you think your fabricator friend will cave to Mr. and Mrs. V?"

"As I say, we're fighting it. Or at least the terms. Seems Mr. V. and the fabricator, our friend, once had shady car deals that landed them in court. Became enemies. Apparently are on speaking terms again."

"Altered VIN," I said.

He looked up sharply.

"So you know about that. Figures."

"I used to be a reporter."

"Still are," Tulip said, nodding.

I wanted to squeeze more information from Tommy Lee. But the show café was starting to thin out. I looked at my watch. Shoot! Nearly one. Had to get back into this horse show. Not to mention opening the Horsehouse tack trailer. People would think we'd died. We'd left a note on the door saying we'd re-open that afternoon. But we couldn't afford to lose a cent of business.

"Well, good luck with your deals, Tommy Lee," I said, pushing back my chair and rising. "Gotta get back. Thanks for lunch."

"Anytime, Reba," he grinned. He pulled Tulip's chair for her. She glanced up, winked, and stood up, fluffing her hair with one hand.

When had my best buddy become a winker?

"Nice to see you all again," she said to Tommy Lee.

It sounded as if she really meant it, and was angling for more. Was she serious?

He drew himself up, took a breath, and dimpled extravagantly.

"Like to meet later, discuss lookalike gigs?" he said to her. "Maybe over dinner?"

"Um," she hedged, giving me the eye. She'd noticed I'd noticed.

"That's very flattering, Tommy Lee. But things get busy in a hurry at a show."

"OK," he said. "Change your mind, let me know." His turn to wink.

"Tulip," I said, as we left the café and Tommy Lee. "Are you out of your mind?"

"Cut a girl some slack," she said. "Can't blame me at least for thinking about it."

***

The heat had ratcheted into the nineties by the time we reached our stall row. We checked our horses' stalls and their water buckets, and greeted a few buddies preparing themselves or their horses for the next events.

Tulip and I had no events that afternoon. It was all English. Not our thing. Boots too tight, ditto the breeches, and we didn't get to wear bling. Strictly classic hunt attire.

Approaching the Horsehouse trailer, I saw several notes flutter from magnets on the metal side of the whiteboard near the door. My heart rate speeding up, I peered at each one. Tulip was opening the Horsehouse door, which this time had been well locked.

"Anything interesting?" she said as we climbed inside.

"Lana needs a bottle of fly-spray," I said, "and Little Stewie's mom wants to buy him some new spur straps. One of his tore off." I was studying the handwriting.

"I can take all that that stuff over to them," Tulip said. "Just take a jiff."

"Hey, wait a minute!" I said. "Here's one from Marietta. At least I think it is."

"Really?" said Tulip, leaning over my shoulder. "Oh yeah, 'MVS'."

"Wants some tummy-smoothing black show leggings she saw here, the kind with belt loops and shiny fabric. Check out the handwriting."

Tulip peered more closely. Her eyebrows shot up. Then she drew back.

"Whoa!" she said. "Same blocky handwriting as on our warning sign, or I turn in my unofficial private eye license."

"Wish we had that sign right now." My mind raced with the possibilities. "Because I think she's our horse killer."

"Seriously?"

"She, or maybe, remotely, Patsy Ann," I said. "Harley Schwartz told me of a car leasing operation he had with her that went south, and also mentioned her gambling debts, which a few people have brought up. She needs the money from her horse insurance, could have arranged for the tack stealing, all of it."

"But she came to the show after we arrived. In her RV with Patsy Ann driving."

"Maybe yes, maybe no. She knew about when we'd arrive and could have come over and set it up well in advance. If she desperately needed money, and her husband threatened divorce, and the killing for insurance money would erase her debt and put down payments on a car business as well as a great new horse, well, why not?"

"How would she be behind our store burglary," Tulip said.

"Maybe she knew Cherie the barrel racer, our suspect, and had her do the job."

"Lotta maybes," said Tulip.

"Or maybe it really was Marietta who did that crime as well, snagging herself another fifteen, twenty grand from resale. How do we know she was in Reno when she said she was?"

"Wow," said Tulip. "No wonder you were a star reporter." Tulip studied her painted nails for a moment. Then she slowly raised her head to look at me. She nodded.

"I think you just hit a home run."

***

A steady stream of customers flowed through the Horsehouse that hot afternoon. We rang up something like a thousand dollars in sales. Plenty of silk shirt sales.

About three I managed to take an hour off to work my horse on trail patterns and over a few obstacles, such as a low bridge and poles on the ground. It was hot, sweaty, dusty work. But I felt Choc and I had fine tuned our skills enough to knock 'em dead in the next day's trail class. Or at least place somewhere in the Top Five.

I then allowed Tulip a couple hours for horse work and cleaning. I kept my revolver conveniently under the counter, for I felt we were real close to solving our crimes. Even worse, I felt the suspected perpetrator knew it. That made her even more dangerous.

Carlos, Freddie's new friend, or possibly ex-friend, dropped in for a few minutes after Tulip had left with one of his employers' credit cards. Royce had bought all three shirts.

"Absolutely loves them," said Carlos, that day in a lavender, not purple, tee shirt and tight jeans. "Raved and raved."

I ran his employer's card and wrote out a receipt for Carlos to sign.

He jotted a quick signature, touched his hat, and left.

Then it was quiet again.

I glanced at the store copy of the transaction. But I was past studying his writing. I didn't have the parking sign-warning note to compare it with anymore, and had little else to go on either for him or his employers as persons of interest.

I supposed Carlos might have taken the sign, or even Freddie, while under Carlos' spell. But that seemed remote now. I wasn't feeling it.

It seemed more and more likely to me that Patsy Ann or Marietta had taken the sign and note. Both women were present when Tulip had stashed this evidence under the Horsehouse trailer counter. Both had reason to kill a valuable, highly competitive show horse, and therefore reason to threaten me, as unofficial lead investigator.

I felt a growing, gut-gnawing urgency to find the warning sign and other evidence. I was more and more certain they'd help me crack the case.

I sat staring at nothing down the long narrow trailer. The back ramp was up and locked. Nothing but a black wall. A heavy feeling rose up from my feet and filled me with dread.

Tonight.

I knew it would be tonight.

34

Feeding time that day came late, well after six o'clock. Dutch and Donna had been coaching Suzy and Jill, as well as Little Stewie, in the English classes, and the latter had taken forever. Lately these classes in the little flat saddles had become more popular, with everyone trying their hand, as it were. After all, a person could ride two-handed, unlike in most one-handed Western classes, and therefore potentially control one's horse to the max. One also got to go faster than in Western, in which the gentle rocking-chair lope had morphed into an even slower, more collected version of that three-beat-gait.

Tulip returned and we buttoned up the Horsehouse about six, just in time to watch Freddie in his Hunter Hack class. Looking terribly dashing and dapper in his black cap and hunt coat, tan breeches and tall black boots, he trotted and cantered his new leased horse around the arena. He then took it over a few three-foot jumps without ticking a pole. Came as no surprise that he placed first. There were only two horses in the event. So what? Years from now no one would know. All they'd see was a champion buckle.

The arena was mostly empty of onlookers, except for a few family members of competitors. The day's show was drawing to a close. Soon everyone would be hosing down horses, changing into civvies and giving stalls a final muck before heading for dinners or beddy-bye. Exhaustion, but the nervous kind, was creeping into my bones.

It was after eight. Twilight was settling over the scene. A satisfied buzz animated the show grounds. People and horses seen outside of stall rows and trailers dwindled down to those you could count on both hands.

I closed the door to our trailer. Tulip already was on the pull-out couch, watching some nonsensical sit-com on TV. She gave me a tired wave.

"Saw Marietta still in the ring with Royce, trying out that new horse again," she said. "That woman is obsessed. And supposedly she can't afford it."

"I know," I said. "I just can't stand it. She's getting away with murder. Equicide, anyway. I'm sure of it. And if I'm not careful, it could be a homicide."

"I know," Tulip said. "I feel none too safe myself. Sleeping down the stairs from you here. Wish I had a weapon, too."

"You do," I said, heading for the mini-fridge under the kitchenette counter. I hadn't realized how hungry I'd become, until now. Anxiety made me ravenous.

"I do?"

"Isn't that softball bat still under the couch where you left it after we took the trailer to an out of town game last year?"

Tulip lifted up the bench seat, went inverted, rummaged around, and came up with the double-walled steel bat. She waved it overhead like a trophy.

I pulled a box of frozen strawberries and a carton of yogurt from the mini-fridge, ice cubes from the freezer tray, and a glass blender out from under the counter. I began to crush myself a super smoothie, with an egg thrown in for good measure. A sprinkle of granola completed my late dinner.

It had been a good eight hours since our lunch with Tommy Lee. By the way, where was he? He said he'd be back tonight to deliver the Lambo to Marietta.

Wait. Tulip had said she just saw Marietta. Riding in the arena. Events were over for the day. Everybody else pretty much turned in for the night. That gave me an idea.

I slurped down my smoothie. Then I pulled on my baseball cap. I got up, slid my revolver under my back waistband, and went to the door. I looked back at her.

"Be gone for a bit," I said. "Need to take care of something. Check in on Choc, see if Dutch is still playing night watchman."

"Okay," Tulip said, yawning. "But just be careful. Wait. I'll go with you."

"Someone should stay in the trailer," I said. "And keep the locks locked. Bat at the ready. I think this thing's about to come to a head."

I opened the door and looked out. Almost dark. As I stepped into the parking lot, and swept my gaze around the pavement and trailers splashed greenish white from the overhead utility lights, I heard that small dog yipping again. The desperate, ultra-annoying sound appeared to be coming from Marietta's motor home across the lot. I looked across. A strange new motor home sat next to it. Patsy Ann's.

As I walked forward—the only person in the parking lot—I noticed a small, dark, blockier car partially obscured by Marietta's motor home. Had that been there before? I couldn't be sure. I'd never been at the right angle, or close enough, to have seen it.

My heart rattled in my ribcage. My cheeks felt hot. Fear began to creep through me. My hands became clammy and cold, as like last night, a slight fog drifted.

I was sure that dark car by the motor home was a fancified Jeep, or Range Rover. A dark blocky SUV. Like the one seen at the Brassbottom neighbors', and near our store the night of the burglary.

Was I conjuring demons? Maybe Marietta or Patsy Ann had company—possibly a husband or two. Or maybe the new vehicle simply belonged to unrelated late comers.

My brain was in overdrive now, besotted with long days and that stupid smoothie, to which I had added a few drops of marshmallow vodka.

Although each motor home had a porch light, interior lights in both vehicles were out. Marietta's, however, showed a faint glow in one window. Possibly a night light meant to calm the yipping dog.

Hello? That plan wasn't working. The dog was still yipping.

The noise now had reached a hysterical pitch. It cut right through me. Marietta must still be out with Royce and that new horse she was trying. And her husband must not be present, or he would have quieted the pooch.

If Patsy Ann and Honey were in the newly arrived RV, delivered by whomever, surely they would have come over and tried to stop the yipping or somehow made their presence known. It was that loud and annoying, a high-pitched fugue in hysteria.

Yet there were no shadows or faces at the windows, no people on front steps, no other signs of life.

At that moment, as I stood in the eerily lit parking lot with the dog still carrying on, a thought shot into my brain with the brilliance of a home-run ball hit into the sun.

Not one of these women, nor their trainers, or whatever, looked or sounded as if they had a care in the world, whether dead horses, gambling reverses, asthma attacks or stolen tack. Not one had given me a clear reason to take the obvious next step.

Yet I did.

35

The dog's yips turned to shrieks as I tried the door to Marietta's RV. Something crashed to the floor inside. That silenced the dog. Then it began barking again.

I fiddled with the door handle. Amazingly, I found it unlocked, maybe because the Rottweiler inside was supposed to warn off intruders. A Rottweiler, I soon saw, whose parents must have been the foster kind, but whose birth parents hailed from Yorkshire, complete with pink topknot bow.

Holding the door open a few inches to protect me from the killer fluffy, I pulled the remnants of a breakfast bagel from my jeans pocket. Those pockets had come in handy for any number of uses lately.

I tossed the pup the treat, which he gobbled. Then I closed the door, locked it behind me, and began my search. I would first look for the parking sign and warning note. Marietta and Patsy Ann had seen Tulip stash them beneath the counter as the women entered our shop that morning.

After that, I didn't know what else I hoped to find. I only knew I had to look. And fast. Who knew when anyone would return. It could be in an hour, or in the next minute.

First I did a walk-through of the airy double slide-out main salon, as well as the two baths, kitchen and bedrooms. The air was redolent of lemon air freshener and the surfaces tricked out in dark wood, terrazzo and leather. I noted all the rooms, even the two bathrooms, had wall-mount flat screen TVs. Nice.

The little dog tailed quietly after me. He looked up expectantly for more treats.

My pulse throbbed in my throat with an odd combination of fear and exhilaration. I hoped this clandestine search would yield the answers I sought. I also hoped I could complete it without interruption, particularly the deadly kind.

After the walk-through, I searched the contents of trashcans. I also looked inside the stove and fridge that were so clean they appeared never to have been used.

Coming up empty in the obvious places to toss or hide things, I thought, what else could I possibly expect? That what I sought would be placed in plain sight? Maybe I was like that cute annoying Yorkie at my heels, sniffing up the wrong tree.

However, since I'd already broken and entered – well, not literally broken, but certainly entered, I had to make the search thorough and faster, if possible. I'd already been in the motor home six or eight minutes. Who knew when Marietta, possibly her husband, too, would return? If they caught me here there would be the Devil to pay.

My mouth felt dry from stress and thirst. I ran water from the kitchen faucet, bent over and gulped it down. The Smith & Wesson popped from my back waistband and clattered across the floor.

Dang! I should have stashed it more carefully. I stooped to pick it up, and then inserted it up to the handle between my panty and jeans waistband, just ahead of my right hipbone.

I also checked my cell phone in the opposite back pocket to make sure it was secure.

While near the door, I spread open the blind slats with my fingers and peered out. So far the coast was clear. Someone was walking from the Grandeen trailer to our stall row. It was only Donna. Probably making sure Dutch was settled in.

I went back to my search. Going faster now, my pulse pounding in my ears, I opened drawers and cabinets in every room. Even those above the faux-fur covered king bed in the master bedroom.

I'd already canvassed Marietta's intricately carved pecan nightstand, or what I guessed was her nightstand, on the right side of bed. The small, curleycued antique held a pharmacopeia of pills and potions.

My eye was drawn to one black and one white 100X beaver felt cowboy hats on the dresser. Thousand dollar hats. At least.

At first I'd merely swept my gaze over them. Now I saw that the black one sat on its square shaped brim, while the white topper sat low on … a short-necked antique wooden mannequin head.

Breathing shallowly, I walked over to pick up the black hat. Underneath I could see a clean round spot on the pecan dresser with a film of dust all around. That hat once sat on a wig or hat stand like the black one.

The enormity of my discovery made me a little giddy. So it was Marietta. Or could be. Though it was still possible Patsy Ann or someone else took the head for the warning setup last night in the parking lot.

I had to wonder, though. Was it possible one of these women, or someone close to them such as Richard Von Sustern, had planted clues, such as the wig stand, the salon-cape fragment on the Brassbottom neighbor's fence even the earring fragment from Vader's stall, to suggest that Freddie Uffenpinscher had killed Vader?

I didn't believe Freddie had killed Vader. He certainly had motive and opportunity to do that, as well as to steal Patsy Ann's saddle and bridle. He did need extra money to swing that salon purchase that suddenly became possible. He knew where we hid the key.

My head began to throb. It just couldn't be our fine, funny, flaming Freddie.

I turned to the bedroom's larger closet to continue my search. I needed more. If Marietta, Patsy Ann, or even an accomplice had set out the mannequin head, parking cones and signs, the guilty one must have come early to do so, perhaps in another vehicle. Such as the Jeep or Range Rover outside. Then made an official and very public entrance for all to see today in this rolling Xanadu.

The Yorkshire terrier who'd been quiet at my feet through this search suddenly barked. He leaped in the air and did a one-eighty, claws furiously clicking, bound for the front door. There he sat on his haunches. He began scratching at the door.

I hadn't a moment to lose. The dog's mistress, and possibly her husband, were undoubtedly on their way to, if not directly outside of, this motor home.

Luckily I had noticed there was another door, smaller than the front, next to the white leather sofa in a small den adjoining the main salon. I'd have to try to use that for my getaway. If there was to be a getaway.

I tore through the closet, flinging aside clothes and boots. Three Louis Vuitton suitcases with "MVS" embroidered on each leather handle patch, were stacked behind a full length leopard coat. I threw the cases open.

The smallest case held nothing. Neither did the second.

But in the mesh lingerie compartment of the third was a folded black nylon cape which, as I pulled it out and held it up, read, "Manes 'N Tales Salon." It had a tiny rip on the right chest, a hole the size of a thumbnail. Out from its folds tumbled a gold hoop earring missing its ear hook. Underneath lay the crumpled parking-lot sign and note.

Just then my cell phone rang. The Yorkie whined louder. On my knees, in a panic, I struggled up and walked toward the den door as I tore the phone from my waistband.

"Where are you?" said Tulip. "There's someone here --"

I tucked the earring in a pocket, wadded the cape and dashed into the den.

"Marietta's RV," I gasped. I stuffed the phone back in my waistband. As I did so, I caught my bum toe on a desk corner. Pain scalded the toe and ran fast up my leg. I cursed. Loudly. But I reached the door. I was almost outside.

That's when I heard the dog stop whining. Someone tried the front door. A few metallic clicks, a muttering outside. Luckily I had locked the door when I'd entered.

Then came sound of a key turning in the lock.

36

The motor home's front door opened before I could escape out the den door.

"Richard?" It was Marietta, calling for her husband. "Why did you lock the door? You knew I ..." She broke off as she greeted her yippy Yorkie.

I tried to be as quiet as I could, turning the handle of the den door. The bolt cleared the latch. I pushed the door open. Humid night air hit me. Almost out.

"Why, Pepper," said a cold voice from behind, before I could step down.

I froze, but did not answer right away, willing myself to think this through. Before I could speak or act, I heard the floor creak as Marietta took a step toward me.

"What brings you here?" she said. Almost a growl.

"I think you know," I said, still not turning, but flashing through what to do next.

That split second of considering my options should have cost me my life. One of Marietta's strong hands took hold of my hair and pulled my head back. The other hand clutched my throat. Sharp nails pressed into my neck.

Marietta yanked me back, forcing me off balance. I swore, and swung my arms in a wild attempt to stay upright as the black salon cape slipped from my hand.

"Ooomph," grunted Marietta, holding tight despite my flailing. With a mighty effort I managed to jerk her off balance, too. Her stout body stumbled backward with mine, but stabilized. She pressed her nails deeper into the left side of my neck, and brought her other hand around to choke me from the right. One of her knees, strong as any man's, jabbed the back of mine. My legs buckled. I felt shooting pains, but wriggled from side to side, managing to stay more or less upright.

There was a pause of no more than a split second. That's when I thought, it's now or never. Don't let her get too deep into this.

At the thought I could lose my life here, in the night, in a luxury RV, at the hands of a woman smaller than me, adrenalin shot through me like a drug from a horse syringe. My cheeks burned. I felt a surge of power.

I raised my right leg and stomped down hard on Marietta's foot. Her boot and her high emotion protected her from feeling too much pain, but the act and the impact distracted her. I felt her grip loosen.

Immediately I raised my hands to my throat. I wrapped them tightly around her fingers and squeezed down with all my might. The effort took my breath away, but I heard a gratifying crackle. A long screech ripped the air as the hands went away.

I coughed violently a few times and my ears rang for one long moment.

Then I spun around to see Marietta doubled over, moaning in pain and cradling her hands protectively in her crotch. As she saw me staring, she narrowed her eyes to pantherine slits, and drew back slightly. Did she now fear me? Had she given up?

While I was feeling relief and pride in my actions, she hit me like a two-hundred pound base runner knocking a catcher off home plate.

I went down hard. My shoulders banged against the metal threshold, sending rays of pain through my neck and back. My eyes rolled, then focused. My head hung out the doorway. I smelled warm asphalt below, and a weird amalgam of horse sweat and gardenia perfume, above.

Marietta's face was purple, and her pupils huge and black. Anger twisted her full, Slavic features. As she held me down by the arms, and jabbed one knee into my gut for good measure, robbing me of breath and sending a dull ache through me, her eyes dropped to my waistband. Her right hand followed.

I blinked as I realized her intention. Time stood still. I felt hollow, and completely powerless as it hit me.

No. Not the Smith & Wesson.

This insane bitch was going to kill me with my own gun. Point blank. No more horses, no more buddies, no more lemon pie for lunch or grilled burgers in the violet night. No dogs licking you awake. No lovers kissing you asleep. No more nothing.

It had come down to this. Nosy ex-reporter Pepper Kane killed for being nosy ex-reporter Pepper Kane. And Marietta would skip because an intruder had attacked her.

She had the gun now. She slowly raised the barrel into position six inches from the space between my eyes. I stared into the skinny black cylinder. This was it.

Come up with something, I thought. *Anything. Now!*

"Hey, Marietta?" I said, quickly, with a cheery confidence that was the farthest thing from what I felt. I looked into her intense dark eyes. The word confidence was not even in my dictionary at the moment. But I tried to project it, just as I did in a big horse show class filled with competitors riding way better horses and out for blood.

I noticed pink returning to the white knuckles of her hand gripping the gun. She was relaxing her hold, if only momentarily. Her eyes showed confusion, a question. She might even have cocked her head like her dog.

The moment was for me to use or lose.

I swallowed to moisten my dust dry mouth.

"Before you ...," I began. "Just tell me why, Marietta. You owe me that."

"Why what?" she said in a monotone, still pointing the gun. Her Yorkie pattered up to us on the floor, sniffed the warm air rolling in the open den door, then licked Marietta's arm. She brushed the dog away, but it came back, and licked her again.

"Why you killed your own horse?"

She took a breath and looked away. When she looked back she had more anger in her eyes, a different seeming anger. She was thinking of something else, perhaps. Something that had been eating her up.

"Shut up, bitch," she said. "Shut effing up." She held the revolver closer to my face. But it trembled slightly.

Another opening. Just a crack, but enough to wriggle through.

"You can kill me if you want, but I have to know. The nosy reporter, as you say. Grant me that last wish."

I heard a clock strike ten in the main salon.

Then the gun barrel dipped. The Yorkie nudged the arm holding the weapon. The gun dipped some more. It still pointed at me, though. I was very aware of that.

"I didn't want to," Marietta spoke in a whisper. "I almost had enough scraped together. But then I lost some more, and Richard found out, threatened a divorce, and worse. As if he didn't have his own problems."

"What did you lose, Marietta?" I prodded, as gently as I could with a gun pointed at my head. "You can tell me. Then I'll be dead, and won't tell anyone."

"Gambling," she muttered. "I kept winning some back, but going deeper in the hole. I thought I could buy the horse for fifty K, insure him for one-fifty, collect some more on Patsy Ann's tack, come real close to paying back what I owed. Then buy the replica cars and have a real sweet deal. I had it all planned out. Freddie all set up to take the rap. Clueless little shit. Or Patsy Ann, for my backup plan. I had that figured out, too."

"I guess you did," I said, remaining at least on the surface, sympathetic. "You could get help for your problem, you know. Might even be a partial defense."

She stared just over my head, as if considering this. She licked her lips. Then she brought the gun barrel back down and forward until it pressed into the hollow above my nose. She inched it slightly higher and increased the pressure.

In an instant, with a heavy thud in my gut, I knew my plan had not worked. I was not going to talk her down. No, I was going to die. No mistake. The cold steel of my own gun would be the last thing I ever felt.

I took what I thought would be my last breath. I made it long and deep. Resigned. Said a prayer for everyone I loved.

Between that breath and prayer, something changed. I couldn't believe what I did next. I sucked back and with a violent thrust I head butted the gun away. I then did a burlesque bump to dislodge her knee. Marietta shouted in surprise as she fell off.

I uncoiled into a kneeling position, ripped the gun from her hand and turned the barrel to face her chest.

She had landed on her elbows and bottom. Her eyes widened as she saw me pointing the gun. Her lips trembled. The Yorkie beside her began to growl.

It was such a high and pitiful sound, like that of an enraged mouse, that I had to smile. I may even have laughed. That laugh went on a little long. Surely one of relief.

It almost masked the sound of heavy footsteps coming through the front door. Then other footsteps. I felt the motor home floor vibrate beneath my feet.

What now? I thought. *Don't tell me I have to face Richard Von Sustern.* Had I escaped a home-base tag only to be called out for missing the plate entirely?

Two familiar shapes loomed in the hall archway. Sonny Chief. And Tulip.

"I was worried," Sonny said, glancing at Marietta, who slowly rose. "Then I heard you laugh. I knew you had everything under control."

37

Sonny stepped into the RV den, Tulip behind him in the hall. He took my non-gun hand and squeezed it warmly. Then he leaned down and laid a light kiss on my cheek.

"Want to tell us what happened?" he said, as if I'd just spent a day at the beach.

"Good God, Gert," said Tulip, eyeing me and Marietta from the doorway. "You OK, Pepper? What all happened?"

"I was just doing a little investigating, on my own," I said, still aiming the revolver.

"You call it investigating, I call it bald-faced snooping," Tulip said. "Knew it when I called. Gonna get you dead, some day. I'm calling 9-1-1." She tapped her phone.

"How'd it go down?" said Sonny, releasing my hand. He looked at me with concern, his brows drawing together. "I've got this. You relax." He took over, aiming the gun at Marietta.

I thought that sweet, that he looked concerned. But then he often looked at me that way. He sometimes had good reason to look at me that way.

"Marietta came in," I said. "We fought. She confessed to killing Vader, making it look like Freddie did it. Scared of her husband, has bad gambling debts, maybe a drug habit. Thought Vader's insurance and the saddle theft were the answer. She'd off me, being an intruder, and no one would be the wiser."

I rubbed the back of my neck, pretty sore from where she'd got me down against the den door threshold. My belly hurt, too, and my fingers.

"You do look a little roughed up," said Sonny, visually giving me a whole body scan. "Bet you gave as good as you got."

I liked hearing him say that. I might have gone up a notch in his opinion, in the capable-woman department.

Or maybe he was just letting me know he'd always thought me capable, and just liked to rattle my cage, as he knew that attitude got to me. Whatever. I was just happy he was there at that moment. Happy about just about everything, in fact.

Marietta came out of the den, at Sonny's suggestion, and sat on the white sofa. She hugged her Yorkie and stared at the floor.

Outside, I saw lights on in nearby trailers and motor homes. A cluster of people stood over by the Grandeen trailer, probably speculating on the commotion.

"Everything all right, Pepper?" called Donna across the parking lot.

"All under control," I said. "Sorry to disturb you. Explain in a bit."

I looked a question at Sonny. He nodded.

"Go on," he said. "I've got this. You need to go be with the buddies."

I did need to be with the buddies after one of the most scarifying encounters of my life. And they needed to hear what I had to say, and see that I was in one piece.

Someone, I think little Stewie, reporter in training, while stargazing out their own motor home window, had seen me enter Marietta's motor home and thought little of it. Little, that is, until Marietta came back and set off banging, yelling and barking.

"Then what happened?" Stewie kept saying, his eyes big as saddle conchos.

During my explanation, with Tulip by my side, I noticed Harley Schwartz striding purposefully toward Marietta's motor home on the other side of the parking lot. Sonny met him at the door, and pointed toward me. A short time later, a sheriff's car arrived, lights silently flashing. Two officers got out. One went into the motor home, and one stayed near the car but kept looking over at me. When the first deputy came out with Marietta and put her into the squad car, the second one walked in my direction.

I was winding down explaining things to my astonished Brassbottom buddies.

"Really?" Victoria kept saying while patting her hair. "I could never do that."

Oh, you could, I thought. *You could if you faced someone like Marietta. Anyone could do what I did. Without thinking twice.*

Dutch rambled up at one point, his eyes red. Probably hadn't had a wink of sleep.

"What a story," he said. "You should write about it. You being the ace reporter."

I had only given these people a Reader's Digest Condensed Version of events of the past days. I hadn't put in my most personal thoughts and feelings. Except for one.

"But weren't you scared?" said Stewie, shaking off his mother's hand on his arm.

"You'd better believe it," I said. "That's how I did what I did."

"Huh?" he said. "I don't get it."

"When you're scared," I said, "you can do things you didn't think you could. As John Wayne said, "Courage is being scared to death but saddling up anyway.""

"Oh," he said. "Just like when you're showing a horse. And then you win."

"Just like that, Stewie," I said. "Just like that."

The buddies said their good nights and good lucks, and left just as the second deputy, followed by Sonny Chief, reached Tulip and me.

The deputy, a buzz-cut Rambo with an impressive swagger and low-slung slacks, pulled himself up importantly. He greeted us, took me aside and asked for my story.

Sonny and Tulip hovered supportively in the background. They eventually had their say-sos, too. Then the deputies, and Marietta, left the show grounds.

Harley Schwartz was coming our way when the low red Lambo rolled up to Marietta's RV. Its high-pitched snarl nearly approximated that of the real deal.

A man with dark hair, likely Tommy Lee, sat in the driver's seat. Two blondes, probably Patsy Ann and Honey, got out of the passenger side. How the three of them had managed to squeeze into that swellegant Italian two-seater I couldn't fathom. Maybe Honey sat on Patsy Ann's lap. A deputy greeted them.

Tommie Lee half-opened the car's door and turned slowly to look over at us. He seemed to be focusing on me, then on Sonny.

"Well, I'll be dipped," whispered Tulip, moving out to get a better look.

"What?" I asked, worried what she might say. I rubbed my arms as if chilled.

"Tommy Lee must have been giving Patsy Ann and Honey a joy ride," Tulip said. "Or taken them to dinner."

Sonny stood by me and stared at the car and driver. A muscle moved in his cheek.

Harley went to talk with the man in the car while the women listened. Patsy Ann was now gesturing, having her two cents' worth. Honey only stood and stared.

"—don't believe it," said Patsy Ann. Some of her words had carried on a sudden breeze that came up. Apparently Harley was bringing her up to date on her gal friend.

Harley gestured over at us once or twice. Patsy Ann gave a tentative wave, then took her daughter by the arm. They went into the new motor home by Marietta's. Patsy Ann opened the door and let Honey in.

"So that was Patsy Ann's RV," I said. "Maybe her husband drove, or Von Sustern."

"The guy in the Lambo?" said Sonny, a little too casually.

"Oh," Tulip said, giving me a let-me-handle it look. "That's the cute lookalike actor I met at a café in Red Bluff. Said he was delivering a Lambo to a client here. Marietta Von Sustern, matter of fact."

Sonny was mostly silent. He startled me when he finally spoke.

"She won't need it now," he said. "Maybe he'll give you a ride, Tulip."

"Yeah, right," she said. "Maybe later."

Sonny looked at her and nodded.

Harley waved Patsy Ann and Honey good night, had words with Tommy Lee, then walked to his pickup. He'd parked it between the two RVs but on our side of the mini-Hummer or Range Rover.

Now he pulled away, giving me a better view of that squat vehicle. I looked harder at it. The way it was outlined in the artificial light, it could be mistaken for a Jeep. A chromed out luxury Jeep, but a Jeep just the same. A vehicle Marietta could have used the night she slipped away from Tahoe and drove to Oregon to kill Vader.

Tommy Lee got back into the Lambo. Then he fired up the engine, doubtless reawakening everyone at the show all over again, and drove away.

I took both Tulip and Sonny's hands as we turned to go back to the Horsehouse, most of the night's excitement being over. There probably were more questions in our future, but we were done for now.

I told them my thoughts about the Hummer-Jeep.

"I think you're right," said Tulip. "Sheriff Jack can check it all out."

Sonny stayed lost in thought. So I asked him about his drive, and about Serrano's handling of all things Kane including my home, store and parents. All fine. He asked me a few questions about the show. Did he really want to know?

We three each took about two minutes to shower. Then we retreated to our beds for some well-earned, thoroughly craved rest.

Sonny, climbing in next to me and smelling of my lavender soap as well as his own exclusive natural perfume, took my chin in his hand and looked down at me. "I have one more question," he said in the dark. "Answer only if you feel like it."

He posed the question with his lips and tongue, as well as his fingers and toes, while trying to avoid my body's sore spots. He acted as if he already knew the answer, although no words left his mouth.

I soon, and with great pleasure, gave him the answer.

~*~*~*~

Meet our Author

Carole T. Beers

Born in Portland, Ore., to descendants of Oregon Trail pioneers, Carole T. Beers fell in love with writing as soon as she could read, and with horses as soon as she could ride. After earning a B.A. in Journalism at University of Washington, she taught at a private school, wrote for true-romance magazines and worked 30 years as a reporter/critic for the Pulitzer Prize-winning Seattle Times newspaper. Several of her pieces won awards. Along the way she competed on a women's shooting team and earned a pilot's license. She also worked in marketing and retail -- great sources of story and character ideas!

Carole now lives in Southern Oregon, where she enjoys writing mystery books and stories. Her debut novel, "Saddle Tramps," centers on two 50-something women who show horses and solve crimes. These sassy ladies are ever seeking the perfect mate and the perfect horse, neither of which, they suspect, exists.

In the pipeline is a sequel to "Saddle Tramps," as well as "Blood Rider." The latter is about a horse-loving teen and a circuit-riding minister who's her triple-great grandfather. Each hunts down a killer a century apart. Soon Carole will publish a 16,000-word novella, "The Stone Horse," inspired by Zuni carvings of spirit animals. Years ago she mentored Indian youth, sang on a drum and danced in pow-wows, with the support of Lakota, Cree and Northwest Coast friends. She still holds these friendships dear to her heart.

Carole's free-time pursuits include dancing, playing games and watching the Seattle Seahawks along with her husband, Rich Peterson. She also likes to attend Bethany Presbyterian Church, visit friends, hang with her Boston Terriers, and ride her American Paint horse, Brad. Though retired from showing, she still rides as if she may show next week.

You may reach Carole at:

www.facebook.com/caroletbeers

www.caroletbeers.com

Made in the USA
Coppell, TX
11 October 2020